I0824391

# THE BOY FROM MARS

BOOK ONE IN THE BOY FROM MARS TRILOGY

ROBERT DeLAURENTIS

RARE BIRD
LOS ANGELES, CALIF.

THIS IS A GENUINE RARE BIRD BOOK

Rare Bird Books
6044 North Figueroa Street
Los Angeles, CA 90042
rarebirdbooks.com



FIRST HARDCOVER EDITION



For more information, address:
Rare Bird Books Subsidiary Rights Department
6044 North Figueroa Street
Los Angeles, California 90042

Set in Garamond
Printed in the United States

10 9 8 7 6 5 4 3 2 1

Library of Congress Cataloging-in-Publication Data available upon request

*For Serafina and Domenica, our future.*

"When all else is lost, the future still remains."

**—Christian Bovee**

# MARS

# CHAPTER 1

IT HAPPENED EVERY NIGHT. For a few precious minutes, Thomas found himself on Earth.

He stood on a steep mountain with three jagged peaks like the crown of an ancient king. He could see his breath in the oxygen-rich air, which along with the solitary moon, were sure signs he was on the origin planet. Even in the near darkness, the colors were bold, untainted by the reddish dust that covered everything back on Mars. Earth was not a planetary corpse buried in floodwater, as his professors had warned, but a spectacular fantasyland.

Thomas walked through the glade of towering trees into a field of snow. Directly in front of him, he saw an animal, a creation unknown on Mars. The large four-legged creature disappeared into the trees, passing a shadow. The shadow began to move forward, enough to reveal the outline of a man. Another step revealed a thick beard, wild and untamed. The man held out a hand, searching for a lifeline, reaching for help.

But then he began to fall.

And in that moment, the man, along with his world, vanished.

✦✦

THOMAS JOLTED UP IN his small cell on the Mars Station. He'd been under the spell of the same nightly vision he'd had since childhood. The Station doctors had explained that it was a dream, a psychological disorder that had plagued his ancestors back on Earth. They gave him medication to banish it from his sleep. But the dream persisted so that now, at the age of fifteen, it felt like an old friend.

He glanced out his portal to see the twin moons of Mars watching him like a pair of ghostly eyes, as if they knew what he was about to do. Below him, his counterpart Eno snored loudly on the lower platform. Even in deep sleep, his face was wrinkled into a scowl, as if something didn't quite meet his approval. He had the same expression when they first met at the age of six, when the hundred children in their birth class (fifty boys, fifty girls) left their small nursery pods to begin serious academic life.

When Thomas looked at their two faces in the portal's reflection, he couldn't help thinking what an odd pair they made, as if someone had gone out of their way to put together the two most mismatched boys on the entire planet.

The taller of the two, Thomas, had the standard buzz cut with a widow's peak that pointed toward his unusual eyes, which were the color of amber. In the rare instances when they came into contact with natural light, they seemed almost gold. Lean and muscular by nature, Thomas constantly found himself at odds with his own limbs, which longed to run, jump, and climb, all of which were strictly forbidden in the narrow confines of the Station.

Eno, on the other hand, moved slowly and cautiously, alert to potential danger at every moment. He was always a step behind, partly due to a weak lung that caused acute asthma, which turned his cheeks brown-red, like metal in the first stage of rust. Since all the children on the Station were genetically designed to be a perfect white, it marked him as flawed. His hair resisted the traditional cut and fell against the top of his forehead like an inverted bowl. It reminded Thomas of the religious society called monks he'd read about on Earth. Like all the children, his eyes were the standard gray, though one had malfunctioned at an early age and required a replacement, which made him a regular visitor to the infirmary.

Thomas checked his wrist pod. It was 3:56 in the morning. He would have to wait another four minutes, until the night guards changed shifts, before he could risk leaving the Boys' Quarters and trespassing into the Station proper. His heart thumped with restless energy, and he felt the familiar pang of emptiness that always accompanied waking. It was not so much hunger but the sensation that something inside him was missing, as if someone had removed an internal organ in the middle of the night.

Thomas knew there was only one thing that could alleviate the feeling. Months ago, after breaking into the Information Archives to retrieve a classmate's radiation pills, he discovered a paper document containing an Earth dictionary. Starting with the first letter of the alphabet, he copied several of the antiquated words, along with their meanings, on his work pad. Back in the safety of his cell, he pared the list down to his favorites, and whenever he couldn't sleep he'd scroll through it, silently mouthing each mysterious one: *accordion, butterfly, chimpanzee, dandelion, elephant, firefly, gondola, jacuzzi, karaoke, miracle, popsicle, razzmatazz.*

Recently, he'd reached the letter "S," which was filled with a treasure of exotic words: *saint, sandwich, serendipity, skateboard, skyscraper, snow globe, spaghetti, and soulmate.*

When he had time, he would study the definition of each. But for now, the very act of repeating them helped to relieve his emptiness. The minutes quickly disappeared, and his heartbeat returned to normal.

It was time to go.

Thomas slid off his sleep platform and changed out of his red pajamas into his day uniform (a darker red). Carrying his rubberized shoes, he crept through the Boys' Quarters and into the Station, where the only sound was the faint hiss of the oxygen regulators.

For the first few seconds, he could barely see. In the constant effort to conserve energy, the Station's corridors were unlit at night. Since no one ever trespassed (the penalty was prison for adults, isolation for juveniles), the night guards quickly tucked themselves into the dark spaces where the walls curved and slept until daybreak.

The Station interior was a dizzying maze of overlapping circles linked by seemingly random connectors. One day, Eno explained how it was laid out with a simple algorithm. By translating it into steps, Thomas discovered that he could navigate perfectly.

Scattered around the Station was a collection of observation towers, the last of which, Tower Twelve, had the best view of Earth. Thomas went there as often as possible. Since the planet was only visible during the day, he timed his arrival to coincide with the rise of the sun. But since he'd need to get back before the morning summons at six, he used his wrist pod to calculate the precise distance and time. It was 1,487 steps away—exactly nine minutes and eight seconds.

Thomas started to jog. He could feel the blood pumping into his arms and legs, his whole body coming to life. But as he passed the 900-step mark, he heard the sound of voices. Startled, he flattened himself against the wall as five boys came into view. With the exception of a smaller one in the back, Thomas guessed that they were a couple years older, around seventeen.

As they came closer, he was surprised to recognize the lead boy.

"Josef?"

"Thomas? How are you? It's been years. Not since Ten-Cube."

Thomas nodded, recalling how generous Josef had been in teaching him the subtleties of the boys' only sport.

As he stepped closer, Thomas was shocked to see two long scars running down his face. Josef must be stationed in the Mirror Factory, Thomas thought, making panels to reflect Mars' meager sunlight to heat its frozen surface. The fragile glass was known to break often, scarring anyone who worked there. Thomas noticed that one of the boys had even lost an ear.

"I wasn't sure you'd recognize me," Josef said, fingering his scars.

"No," Thomas lied. "I'm just not used to seeing anyone out here."

"Actually, we were hoping we'd run into you."

The other boys nodded. Except for the smaller one, they were all the standard Station height for their age. Perhaps the smaller boy had growth issues, like Eno.

"We heard what you did for Poke," the one-eared boy added.

"Poke?" Thomas replied. He trusted Josef but didn't know the others, and if word of what happened ever got out it could land him in one of the weightless detention chambers, which the boys avoided at all costs. The nausea and back pain suffered in a single one-hour session often lasted for days after it was over.

"He left his wrist pod in the Planetarium," Josef reminded him.

"You broke in and got it back for him," the one-eared boy added.

Josef nodded toward the one-eared boy. "Zev isn't wrong, right?"

Thomas gave a noncomittal shrug. Over the years, he'd scavenged the Station's repair zones for scraps of magnetic metals, which he used to construct a special pick for unscrambling lock codes. He'd not only gotten into the Information Archives but also the Artifacts Museum, the Planetarium, and even the Birthing Lab.

"I get it, the last thing you want to do is admit something like that," Josef said. "Besides me, you don't know us, and we all understand what the penalty would be if you were found out."

Thomas didn't respond. The incident had triggered requests from many of the boys in the weeks that followed and earned him a reputation as a break-in specialist.

"Word is you can get into any place in the Station," Josef said.

"I wander around at night." Thomas shrugged. "Sometimes I find things."

Josef smiled as if he had gotten the answer he was hoping for. "We were wandering around ourselves and got lost. We're lucky you found *us*."

"Where are you trying to get to?" Thomas said.

Josef glanced at the others as if to get approval, and the smaller boy at the back spoke. "The Propellant Depot."

Thomas couldn't hide his reaction. Everyone knew that the depot was off-limits because it stored the volatile fuel used to run all the Station's vehicles.

"Don't worry," Josef added. "I'm not asking you to break in, but I lost my labor ID somewhere inside, and I'll get detention if I can't find it."

Thomas knew there was risk involved in helping Josef, but he wanted to return the generosity he'd show years ago. "Turn left at the next connector and walk toward the Artifacts Museum. Take the third right, and the depot will be forty-three steps away."

"Forty-three?" Josef repeated.

"Exactly."

Josef nodded to the others, as if to confirm Thomas's expertise. "Thanks, Thomas. It was good seeing you."

The boys quickly receded into the shadows, and Thomas hurried forward, hoping to make up for lost time. In less than three minutes he reached Tower Twelve, which had recently been closed by order of the High Governor in response to a small group of rebels known as the Returners, who wished to return to the origin planet. Several tried to flee the Station, hoping to join a secret community created to protect the last child born on Earth—a child who would someday lead them back to their rightful home. Most were captured or killed, yet they continued to flee. In an attempt to discourage them, the governor declared Tower Twelve off limits.

Thomas vaulted over the protective barrier that now stood in front of it and raced up the eighty-eight steps to the observatory. He slid his pick into the door and worked the lock free. Inside, the silver titanium panels that formed the exterior soared overhead. Designed to make the Station look like a diamond in space, years of dust storms had reduced them to the same reddish brown as the rest of the planet. Four thick legs, housing the Station's water, food, power, and research facilities, held the Station aloft, reminding Thomas of one of the prehistoric lizards that once roamed the origin planet. On the lizard's back sat a glass dome housing a fleet of Ramjets.

In the center of the fleet was a sleek black aircraft known as the Mastership. With its sharp laser probe and a dozen independently operated legs, it looked like a spider on the lizard's back. Originally built to patrol the asteroid belt, it was now used to hunt down Returners.

Directly behind him sat Olympus Mons, a volcano several miles to the west—the biggest mountain in the solar system. A dust devil, one of the massive storms that plagued Mars, gathered at its base. Since they often lasted for weeks and obscured everything, Thomas knew that it could be his last chance to gaze at the origin planet for a long time.

He pulled down the observatory telescope and swiveled it toward Earth. Set against the black canvas of space, the small blue sphere glistened like a precious jewel. The sight filled him with joy, though it also produced another emotion, not unlike the one he often felt upon waking. It was as if he had lost something special but couldn't remember what.

During one of his nightly expeditions, Thomas had found a small hunk of blue magma known as hematite. By smoothing its edges, he fashioned a crude replica of Earth. He reached for it now, as if to connect him to his ancestors.

But as he did, a piercing alarm echoed in the Station, most likely from a radiation leak or runaway meteor. Then again, it could be for him. If Josef and his friends had been caught violating curfew, one of them might have given him up for a reward.

Thomas knew that the boys would be filing into the Common Circle for a head count at any moment. His only chance was to get back in time to join them.

He took one last look at Earth and ran for his life.

# CHAPTER 2

THOMAS TOOK THE STAIRS three at a time, using the last landing to launch himself to the floor, where he broke into a full sprint.

When he came around the first circle, Thomas heard footsteps and spotted the shadow of a large man with massive shoulders. He dove into the nearest connector as the footsteps came to a stop. Thomas held his breath and peered out. Surprisingly, the man was no longer there. He seemed to have simply vanished.

But there was no time to solve the puzzle. Trusting his good fortune, he bolted out of the darkness toward the Boys' Quarters.

After a few minutes, Thomas heard the hum of voices and knew that the four hundred boys were gathering. As he came out of the last connector, he saw them shuffling toward a flickering wall of light like a crowd of sleepwalkers. They wore their matching red pajamas, and Thomas hoped no one would notice he was wearing his day uniform.

Arriving at the Common Circle, he could see that the light was coming from the hundred-foot-high Magnum Screen used for Station announcements, mostly meteorological alerts. Thomas spotted Varik, his nemesis, standing at the front of the pack, directly below the screen. The tallest and thinnest boy in their class, Varik had an intestinal disorder that restricted the absorption of food, so his bones were almost visible under his flesh. In the harsh glare of the Magnum Screen, he looked like a skeleton come to life.

Flanking Varik were his constant allies, Simon and Bruno, who had the opposite disorder. Everything they ate was immediately converted to fat, making them look inflated, like the columns that marked the Station boundary. In Two-Class, the boys learned that Mars' two moons were named after the Greek gods Phebos and Deimos, signifying fear and terror. From then on, Simon and Bruno, the school bullies, became known as the Moons.

Thomas maneuvered through the crowd until he could see the screen. It displayed a shot of the barren red landscape outside the Station perimeter. At the top of the frame, he caught a glimpse of the dust devil he'd seen from Tower Twelve and was reminded of one that struck two years earlier, causing a weeklong power outage. Perhaps the alarm was for the storm.

He saw Poke, the boy Josef had talked about, standing by himself, and Thomas slid in next to him. "What's going on?"

Poke kept his eyes on the Magnum Screen. "Returners."

Thomas breathed a sigh of relief that he wasn't the cause.

"Two of them hijacked a water tanker from some perma-dig," he said, referring to one of the frozen permafrost mines that supplied the Station with water. "But they're not in camera range yet."

Thomas understood that it would be up to the Ramjets, with their sophisticated tracking equipment, to provide the video feed.

"It shouldn't be long now," Varik shouted, unable to hide his exhilaration.

Escape attempts had occurred before, but only recently were the boys permitted to watch live coverage. A forty-wheel water tanker appeared on the screen along with a digital time code. It was headed toward the Valles, the subterranean canyons that stretched for miles between the Station and the towering Olympus Mons.

A pair of Ramjets shot into view at the six-second mark. Varik led the boys in a cheer.

"Oh, dear," came a voice from behind Thomas. "Another one?"

Thomas turned to see Eno, still in his eye patch, which he wore whenever his replacement eye was in docking mode. He slid in between Poke and Thomas.

"You got here fast," Eno said. "I'd barely opened my eye and you were gone."

Thomas shrugged, not wanting to discuss his absence.

"I can't quite believe we're being required to watch one of these dreadful things at this hour of the morning."

"Your presence isn't required," Poke said, without turning back.

"I beg to differ," Eno said. "Only last week Professor affirmed the necessity of bearing witness. He said the escapes had civic import."

Thomas glanced at his counterpart. "What's so important about seeing outnumbered men hunted down by superior forces?"

Before Eno could respond, the Ramjets began to descend, and the boys got their first glimpse of the two men in the tanker. They wore the protective gloves of drillers, and both appeared to be in their forties, though Thomas guessed they were probably younger. The radiation exposure caused by working outdoors, even in protective gear, inevitably took its toll.

"They're heading toward the Valles," Poke said. "I wonder why?"

"If they could climb far enough into the canyons," Thomas said, "they'd be beyond the reach of the Ramjets."

"Sounds like you've given it some thought," a voice called out.

Thomas looked over to see Varik staring at him.

"It doesn't take much to see the obvious," Thomas said.

"Even if they could get there in time," Varik said, "the Mastership can see everything."

"It can't see through rock," Thomas said.

A few boys laughed, but when the Moons glared at them, they fell silent and went back to waiting for the arrival of the Mastership, which was an event in itself. Coated with a rare composite that produced a perfect reflection of its surroundings, it was constantly camouflaged. At night, it seemed to be wrapped in the darkness itself. The boys let out a gasp of awe whenever they saw it.

"There it is!" shouted Varik, thrusting a fist in the air.

The Mastership leveled off and took on the reflection of the Martian landscape. The color reminded Thomas of dry blood.

It held its altitude while the Ramjets began descending over the tanker, which wove back and forth in an attempt to evade the jets.

"Shoot," shouted Varik. "Now!"

As if obeying his command, each Ramjet fired a mini-missile, blowing out a bank of tires and forcing the tanker into a violent roll.

It came to a rest roof-side down with its wheels still spinning wildly. One of the doors burst open, and the two Returners rolled out of the cabin. The moment they hit the ground, a digital time code appeared beneath them.

"Eight seconds and counting," Poke said.

"Why do they put that up, I wonder?" Eno asked.

"For our benefit," Thomas said. "To show us it's useless to run."

"The record's forty-one seconds," Varik said.

A pair of vertical aircraft dropped into the frame, stopping just a few feet from the ground. Their hatches opened to reveal a team of Commandos in hazard suits and combat gear. Riding single-wheel motorized terrain bikes, they shot out of the verticals and sped off in pursuit.

"Twenty-eight seconds," Varik called out.

A pair of bikes zeroed in on the first Returner. One of the Commandos swerved behind and struck him on the back of the head with a baton. As the Returner skidded across the frozen ground, another cheer echoed from the boys.

"That's your survivor," Varik said. "They always take one alive, so they can get information on the others." The Moons bobbed their heads with relish.

The Commandos turned toward the driver, firing their laser guns. Two shots tore into the driller's hazard suit, one at the ankle and the other near the shoulder.

"His suit's torn!" Varik said. "He might as well give up now."

Everyone understood that the driver was now vulnerable to Mars' sub-zero temperature. He wouldn't survive more than a few minutes in the freezing cold.

But, for some reason, the Returner kept running toward the rim of the Valles.

"He'd better slow down," Varik said, "or he'll go over the edge."

The canyons were thousands of feet deep, and it was unlikely anyone could survive the fall. As the driller came within fifty yards of the rim, he glanced back at the Commandos, revealing a thin layer of permafrost on his face. He was turning blue. As the camera came closer, Thomas recognized him as one of the Nursery Prefects from many years ago.

"It's Benjamin."

Eno squinted with his good eye. "It can't be."

"No," Poke said. "Thomas is right. It's him."

Benjamin had been removed from the nursery pods the year after the boys started school and sent to work in the drilling fields. It was a cause of great confusion to the boys at the time, as no one could understand what he could have done to warrant such a demotion. They watched with renewed interest as Benjamin began to slow.

"He knows he has no chance," Varik said. "He'll surrender soon."

But suddenly Benjamin summoned a final burst of speed.

"What's the fool doing?" Varik asked.

Benjamin reached the edge of the rim and leapt into the air, flying over the dark abyss of the canyon. For a few terrible moments, his arms and legs flailed against the thin Martian atmosphere, and then he disappeared inside as if swallowed by a black hole.

The Magnum Screen went blank.

A hush fell over the boys. No one could quite comprehend what they'd just witnessed. Finally, the silence was broken by the voice of a One-Classer so small he was barely visible in the crowd of older, taller boys.

"What happened to him?" the boy asked.

"He killed himself," Thomas said.

"But why?" asked a Two-Classer, even more confused.

Everyone turned toward Thomas as if he alone could explain the mystery.

"Because he'd rather die than be taken alive," Thomas said.

"How do you know that?" Varik asked in a demanding tone. He headed toward Thomas and Eno, as the Moons cleared a path with their beefy arms. Eno's breathing quickened.

"Well, Thomas, we're waiting for your explanation."

"It's pretty clear," Thomas said. "Not everyone thinks life on the Station is so wonderful."

"Does that include you?"

Eno began to wheeze. "I think what Thomas is trying to say…"

"Shut up," Varik said. "No one asked you."

Eno lowered his head, as if hoping to hide. As the smallest boy in their class, he'd always been a favorite target. Once, after he'd made a class presentation about the uselessness of certain bodily appendages, Varik cornered him in the Boys' Quarters and ordered the Moons to cut off his little toe. Thomas had arrived just in time to prevent the surgery, but since then, Eno couldn't look at Varik without a shiver of panic.

"Benjamin is a traitor," Varik continued. "And if you have any sympathy for him, you're no better. Perhaps you're a Returner in the making."

Varik took a final step forward, nose to nose with Thomas, who stood his ground. Eno put his hand to his chest, wheezing loudly now.

"For all we know your little counterpart's one as well!"

Eno gave out a final wheeze, accompanied by a groan, and fell to the floor.

A pair of Prefects appeared at the edge of the crowd and ordered the boys to return to their quarters. Thomas dropped to his knees and reached into his pocket for the chemical patch he carried for emergencies. He pulled Eno's pajama top up and placed it over his bad lung, a procedure he'd performed so many times he could do it with his eyes closed.

Varik, no longer able to command Thomas's attention, turned and walked away. The rest of the boys in his immediate circle took his cue and did the same.

After several seconds, Eno finally opened his eyes and took a few deep breaths.

"Are you all right?" Thomas said.

Eno nodded, and Thomas helped him to his feet.

Alone, they walked slowly and silently back to their cell.

# CHAPTER 3

In the aftermath of one of his attacks, Eno always fell into a deep sleep. Thomas, haunted by the image of Benjamin going over the cliff, remained wide-awake. He couldn't help thinking about what Varik said. Indeed, he'd always felt sympathetic to the Returners and couldn't understand why the Station reacted to their escape attempts by hunting them down. But sympathy for their cause was one thing and being a Returner was another. While he couldn't deny his fascination with the origin planet, it had never occurred to him that he might want to leave the Station, even if that was possible.

Thomas turned on the monitor above his sleep platform, hoping for news. High Governor Balthazar, flanked by the ten members of the Governor's Council, was making an address. After every remark, the council nodded its approval. The only exception was a man at the very end, with close-cropped, gray-black hair and beard. Thomas guessed he was approaching fifty, old enough to have been born on the origin planet, and recalled that he was the sole council member from the original settlers. His shuttle, the last to arrive from Earth, had crashed upon landing, and he managed to survive several weeks on the harsh Martian landscape before reaching the Station. He leaned on a cane, his eyes cast downward, as if he found the governor's speech difficult to tolerate. And when it ended, he didn't join the council members in their enthusiastic applause.

Thomas turned off the monitor and tried to sleep.

At 2:00 a.m., he gave up and got out of bed. The Eight-Class Annuals, a yearlong report that counted for half of their final grade, were due the next day. Each student was required to compare an aspect of Station life—such as waste removal, food production, or incarceration—with its counterpart on Earth. The objective was always the same: to demonstrate the Station's superiority.

Thomas's chosen topic was transportation, and he'd devoted much of his report to the train system on Earth. He'd been enchanted by the powerful-looking locomotives ever since he saw an image of one in the Artifacts Museum. On one of his nightly forays, he located some maps that revealed a vast network of railway routes. Some included photographs of trains crossing rivers or climbing mountains. Despite their primitive engineering, they gave off a dazzling appearance and made the Station's fleet of vehicles seem dull by comparison.

At 6:00 a.m., the first summons—a pulsing orange light—invaded their cell.

Eno rolled over and opened his good eye. "Thomas, what are you doing up so early?"

"Working on my Annual."

"The one about supply carriers on Earth?"

"They're called trains. And they carried passengers, too."

Thomas knew that Eno didn't share his affection for the origin planet and expected some snide comment. But Eno was silent as he removed his prosthetic eye from its docking chamber and slid it into his empty eye socket. "I assume these *trains* were restricted to adults?"

"No, somebody our age could ride one, too, as long as he had a ticket."

"And if he didn't?"

"Then he'd have to ride in the freight compartment with the hobos."

"*Hobos*?"

"A secret society of train travelers, who built fires in the woods for cooking."

"Fires, of course. They were quite fond of those on Earth."

Thomas knew that Eno was parroting the official Station view. Their professors never tired of telling them how their ancestors, unable to curb their use of fossil fuels, warmed the origin planet, eventually causing the great floods.

Thomas preferred to let the conversation die, but Eno continued to give it life. "Was there no penalty then, for not having a ticket?"

"Of course. If you were caught without one you were tied to the tracks. And then the train drove over you until you were pulverized."

Eno raised his eyebrows so high that his replacement almost popped out.

Thomas couldn't hold back a laugh.

"Very humorous," Eno said. "Let's hope Professor finds it more amusing than I do."

✦✦

THE BOYS WALKED TO the Nutrition Court in silence. Like the Station itself, the tables were arranged in a series of concentric circles. Varik and the Moons always commandeered the innermost circle, which only seated ten boys, forming their own little ruling council.

Thomas and Eno took their trays and passed through the automated line. There was no choice in the daily menu; each meal contained a blob of spirulina, the blue-green algae that provided the boys with protein. The remainder consisted of freeze-dried segments of the six items grown in the Martian terrafarms: squares (soya, spinach), circles (rice, onions), and triangles (tomato, potato). The food was sprayed with a light mist to add water, resulting in what Thomas thought was a soggy, tasteless pulp.

Thomas and Eno took their seats at the outermost circle. Continuing an arrangement established in One-Class, they silently traded soya squares for tomato triangles. But before they could take a bite, a commotion erupted across the room, and several boys rushed to the portal as a red light flashed outside. Varik and the Moons pushed their way to the front.

Thomas stood up, though Eno stayed seated.

"What's going on?" Eno said.

"Not sure," Thomas said. "But I can see an ambulance outside."

"What on Mars for?"

Eno stood up to see two attendants slide a gurney containing a frozen corpse out of the ambulance. The man's hands were enormous, and Thomas realized that it was Benjamin, still wearing his drilling gloves. The ambulance pulled away.

"It's the Returner," Varik said, "the one who was driving."

"Why did they leave him here?" asked one of the Seven-Classers.

"There's a problem at the morgue," Varik said. "Can't any of you read?"

In unison, several hundred heads checked their wrist pods for news.

Eno whispered. "Apparently they ran out of the chemical used to dissolve corpses."

"So, they had to leave his body where everyone can see it?"

Varik swiveled toward Thomas and spoke loud enough for everyone to hear. "It's a demonstration of what happens to traitors."

Thomas shouted back. "We had a pretty good demonstration last night. That seems like more than enough to me."

"Perhaps you should confide your dissatisfaction to the authorities."

"And save you the trouble?" Thomas said.

Varik and the Moons started toward Thomas, and Thomas pushed his tray to the side, ready to defend himself. But the third and final summons, announcing the beginning of class, flashed in the background.

Varik stopped, then turned, along with the Moons, and made his way out. Thomas started after him, but Eno grabbed him by the arm.

"Let him go, Thomas. He's not worth it."

✦✦

THE BOYS WERE BARELY seated in class when Professor entered, looking more serious than usual. "I've just received an urgent communication from the governor's office concerning suspicious activity in the corridors last night. A boy was seen leaving Observation Tower Twelve after curfew."

Professor gave the announcement time to register the predictable shock from the boys, scanning them for some sign of complicity. "Does anyone have information regarding the identity of this person?"

Varik's bony hand leapt into the air. "I was watching the defection last night when Thomas appeared. Everyone was in their sleep uniform except him, and he was wearing his daily."

"Is that true, Thomas?"

"Yes," Thomas said. "I woke early to do some extra work on my Annual and got dressed. As far as I know, there isn't a rule against that."

Professor nodded thoughtfully. "Very well, I'll submit your excuse officially."

Thomas gave Varik a victorious smile and slid back into his seat.

"And now," Professor said, "if you would all direct yourselves to unit seventy-eight for a review of the Third Unified Field Theory."

✦✦

The rest of the day passed uneventfully, though Eno was unusually quiet. Thomas wondered if he was beginning to think Varik's suspicions about him might be true, that Thomas was the boy at Tower Twelve. His counterpart had always been a loyal cellmate, but he was equally loyal to the Station. Thomas had no real idea what Eno would do if the two things came into conflict. He hoped Eno would at least confide his suspicion and give him the chance to explain. But there was no way to know for sure. And Eno never said a word about the matter as they climbed into their sleep platforms that night. Within minutes, he was snoring.

Thomas reached for his hematite sphere, which always had a calming effect, but when he slid a hand under his sleep pad to retrieve it, he discovered that it was gone. It must have fallen out of his pocket when he bounded down the tower stairs the previous night. If it was found by the guards, it could be tested for DNA and traced back to him from the Station medical records.

Under the circumstances, he had no choice but to act. Thomas quickly slipped off his platform, out the door, and into the darkened corridors. He ran as fast as he could, but as he approached the connector near Tower Twelve, a shadowy figure stepped out in front of him, cutting him off.

Thomas froze as the boy revealed himself.

"It's me again," Josef whispered. "I need to talk to you in private."

"What about?"

Josef hesitated for a moment, as if he were about to share a terrible secret. "My friends and I…we're planning an escape."

Thomas was stunned. No one under the age of thirty had ever tried to flee the Station.

"When?"

"Tomorrow night, so we can use the big dust devil for cover. We've been waiting for one like that for weeks, so now that it's here we can't waste our chance."

Thomas nodded. "How will you do it?"

"We'll take one of the small vehicles that service the mirror fields. They're equipped with cables and weighted boots, which we can use to climb into the Valles. Before the Ramjets arrive, we'll be in the canyons, moving in four different directions. They won't be able to cover us all."

Thomas didn't understand. "Four different directions, for five people?"

"Lina will be with me," Josef said, turning back to the dark recess where the circle joined the connector. "The two of us will make it together or not at all."

The smaller boy from the previous night emerged and pulled off his cap. A spiral of hair tumbled free, and Thomas could see that the boy was in fact a girl.

"She's a Cerebral," Josef said with pride, referring to one of the rare students chosen for special careers at the Station. "We met when she was sent in to oversee work on the new mirror satellites."

The girl reached over and linked hands with Josef. Thomas couldn't help staring. He had never seen a girl touch a boy like that. "I hope it doesn't shock you," Lina said. "But on Earth, boys and girls often pair up for life, even at our age."

Thomas knew little about mating rituals on the origin planet. Professor had covered the topic in Six-Class biology, but only barely, dismissing the behavior as barbaric.

"We need your help," Lina said, "to get into the Propellant Depot."

"What is it you want me to do?" Thomas said.

"The vehicle we need is parked in the bay outside the Mirror Factory," Josef said. "But the drivers remove the fuel canisters after their shifts. They pick up a new supply every morning at the Propellant Depot. We want you to get us inside."

It was one thing to be sympathetic, but another to aid a criminal act. Thomas hesitated.

"Think of it as an act of patriotism," Lina said. "For everyone who wants a chance to return to Earth. We know in your heart that you're one of us."

Lina's words ricocheted around Thomas's brain, as if they couldn't find a place to settle. If that was true, it meant that Varik was right after all. But there was no more time to wonder. Thomas had to make a decision, relying on nothing more than instinct.

"How much fuel do you need?"

"Only ten gallons." Josef smiled. "It's a one-way trip."

# CHAPTER 4

THOMAS SNUCK BACK INTO his cell but couldn't sleep. His mind was still vibrating with the decision to help Josef escape. He scrolled through his wrist pod for his "S" words and came across a new one. *Sandcastle.* It referred to a structure made from soft silicate that was part of the terrain adjacent to an *ocean*. As he mouthed the word, he tried to picture himself on a *beach,* making his own *castle*, until the light of the filtered red sun crept into his cell.

A low hum echoed outside his portal, and he turned to see the dust devil forming on the horizon. Josef was right. It would make a perfect cover for an escape. Directly above it, the Martian moons glared at him, as if watching his every move. A voice startled him.

"They say it's going to be a monster," Eno said.

Thomas looped his head over his sleep platform to see Eno sitting cross-legged, staring out the portal. "You mean the devil?"

"It could reach a height of five miles."

"I guess we won't be seeing the Mons for a few days, huh?"

"We won't be seeing anything," Eno said.

Thomas flopped back onto his pad with a thud.

"Are you all right?" Eno said.

"All right?" Thomas repeated, surprised by the question. He couldn't remember the last time Eno inquired about his personal well-being. "What do you mean?"

"The incident with Varik in class yesterday. You must be at least concerned."

"Not particularly," Thomas said. "Why should I?"

"That sort of accusation isn't taken lightly by Professor. And these sorts of things have a way of working their way up to the authorities. They already know about your feelings regarding Earth. I'd hate to see you get a bad reputation."

"I'm not worried about my reputation."

"It's not only that," Eno said. "I'm starting to worry that it's corrupting your mind."

"What are you talking about?"

"We've been living together for ten years, Thomas. Do you think I don't know about your night spasms?"

"You mean my dreams?"

"Whatever they're called. I hear you mumbling in your sleep. I assume your 'dreams' are about Earth?"

"Well, yes, if you must know."

"What happens?"

"Nothing much. I'm just walking on a mountain, that's all."

"How do you even know it's Earth?"

"I look at the sky."

"Ah, the solitary moon. Of course. And then what?"

Thomas thought about telling Eno the truth but quickly realized it would be a mistake. "Nothing. I wake up."

"With the recent spate of escape attempts, I just hope you're careful."

"I'll do my best. Promise."

Eager to avoid another encounter with Varik, Eno suggested skipping breakfast, and Thomas readily agreed. Today of all days, he couldn't risk a confrontation that might land him in detention. They went directly to class where Thomas spent the entire time going over Josef's escape plan in his head.

He would leave the Boys' Quarters at three o'clock that night to meet Josef at the Propellant Depot by 3:13 p.m. After retrieving the fuel canisters, they'd rendezvous at the Mirror Factory at 3:23 p.m. This would give Josef and his friends seven minutes and forty-two seconds to reach their escape vehicle. Thomas would have the same amount of time to get back to his quarters.

As class ended and the boys were filing out, he rose to follow, but Professor held up his index finger. "Thomas, I need to speak with you."

"Yes?"

Professor waited until all the boys had filed out and closed the door. "I've been reviewing your Annual reports from past years, and I regret to say that there appears to be a problem."

From the look on Professor's face, Thomas found it hard to believe he had any regret whatsoever.

"I'm referring, of course, to your interest in the origin planet, which seems to border on obsession. Your reports seem to exhibit a sense of 'nostalgia.' Are you familiar with that term?"

"No," Thomas said.

"It's a yearning for something in the past—or in the case of Earth, a place."

Thomas averted his eyes for a moment, so as not to betray the truth of the accusation.

"Trust me, no one ever mistook you for a Cerebral. But your skill in games is well known, as is the fact that for some reason the younger boys look up to you. These qualities earmark you as a potential candidate for a position in the Defense Dome, perhaps even on the Mastership itself. Another Earth-centric report could destroy all that. I encourage you to make certain it reflects a commitment to the Station and its values. Your future depends on it."

✦✦

Thomas left the classroom in a daze, wondering if the authorities already suspected that he was the boy at the tower and were watching him. When he reached the Common Circle, he saw Varik and the Moons standing off to the side, whispering to each other. Avoiding them, he turned in the opposite direction, leading to the Planetarium, passing a group of Eight-Class girls. With their regulation hair, they looked indistinguishable. He couldn't help thinking of Lina and what courage it must've taken for her to pair off with Josef. It seemed almost as daring as the escape attempt itself.

As he approached the Planetarium, he spotted a large man standing just inside the connector. Thomas couldn't be sure, but it looked like the same man he'd seen two nights ago. He seemed to be waiting for something or someone.

Thomas turned and pressed himself against the wall, hoping to let some time pass before he went back to the Boys' Quarters. Hopefully Varik and the Moons would be gone by then. But a few moments later, a beeping sound echoed from his wrist pod. It was the code he'd set up with Eno in case of an emergency. Coming from the cell they shared, it meant that Eno was in distress. Thomas turned back toward the Boys' Quarters, but in doing so, glanced over to see that the man had vanished, just as before.

He jogged down the hallway and as he neared the Boys' Quarters, he heard muffled cries. They grew louder as he sprinted toward his cell. When Thomas reached the door, he threw it open to see Eno face down on the floor. Varik was kneeling over his neck and the Moons holding down his arms and legs.

"What are you doing!" Thomas demanded.

Varik ripped his hand from Eno's face, causing him to scream in pain. Thomas pushed the Moons off Eno as Varik jumped to his feet. The three of them stood back, circling Thomas, who knelt next to Eno and tried to see what was wrong. But Eno hid his face.

"What did you do to him?" Thomas said.

Varik grinned with mock innocence. "We merely came down to play a little game and found ourselves without a ball, so your counterpart was nice enough to volunteer his."

Varik held Eno's eye aloft in his bony fingers. "Care to play?"

Thomas held out his hand. "Give it to me!"

"I'll take that as a no?"

Varik tossed the eye over Thomas's head to Simon, who threw it to Bruno, who tossed it back to Varik, who made an awkward attempt to catch it, but in his clumsiness, missed. Thomas could only watch, helpless, as the fragile acrylic eye hit the floor.

For a moment nobody moved as the gel-like interior slowly spread across the floor in a small puddle. The Moons hurried past Varik and ran out, leaving their leader behind.

Thomas stood up, furious. "You won't get away with this."

"I beg to differ," Varik said. "If you dare mention this to anyone, I'll tell the authorities about your traitorous comments last night."

"Get out of here," Thomas said. "Now!"

Varik backed out of the room and closed the door. Thomas turned back to Eno, who continued to lie face down on the floor.

"It's all right Eno. We'll get you another eye right away."

But Eno still didn't lift his head. Thomas put a hand on his back as he began to sob.

MOMENTS AFTER THEY CHECKED into the Infirmary, a male nurse arrived to lead Eno and Thomas to the Eye Clinic. In the waiting room were several other boys, most no older than ten, all wearing eye patches like Eno's.

They had barely taken their seats when the door opened and an older man in a white smock appeared. His skin was dark brown, one of only a few with a non-white complexion on the entire Station, all from the original group of settlers.

The doctor stopped. "Eno? I didn't have you down for an appointment."

"It's an emergency, Dr. Jax." Eno said. "I'm afraid I need a replacement."

Dr. Jax glanced at Thomas. "And this would be?"

"My counterpart. He brought me in and I was hoping he could stay for the procedure."

"Of course," Dr. Jax said. "Follow me."

He led them into an exam room where Eno laid on the table and pulled a metal brace from the wall to hold his head in place.

"What happened to the G-22?" Dr. Jax asked, removing Eno's eye patch.

"I dropped it on the floor and it shattered. You know how clumsy I am."

Dr. Jax nodded, though the look on his face made it clear he knew Eno was lying. "Well, your timing is good. There's an upgrade available. The G-23 has better peripherals and not nearly the same reflection issues."

Dr. Jax pulled a cord from underneath the table and attached it to Eno's neck. Within seconds, Eno was unconscious.

"Is he going to be all right?" Thomas asked.

"More or less. The replacements keep getting better, though there's still no substitute for the real thing. It's the price of genetic engineering and our great cosmic joke. On a planet with nothing to see, the eyes are the first to go."

"I guess I'm lucky to have my originals," Thomas said.

Dr. Jax looked him in the eyes. "Yes, they're remarkably clear. They remind me of my son's, back on Earth."

"Oh, is he…?"

"No longer among the living?"

"I'm sorry," Thomas said. "I didn't mean…"

"No, of course not. Like many of us, I was forced to leave him behind—in Colorado, along with my wife. I was unfortunate enough to be a doctor and required here, while they were not."

Thomas remembered Colorado from one of the train route maps. The name sounded like an adventure unto itself. But clearly it didn't have the same meaning for the doctor.

Dr. Jax turned his attention back to Eno. "I'll need him to stay overnight. There's an extra cot, if you'd like to keep him company. I'll send along a permission pass."

"Thank you," Thomas said, as the doctor left the room.

After several sleepless hours, Thomas drifted off and found himself on a train, headed toward a mountain range. As it climbed up through the trees, he saw the figure of a man standing hundreds of feet above, as if waiting for him to arrive. In the distance, he couldn't tell if it was the man from his usual dream. But despite the fact that the train was moving quickly, he didn't seem to be getting any closer to him.

Finally, the alarm on his wrist pod vibrated. It was shortly before 3:00 a.m. He checked on Eno, who was sleeping peacefully, then slipped out of the Infirmary.

He reached the Propellant Depot at 3:11 a.m., two minutes before Josef was due. Sliding into the shadows, Thomas leaned against the wall and waited. When his wrist pod registered 3:13 a.m., there was still no sign of Josef. Perhaps he was caught leaving the Men's Quarters, Thomas thought, when he heard footsteps. A moment later, Josef appeared, breathless and agitated.

"Zev isn't coming," he said, referring to the boy with one ear. "He panicked and said we were all going to die. I won't blame you if you want to back out."

"Why would I do that?"

"You've heard of Bron the Interrogator?"

Thomas nodded. The boys had all heard stories about the man with the black eyes. It was rumored that he could make people confess with only a look.

"It's only a matter of time before he finds out Zev was involved. He's a good kid, but no match for Bron. He'll turn you in."

"Thanks," Thomas said, "but I'll take my chances."

Josef glanced at his wrist pod. "Then we better get moving."

Within minutes, they arrived at the Propellant Depot where Thomas quickly unlocked the door. Josef located the five-gallon canisters of fuel and lifted one from its stack. Thomas took the second, and together they hurried toward the Mirror Factory, where Lina was waiting.

Thomas handed his canister to one of Josef's friends and used his pick to open the door. He'd only been inside the factory twice. It was like an endless field of mirrors, including several hanging in tiers above, reflecting in every direction.

"This is where we say farewell," Josef said. "The vehicle bay's at the other end of the factory. There's no reason for you to go any farther. Thanks, Thomas."

Lina squeezed Thomas's hand in gratitude.

He watched as the group hurried off, their wrist lights dancing against the mirrors. Thomas turned to leave but pulled up short when he saw a guard enter the corridor. Six others quickly joined him, fanning out around the entrance.

Josef and the others would be at the vehicle by now, Thomas thought. He had to hold off the guards long enough for them to begin the escape.

Glancing at the mirrors above, Thomas saw that they were tied to cables, which allowed the racks to be lowered. He carefully untied one and the weight nearly pulled him off his feet, his fingers burning with pain. But he leaned back using all his body weight to keep them aloft.

The door burst open, and one of the guards shouted into the dark. "Come out right now!"

Thomas didn't move. When the guards charged forward, he released the cable, sending the mirrors crashing to the floor in an explosion of glass. In the darkness, he heard their angry screams and felt a rush of satisfaction that Josef and the others were on their way to freedom.

But the feeling was short lived.

The guards were rising from the pile of broken glass.

It was time to make an escape of his own.

# CHAPTER 5

Thomas ran to the rear of the Mirror Factory and took the exit into the corridor, which led to the Food Preparation Center. As he entered the connector, he heard the guards running behind him.

At Food Prep, he unlocked the door and hurried to the first waste chute, only to find it clogged with garbage. He climbed inside the second chute as the guards burst through the doors and pushed off.

Almost instantly, he heard a squirting sound. Yellow liquid rained down on him. By the smell, Thomas knew it must be some sort of antiseptic, but it had the effect of a lubricant, glazing the chute and increasing his speed.

He jammed his feet against the sides of the chute to slow himself, but within seconds he was in free fall. Out of the corner of his eye, he could see the bottom of the floor coming toward him. He curled his arms around his legs in a tight ball and shot several feet into air, landing on his back with a loud splat. He skidded to a stop, drenched in a coat of slimy, yellow fluid.

A man appeared from the darkness with the same huge shoulders as the one who vanished at the Planetarium. Thomas struggled to get to his feet but slipped in the pool of yellow fluid dripping from his body. The man grabbed his arm and lifted him into a standing position.

"Hurry! We only have a few seconds."

He dragged Thomas toward some waste containers and pulled out a circular section of floor, revealing a dark hollow. The man gestured for Thomas to climb in. Putting his legs inside, he dropped several feet to the ground and was jolted by the searing cold.

Except for a demonstration in science class, he'd never experienced anything other than the Station's temperature, perfectly controlled at seventy degrees.

The man dropped down after him and pulled the hatch closed. Strapping a small headlamp onto his forehead, he held out a face mask and a pair of gloves.

"Put these on. It's thirty below down here, and they'll prevent frostbite. My name is William, by the way."

"I'm Thomas."

"I know."

William led him down a narrow passage to a set of makeshift stairs that dropped several more feet. At the bottom of the stairs was a small rolling car big enough for two passengers. William gestured for Thomas to get in and took the driver's seat.

He handed Thomas a blanket, then turned on the ignition, which activated a pair of headlights. They illuminated a crude tunnel carved out of the permafrost.

The vehicle shot forward, quickly gaining speed as it rattled through the tunnel. Thomas was thrilled by the ride but mystified by the tunnel. The Station's construction was a subject every schoolboy learned in Four-Class. There was never any mention of a tunnel system or where it might possibly lead.

Thomas heard the muffled sound of the Defense Dome retracting. He could hear the rumble of the Ramjets taking off, followed by the low whine of mini-missiles. Moments later, they exploded against the ground above, shaking some of the wall ice loose. A powerful vibration rocked the tunnel, and he knew it could mean only one thing: The Mastership had triggered its quantum engines and was on its way to join the Ramjet fleet.

It was 3:40 a.m., almost seven minutes from the start of the escape. By now, the boys would be gathered under the Magnum Screen to view the chase. His stomach clenched at the thought of Varik cheering the Commandoes as they hunted down Josef and Lina.

After another few moments, William pulled over to a small turnout.

"We're here."

William jumped out of the vehicle and pushed against the tunnel roof. A circular section dropped down, and he cupped his muscular hands together to form a step.

Thomas stepped into his hands and was lifted up and into a dark room.

"I'll be back for you when it's time," William said.

He pushed the circular section into place, disappearing below it.

Thomas pulled off his mask to see that he was in an oval room. It was surprisingly warm, most likely heated by geothermal power. He ran his hands along the wall, locating a switch that illuminated the space. In the center of the room was a small suspension chamber, the kind used by the first passengers from Earth. It was filled with soft bedding, as if it had belonged to a child. Next to it was a strange chair with legs that curved up at both ends. It appeared to be made of some sort of Earth fossil, like wood. As strange as everything was, Thomas was gripped by the feeling that he'd been in the room before.

Thomas put a hand on the chair to feel its surface, and it began to rock back and forth. A small box was on its seat, and Thomas lifted its lid. Music began to play, though it was very different from the monotonous digital soundscape that flooded the Station every night. Oddly enough, he could follow the simple melody, as if he already knew it. When Thomas closed the lid, the music abruptly stopped.

Surveying the room, he saw several shelves carved into a wall, one of which held a glass case containing thin paper books. Thomas opened the case, removed one, and fanned its pages. They pictured small children playing on a *beach* near a massive *ocean*. He immediately recognized the words from the definition of *sandcastle* in his list.

Next to the books was a small yellow box, which held a variety of wax-like sticks, individually wrapped in paper, worn down at the top as if they'd been used. Each was a different color with an exotic name printed on the side, like Cotton Candy. There was even one that looked like the Earth itself, called Sky Blue. It was a color unseen on the Station.

Thomas slid them back into the box and returned it to the case with the books. In the shelf above was a clothbound replica of a small animal. Thomas recognized it from his research on domestic animals. The dog's fuzzy ears flopped over his fingers when he picked it up.

And then Thomas saw something that nearly took his breath away.

On the wall were some framed photographs of Earth. The only images of the origin planet he'd ever seen were taken from space. But these were clearly taken on the surface of the planet itself.

Thomas could that tell that the photographer had been facing a crystal blue lake, looking up at a snow-covered mountain with three separate peaks. The colors were so vivid that they appeared to be vibrating.

The last photo appeared to be upside down. But after a moment, he realized it was actually a reflection of the lake. A large animal stood at the water's edge, looking toward the camera. Thomas felt a chill on the back of his neck.

It was the same animal he'd seen in his dream.

A tapping noise sounded, and a door hidden on the wall opened, revealing a man with a walking stick. It was none other than the man with the gray-black beard that Thomas had noticed during the High Governor's address.

"Good evening, Thomas."

His voice immediately put Thomas at ease. It had a warmth that he'd never encountered from an adult on the Station. Using his walking stick, the man pointed at the photograph of the horned animal.

"Magical, isn't he? In my humble opinion, the mountain goat is the most glorious species native to that part of Colorado."

"Colorado" echoed in his brain. It was the second time in one night that Thomas heard the word.

"I'm sorry we have to meet under these circumstances. I have much to tell you, though I warn you: some of it is quite shocking. Perhaps it's best if we sit." He motioned Thomas toward a small table with two chairs. "My name is Ignatius. I was a close friend of your father's."

Thomas wasn't quite sure whether he heard the last sentence correctly. The word *father* described a relationship that no longer existed on the Station. Biological childbirth had been abandoned as part of the original settlement plan. It was part of a larger effort to weed out the self-destrucive aspects of humanity that were thought to cause Earth's demise.

"His name was Matthew Knight. We actually met when we were boys, and then again many years later as adults. We worked together on a small team of scientists documenting Earth's final days before the superfloods consumed the planet. Our outpost was on the mountain in Colorado, where those photographs were taken. Your mother gave birth to you there, a short time before we left for Mars. Indeed, you were the last child born on Earth."

Thomas felt as if he were jolted out of his body and reflexively gripped the sides of the chair to avoid falling out. Born on Earth? With a real mother and father? How could that possibly be?

"You've no doubt heard stories about the arrival of the last shuttle from Earth? And the crash that killed almost everyone?"

Thomas nodded. Every schoolboy knew the story well.

"What else have you heard? I'm of course referring to the version you're not supposed to speak about."

Thomas hesitated, though like every boy on the Station, he knew it well. "A child survived and was hidden in the Valles so that one day he could return to Earth, to start a new civilization. They say it's a myth, created by the Returners."

"It's no myth, Thomas. I was on that shuttle, as were you and your mother. A child did indeed survive and was hidden in this very room." Ignatius smiled. "That child was you."

# CHAPTER 6

THE WORDS SNAPPED TOGETHER like interlocking parts, one leading directly to the other, each providing a piece of a larger puzzle: *child, birth, mother, father.*

"I know," Ignatius said. "All this must seem unreal. Nonetheless, it's true. Here, let me show you something." He removed a thin leather folder from his pocket. Its binding was cracked with age. Inside was a yellowed photograph of two men and two women. The younger pair sat on a large boulder, while the older two stood behind them. They were on a mountainside, with the lake below. "This was taken the year before our evacuation."

Thomas easily recognized the younger man sitting on the rock. He had the same kindly eyes, the same smile, as Ignatius. "That's you," Thomas said.

"I was only thirty-one at the time. Behind me is your father, who was a few years older. Do you know the phrase 'spitting image'?"

Thomas shook his head.

"It means the resemblance between the two of you is remarkable."

Thomas studied the picture. It was like seeing himself in the future.

"Beside him is your mother, Katherine. As you can see, she's pregnant with you."

✦✦

THOMAS STARED AT THE couple, trying to process the bizarre idea that these two strangers were related to him. But the resemblance was amazing. Thomas noticed the woman next to Ignatius. Trim and athletic, with a dark complexion, she carried a backpack over one shoulder and a long weapon on the other.

"Who is she?"

"My girlfriend, Gabriela. She took the photos of Earth that hang on the wall. After we arrived on the Station, before marriage was outlawed, she became my wife. But unfortunately, she died many years ago."

"I'm sorry," Thomas said.

Ignatius nodded; his eyes filled with sadness.

"What happened to my…" Thomas stopped, unable to utter the word.

"Father?" Ignatius said. "He made the hardest decision of his life: to stay on Earth after everyone had gone. Fortunately, we worked closely with the engineers who built the Station, so we knew about the network of tunnels that were dug during its construction. Several rooms had been created as temporary living areas. After they were no longer in use, your mother chose this one as your hiding place."

"But why did I have to be hidden?"

"Biological children were not part of the Station's master plan. It was decided that the future population would be genetically designed to forego their individual desires in the service of the new civilization. As such, no children under the age of sixteen were brought to Mars."

"What about me?"

"You were the exception, smuggled on the final Shuttle. Once here, we felt it was in your best interest to be with your mother as long as possible. But when she became ill with radiation sickness, we were forced to introduce you to the general population. We created a group of guardians to watch over you. One has been with you almost constantly over the years."

"William?"

"He was your night-watchman, so to speak."

Thomas suddenly began to put the pieces together. William hadn't magically vanished but had merely dropped into one of the floor hatches.

"So, you knew I was helping Josef escape?"

"William was standing by when you broke into the Propellant Depot. Fittingly, the closest tunnel was the one that brought you here, to the very place you spent the first year of your life. After your mother passed away, we snuck you into the nursery with the rest of your birth class, complete with a fictional DNA file. That was fifteen years ago."

A wistful look came over Ignatius's face. "We've lost so much since then, some of our most precious values, and even the words to name them. The things we thought most critical to our civilization: art, romance, and family were rendered extinct in decades. And now, barely a quarter century later, we find ourselves on the brink of losing mankind's very soul."

Thomas recalled the word *soul* as part of the word *soulmate* from his list of 'S' words. He wondered how they might be connected and made a mental note to search for the definition of both.

"But enough of all that. I think you've been subjected to enough shocking information for one night. I'll tell you everything else you need to know when we get together tomorrow."

Ignatius pulled a small antique timepiece from his pocket.

"I must go. After every escape attempt, the High Governor convenes an emergency session to vent his frustration, which only masks his greatest fear: that our little community of Returners will rise up in rebellion. But your father had a very different plan for us. And for you."

Ignatius got to his feet and steadied himself on his cane.

"Try to sleep. The Station's crawling with guards, so we'll have to wait until morning to deliver you back. Before I leave, I want you to have something. It's a farewell gift from your father. I've waited so many years to finally give it to you."

Ignatius moved toward a metal cabinet and lifted out a faded backpack. "I don't know what's inside, but your mother insisted it include a new box of crayons as a special gift from her. Being water resistant, they're one of the few things that survived the floods. She thought it was of great importance for you to remember what a colorful world you came from."

He handed it to Thomas, then limped across the room and was gone.

Thomas sat on the floor and unzipped the backpack. Along with the crayons were a bag of tiny multicolored glass balls, a stack of ringed metal that could be expanded several feet, and a small contraption from which six pieces of metal, including a knife, protruded.

In a side compartment was a book about mountain climbing. Thomas opened it to find a thick paper map. On one side was the United States of America and on the other the state of Colorado. And then the backpack was empty.

Or so he thought.

At the very bottom, he could feel a weight, and discovered a hidden compartment. He unzipped it to find a rectangular box. Inside was a gleaming blue metal object. He lifted it out to see a scale replica of a train locomotive. Its name was written along the side: MOUNTAINEER.

Running his hand under the carriage, he located a switch, which brought the little locomotive to life. Its wheels rotated under his hands, eager to be set free. He put the train down, and it immediately began to circle him with a soothing hum.

It was the last thing he remembered about the night.

An object pressing against his forehead jarred Thomas awake. He saw the locomotive, sitting in the hollow between his eyes and nose, still humming with energy.

Glancing at his wrist pod, he saw that it was almost 6:00 a.m. A section of floor suddenly dropped away, and William's masked head appeared.

"Time to go."

As they drove back toward the Station, Thomas replayed Ignatius's revelations in his mind. For the first time, they made sense of his nightly dream of Earth, and even his fascination with trains. But then he suddenly recalled Josef's escape attempt. "I don't suppose you know what happened to…"

William nodded. "Two made it, two didn't."

Thomas imagined an ambulance outside the Nutrition Court, and the attendants unloading the bodies of Josef and Lina. He pictured Varik and the Moons gloating and felt a lump of anger rising in his throat.

Arriving at the shaft where they had originally entered the tunnel, William made a turn in the opposite direction. A few minutes later, he pulled the car over. As Thomas got out, William reached into his pocket.

"I think this belongs to you, Thomas." William handed him his hematite model of Earth. "I found it in Tower Twelve. You have to be more careful from here on."

Thomas slipped the hematite back into his pocket as William opened a hatch and cupped his hands.

"I'll pick you up here at five a.m. tomorrow."

With that, William thrust him up through the hatch. Thomas stepped back to get his bearings and saw that he was in an Eight-Class bathroom stall. Graffiti was laser-burned into the door in primitive letters: DEATH TO RETURNERS. A crude drawing of a pair of moons marked it as the work of Simon and Bruno.

Thomas came out of the bathroom, joining a group of boys as they filed toward class. He spotted Poke and hurried to catch up. "I hear I missed all the excitement last night."

"Actually, you didn't miss a thing. The dust devil obscured the entire escape. It wasn't worth waking up for," Poke said. "Good thing your counterpart wasn't there."

Thomas wondered if Eno was still in the Infirmary. "What's the latest on the escape?"

"Four older men: three from Waste and one Terrafarmer. All killed."

Thomas couldn't hide his puzzlement. "Older men? Are you sure?"

"Yes," Poke said. "It was repeated several times."

Thomas was about to question him further when he heard a voice from behind.

"Thomas, wait up!"

As Poke continued on, Thomas turned to see Eno hurrying to catch up. Strangely enough, there was a smile on his face. "Beautiful day. The dust devil blew through, and you can see all the way to the Mons. There are even a few rays of sunshine on the old volcano."

For a moment, Thomas thought Eno was kidding. He had never heard him describe a day as "beautiful" or comment on anything so trivial as the weather.

"I hope you didn't mind my leaving you at the Infirmary?" Eno continued. "Dr. Jax said you were still asleep in Examining and I didn't want to wake you."

Thomas realized that Eno had no idea he'd left.

"Thanks," Thomas said, changing the subject. "How's the new eye?"

"Amazing. Dr. Jax was right. The peripherals are a major improvement. Almost like having an eye in the side of my head."

"That's great," Thomas said, glancing back to see Varik and the Moons trailing a few steps behind and fast approaching. "Now all you need is one at the *back* of your head."

Varik fell into line next to Thomas with the Moons flanking Eno.

"We missed you last night," Varik said.

"I slept in the Infirmary with Eno."

"What a coincidence. You seem to go missing every time there's a defection."

"What's your point, Varik?"

"You may have everyone else fooled, but not me."

"Feel free to pass along any suspicion you might have. I'd welcome the chance to tell Professor about your little game with Eno. I can almost picture you and the Moons bouncing around in detention chambers."

Varik stiffened. Like any bully, he backed off whenever he didn't have an unfair advantage. Still, he couldn't resist a final threat.

"Sooner or later you'll slip up, Thomas. And when you do, I'll be watching."

# CHAPTER 7

As Thomas and Eno entered the classroom, they were surprised to see Professor already standing at his teaching platform.

"Boys, I'm extremely honored to announce a surprise visitor. Please stand and welcome High Governor Balthazar."

The doors opened and Balthazar entered, flanked by a pair of Commandos. The boys were awestruck, as he rarely appeared in public.

The few strands of hair on the governor's head were pulled so tightly against his scalp that they looked like black stripes. His razor-thin lips were creased into a frown that resembled a deep red scar.

"As you're all aware, there was a defection late last night. While none of the four men survived, we suspect they were aided by a fifth person, who remains at large. The accomplice was seen near the Mirror Factory prior to the incident, and we have reason to believe he may be as young as fifteen. He could even be among you now."

Out of the corner of his eye, Thomas saw Varik glance in his direction.

"I needn't remind you," Balthazar said, "that anyone who has information leading to the identification of this person is required to report it immediately."

Professor nodded. "Hopefully, they will recall something relevant. I've always taught them the importance of the power of observation."

As if they hadn't heard him, Balthazar and the Commandos made their exit.

✦✦

Thomas spent the rest of the class wondering if and when Varik would report him. He could only hope that Varik wouldn't risk another accusation without proof, particularly in front of the High Governor. If he did, he'd have to face the consequences of Thomas's own accusation about his assault on Eno. In either case, Thomas had no choice but to wait and hope for the best.

Distracted by his dilemma, Thomas was unusually quiet through dinner and barely ate. After dinner, he went directly to the Study Sanctuary and stayed until it closed. Knowing he had to be up early to meet with Ignatius, he willed himself to sleep. He woke at 4:51 a.m. and went directly to the Eight-Class bathroom stall. At 5:00 a.m., the floor opened and Thomas lowered himself down to where William was waiting.

After a few minutes in the tunnel car, Thomas realized he was being taken on a different route. They were heading toward the Government Center, the Station's innermost circle. It was the one part of the Station he'd never visited during his nightly forays, as it was protected by an elite corps of Commandos.

William pulled the vehicle to a stop and jumped out. Opening a section of the tunnel roof, he held out his interlocked hands. Thomas climbed into a large seating area with a desk and two chairs. It had a narrow wall at the very back, which parted, revealing Ignatius. He was standing in an enclosure no bigger than a closet in the Boys' Quarters and made no move to enter.

"Come along," Ignatius said, "we'll be meeting in my private room."

Thomas stood in the narrow space next to him, and as the wall closed, Ignatius pushed a button on his wrist pod and the enclosure swiveled around to face a larger space with a desk and two chairs. Ignatius took a seat behind it. "Make yourself comfortable."

Thomas sat in a chair directly facing him.

"First of all, let me put your mind at ease. We have no indication the authorities know of your part in the escape last night.

We'll continue to monitor the situation, and if we hear a word otherwise, rest assured we have a plan to protect you."

Thomas breathed a sigh of relief.

"Now, I promised you a full account of things, so where would you like me to start?"

"My father's plan for the future," Thomas said. "And for me."

"Yes, quite understandable. But in order to explain that, let me take a step back, to the beginning of the Final Evacuation on Earth. What do you know about that time?"

The topic had been well covered in school. But Thomas had spent hours in the Artifacts Museum reading first-hand accounts from the scientists themselves. Their stories were much more complicated than his Professors said, with many people acting in a heroic way to forestall the death and destruction brought about by the floods.

"The superfloods started in 2051, and the Mars Project was started ten years later, when it was known for certain the Earth would become uninhabitable."

"Correct. During those early years, the powers that be hoped there might be a solution that could alter the outcome. They consulted scientists in various fields, and many concepts were floated, but all of them sank quickly. The person with the most viable idea was your father, who was an expert in the design and construction of Biospheres. Do you know what they are?"

"Artificial habitats, built to mimic planets?"

"Right again. Early in his career, he'd built several that simulated conditions on Mars. But the important ones for the global powers were the ones he built for Earth. They contained all the components of life on the planet, everything from miniature farms to hummingbirds, and it was thought they might be a way for people to survive the floods."

"But they weren't?"

"Unfortunately, no. The carbon dioxide caused by growing food was lethal, so extra oxygen was needed to offset it. And since they'd need to be built at high elevations to escape the floods, even more was required. But your father refused to give up on the idea, and before you were born, he built one on a mountaintop near our last outpost in Colorado."

Ignatius opened the desk drawer and withdrew a folded piece of paper. He opened it to reveal a large sketch. Thomas could see that the glass-enclosed structure was as big as the Station's Planetarium and Birthing Lab combined. In the background were a series of three jagged peaks, and the blue light reflected off the glacier below filled the Biosphere with the same color.

"It looks amazing," Thomas said.

"Yes. It was quite wonderful. Your father even considered staying there with you and your mother instead of going to Mars."

"Why didn't he?"

"Apart from the oxygen problem, you'd be forced to live in isolation at an extreme elevation, with no ability to even go outside, like here. It wouldn't be much of an existence. And certainly not the one he wanted for you."

Ignatius refolded the sketch and put it away.

"But there was another reason as well. As the last of the shuttles left Earth, there was increased conflict over who'd be given passage and who'd be left behind. As the floods worsened, millions were left homeless, including many children who were orphaned. One day a large group of them showed up at our outpost, and your father came up with the idea of sheltering them in his Biosphere."

Thomas felt a wave of disappointment. He couldn't help wondering why his father hadn't chosen to save *him*.

Once again, it seemed as if Ignatius could read his mind. "I know it might seem like your father abandoned you, but the opposite was true. Part of his plan was to ensure your survival. But he also had faith in your potential to help save those children, and ultimately, Earth itself."

"How?"

“Because of the oxygen issue, the Biosphere couldn’t sustain the children for very long, perhaps a year or so. Ultimately, someone would be required to release them before they perished. That person was meant to be you. Assuming of course, you were to agree.”

“And if I do, I’d be traveling back to Earth?”

“Yes,” Ignatius said, standing up. “And that’s where I come in.”

He pulled a small pod from his pocket and pointed it at the opposite wall, which slid open to reveal several rows of shelves filled with books.

“Welcome to my secret library.”

Thomas guessed that there must be at least a hundred books. He had never seen so many, not even in the Artifacts Museum, where most were under protective glass. These were out in the open and close enough to touch.

“Where did you get them all?”

“I brought them from Earth. Most are dedicated to the same subject, and several I actually wrote.”

Ignatius approached the wall and removed a particularly thick volume.

“Time travel?” Thomas said, with a mixture of surprise and disbelief.

“I know, your professors regard it as junk science, as did most scientists on Earth. But when the superfloods arrived, even the most outlandish ideas were given serious consideration. Since I’d done research in the field, I was asked whether it was possible to go back in time and undo the damage done by mankind.”

“Was it?” Thomas asked.

“No. The principles of time travel don’t allow us to undo the past, or at least not the way people think. And I use the word ‘principles’ very loosely, as time itself remains something of a mystery. But I’m getting ahead of myself. As oxygen was the problem for the Biospheres, ‘destination’ was the problem for time travel.”

“Destination?”

"The *mechanics* are relatively simple and have been known for years. One merely needs a lead enclosure of at least ten thousand pounds and a means to attract enough negative energy to traverse a wormhole. But without the ability to pinpoint *when* and *where* one is going, *actual travel* is useless. For that, one needs a map of time and space. And since none existed, I was forced to become a cartographer of spacetime."

Ignatius put his arm into the gap left by the volume now in his hand and removed a square case. He handed it to Thomas and put the book back in the shelf. "Go ahead, open it."

Thomas opened the case to reveal a titanium ball about five inches in diameter. It reflected the library as if it were a small planet itself.

"You can take it out. But be careful."

Thomas removed the ball. It was much heavier than he expected.

"There's a button on the bottom. Press it."

Thomas did, and thousands of shafts of light instantly emanated from the surface in a mesmerizing kaleidoscope. Without stopping, each shaft then began to produce branches of its own and within seconds produced other branches, completely filling the room with pinpoints of light. They began to blink, as if welcoming Thomas.

"Each shaft represents a different location in the space-time continuum," Ignatius said.

"But how do you know which is where, or when?"

"For that you need the companion document, which is kept in a different place so that no one can decipher the code. It's hardly perfect, but ultimately does the trick."

"So, you've traveled through time?"

"Twice."

"What's it like?"

"Other than some vertigo, it isn't particularly uncomfortable, though the end result would be confusing to a novice."

"What do you mean?"

"The globe tracks your general objective in time and space, though the exact *route* can seem random. Time emits a powerful gravitational force—a *tide* so to speak. While I wouldn't say it has a mind of its own, it can seem as if it's delivering you to the place where you need to be in order to connect to your ultimate destination. Do you understand?"

"It takes you where you want to go but in its own way?"

"Exactly. Which means it can often require more than one time-jump to reach your destination. But in my case, I discovered that the journey turned out to be every bit as important as the end point. I came to think of it as the intersection of destination and destiny, if that makes any sense."

"I guess," Thomas said, trying to wrap his mind around the complicated idea.

"At any rate, there are some basic rules you need to be aware of."

Thomas sat up, excited to hear more about the actual travel.

"First and foremost, you can't occupy the same timespace as yourself."

"So, I couldn't meet an older or younger me?" Thomas said.

"No. Each of us has unique time energy, a kind of temporal DNA. And if two identical energies come into contact, the collision produces a volatile reaction. On my first jump, I came into contact with my younger self and was blown out of time, or as I call it, 'timeblown.' I managed to survive, but just barely. In any event, it's to be avoided at all cost."

"I understand," Thomas said.

"The second rule is, as I've said before, you can't alter the past. That's why we can't go back and somehow undo the planetary destruction on Earth."

"But isn't my mission to change the past?"

"No. It's to create a new future."

"I'm not sure I get the difference."

"Think of time as a tree with many branches. The act of inserting a new human presence in any given time forms a new branch, connected to the old at the time of landing and different from the original trajectory of the first branch. An offshoot if you will."

Thomas furrowed his brow, trying to hold the image in his brain.

"In practical terms, nearly twenty years have passed since we abandoned Earth, so we have to assume the Biosphere is filled with carbon dioxide and the children perished. Since we can't bring them back to life, our only option is to return to a time when they're alive."

"But won't the Earth still be flooded?" Thomas said.

"Yes. One of the challenges of the mission will be to navigate the worst of it. But, purged of mankind, the planet will eventually heal itself. The computer models predict that the floods recede by the turn of this century, somewhere around 2100. Your mission will be to reach the Biosphere, release the children from suspension, and take them to the future."

"And do what?" Thomas said, completely bewildered.

"That's the easy part." Ignatius smiled. "Restart the human race."

# CHAPTER 8

MINUTES LATER, THOMAS FOUND himself sitting on the floor, his back against the wall, having blacked out. He quickly realized he'd spent the unconscious time on Earth, in a dream state, wandering around the forest, shadowed by the same animal that always appeared in his dreams. After a while, he sensed that the animal might be leading him somewhere, though he didn't know where. But as he brushed against one of the trees, he felt a tingling sensation on his face, which seemed to wake him. He looked up to see Ignatius standing in front of him with a tray that held a strange looking pot. Steam billowed from the spout, filling the cell with a sharp aroma.

"Are you all right, Thomas?"

"I think so. I was dreaming."

"I've brought you some tea, a beverage that was popular on Earth. I packed a small amount to bring on the shuttle and saved enough for special occasions. I've been waiting to tell you about your father's plan for many years, so this certainly qualifies."

Ignatius put the tray on a table and poured the amber liquid into two cups. He handed one to Thomas, who took a sip.

"It's called 'lemon,' from a fruit that grows on a tree."

Thomas could feel the flavor explode in his mouth, bringing his senses back to life.

"Perhaps we should wait until tomorrow to continue our discussion."

Thomas sat up, anxious to hear whatever else Ignatius had to say.

"No, I'd like to hear more, if that's all right."

Ignatius smiled. "Do you have any questions so far?"

"Well, to start with…why did my father want me to take on this mission?"

"The simple answer is that you were the very reason for its existence."

"I don't understand," Thomas said, taking another sip of tea.

"The only way he could justify sending you away from Earth was by coming up with a plan to bring you back. It was meant as his gift to you, the most valuable thing he had to give—an inheritance so to speak. But of course your legacy is a mixed blessing. If found out, you'll be considered a traitor here on Mars, and we both know what that means. On Earth, you'd be considered an alien, perhaps even a fugitive, hunted and…possibly worse, so…"

Ignatius's wrist pod began to strobe. He checked it with concern. "Hmmm. Seems I have a visitor."

Ignatius turned on a monitor mounted on the opposite wall, which revealed the outer sitting room Thomas had come through earlier. It showed the sitting room door, which opened to reveal the High Governor. He was shadowed, somewhat literally, by a giant of a man. Thomas could only make out his massive torso, towering above Balthazar's head.

"I see he's brought Bron along."

Thomas immediately recalled his conversation with Josef about the powerful interrogator with the deep black eyes. "Should I hide?"

"No, you should stay and watch. It should be very informative."

Ignatius hurried back into his living quarters, as Thomas swiveled the monitor to see him greet the governor. Thomas hoped the Interrogator would take a step closer so he could see his face, but Bron remained in the background, still headless.

"High Governor Balthazar," Ignatius said. "What a surprise."

Balthazar waved a hand in front of his face. "What is that noxious odor?"

"I was applying some medicinals to counter the tribulations of age," Ignatius said, quickly changing the subject. "Did you have some urgent business?"

Balthazar sat while Bron stood in place. "As the only original settler on the council, I'd like your opinion about a piece of legislation I plan to introduce."

"Of course," Ignatius said, taking a seat opposite Balthazar.

"Lately I've been thinking about the future, specifically the turn of the century in less than twenty years. In that regard, I've come to believe we're long overdue in giving our planet a proper name."

"I was under the impression that it already had one," Ignatius said.

"Oh, I have no intention of dropping 'Mars,'" Balthazar said. "We could hardly improve on its history or symbolism. The fact that we're named after the Roman god of war gives us a special potency."

"Yes," Ignatius said. "Though I sometimes wonder *who* and *what* exactly we're at war *with*."

"The past," Bron said, his deep voice booming. "And those who cling to it."

"Indeed," Balthazar nodded. "It's the term 'Station' that's problematic. It implies that we're connected to Earth by some sort of invisible umbilical cord. It's time we severed it."

"An inspired idea," Ignatius said. "Though of course not everyone will be happy about cutting the cord, to use your metaphor."

Balthazar shifted uncomfortably in his chair. "I know you wield great influence with the original settlers. That's why I need your support on the matter."

"You have it," Ignatius said eagerly, hoping to end the reason for the governor's visit. "Was that all?"

Balthazar stood, and for a moment Thomas thought he was about to go. Instead, he began to move in the direction of the monitor. "There is one other matter. You've heard about last night's defection?"

"Yes, though I haven't had a chance to read the daily log for details."

"Up to now, these Returners have been an annoyance. But when they begin to impact the young, they threaten the very foundation of our society."

"I don't understand. I thought the escapees were older men?"

Balthazar stopped abruptly, his head so close that Thomas could see the veins on his scalp throbbing with agitation.

"Actually, they were seventeen-year-olds. One of them was even female."

Ignatius did his best to appear shocked. "I had no idea."

"We chose not to release that information publicly, lest the incident take on larger meaning. The boys were factory workers, but the girl was a member of the Redstar Group."

"A Cerebral consorting with factory workers? What could she have been thinking?"

"Indeed," Balthazar nodded.

Ignatius glanced at Bron. "Have you interrogated her yet?

Bron's body stiffened. "She got away with the ringleader. The other two were killed."

"Ah," Ignatius said. "That means you're without an informant?"

Bron glowered defensively, but didn't respond.

"Most unfortunate," Ignatius said.

"Perhaps not," Balthazar said. "We have reason to believe another boy was involved in the incident. He could prove far more significant."

"I'm not sure I follow," Ignatius said.

"I refer to the legend. That a child was hidden after the arrival of the last shuttle. The Returners believe he'll someday lead them back to Earth. Surely you're familiar with it."

"No. Perhaps you forget: I wasn't schooled here on the Station. In any event, surely you don't believe that nonsense?"

"Of course not," Balthazar said. "But one can't underestimate the gullibility of youth. As we know from Earth history, these childish myths can take on a life of their own. Our society is at a critical juncture. The next century will see us harness the energy of the sun and become the first Type Two Civilization in the history of humanity. But with our limited population, we can't afford a loss of manpower. Consequently, we can't let anyone undermine our future by abandoning our effort for fantasies about the old world."

"What are you suggesting we do?"

Bron suddenly leaned forward, revealing his head, which was dominated by his eyes. They were even darker than Thomas had imagined.

"Find this boy," he said. "And eliminate the myth once and for all."

# CHAPTER 9

Thomas dropped down the hatch behind William and Ignatius, and without speaking, they loaded themselves into the tunnel car. William drove so fast that the car lurched from side to side, barely staying upright. On several turns, Thomas felt his arm brush the tunnel wall and had to grip the car's metal frame to keep from being thrown out. Ignatius sat behind them, barely moving, as if anchored by some invisible force. All Thomas could think about was Balthazar and Bron. He wondered how long it would take them to track him down.

As they rumbled through the tunnel, Ignatius leaned forward to make himself heard.

"Don't worry about them, Thomas. They'll focus their immediate search on Josef's friend Zev, and it will buy us time."

"Time?" Thomas muttered, wondering exactly what he meant.

"For you to make your decision," Ignatius said. "Now that Balthazar has made his intentions clear, it won't be safe for you in the Station much longer. But that's not to say you have to accept the mission. You still have a choice in the matter."

"If you decide against it, you can always live at the Returner Compound," William said.

Thomas nodded mechanically. If he disappeared from the Boys' Quarters, he'd immediately be branded a traitor. It was one thing for Varik to accuse him of treason but another for the authorities to make it official. As for the Returner Compound, living under a volcano might just be another version of life on the red planet. Different, but no better.

Ignatius put a hand on his shoulder, bringing him back to reality. "It's the most important decision of your life, Thomas, and I'm sorry you have to make it so quickly. We'll respect your answer either way, I promise you."

"How much time do I have?"

"We'll pick you up tonight. You can tell us then."

Thomas sighed. A single day, to decide the rest of his life.

When Thomas got back to his cell, Eno was face down on his sleep pad. Using the rail of the bed, Thomas quietly vaulted over him to the top bunk and checked his wrist pod. It was just past five o'clock, and he had to get up in two hours. Exhausted, he fell asleep and woke to see Eno already dressed and hunched over his work table.

Thomas stayed in bed, hoping to avoid any conversation. His cellmate was so engrossed in whatever he was reading that he didn't even look up. He admired how easily Eno could shut out the world. If only he could do the same. But a list of pros and cons had already begun to assemble in his mind, fighting each other for attention.

The most compelling thing in favor was obvious. He'd always been fascinated by Earth, drawn to it in some strange way that he couldn't understand. But when he really thought about being there forever, it was the planet of the past that intrigued him, not the empty wasteland it was now. He'd simply be trading a radioactive world for one that was flooded.

Then again, what kind of life could he expect by staying on Mars? In order to avoid a future in the water mines or Mirror Factory, he'd need to focus on school and abandon his nightly wandering—not to mention his preoccupation with Earth.

Then there was the whole business of his *father*. Other than the backpack filled with random toys, the only thing he'd gotten from him was a lost childhood on a barren planet sixty-five million miles from his birthplace.

Finally, there was the mission itself. Traveling the *tide of time,* whatever that was, on a quest to rescue some orphans and start a new civilization. The very concept was difficult to hold in his mind without shattering into a dozen unanswerable questions. And if he failed, Thomas would not only be responsible for the death of seventeen children but also be forced to live the rest of his life entirely alone—an alien on an alien planet.

Thomas felt his heart sink. He was no closer to a decision than before he slept. The only good news was that he had eleven hours to figure it out. The way things were going, he'd need every single minute.

Eno got up and left the cell without saying anything. He seemed to be just as distracted as Thomas, but then again, it was the first Friday of the month when he spent the day with the Redstar research group. As Eno went out the door, Thomas suddenly had a strange thought. If he were to leave Mars, he'd never see his counterpart again. They'd been living together since they were children, and despite all their differences, Eno was his Martian "brother." For better or worse, it would be strange to suddenly be without him.

Thomas sleep-walked through the morning, ate lunch alone, and spoke to no one during the after-school exercise regimen. At some point, it occurred to him this was the way he spent most days and no one would think he was acting differently. This was life on Mars: boring but safe. But perhaps that was better than a risky one on Earth.

He skipped dinner and returned to his cell with only a few remaining hours to make his final decision. Moments after his arrival, Eno entered, and slid into his bed without speaking. Normally Eno would at least complain about whatever happened with the Redstar group that day. Perhaps he'd had another encounter with Varik and didn't want to admit it. In any event, his behaviour was odd. Thomas was about to ask him about it, when he noticed something unusual.

Outside the portal, the constellation of lights that lit the mirror fields blinked out. A moment later, the lights in their cell did the same, meaning that the power was out in the entire Boys Quarters. The Station was prone to power failures in any one of its stumpy legs but rarely at the same time.

A disembodied voice from Eno's bunk confirmed the situation. "It's a Station wide failure."

"How do you know?" Thomas said.

"We were talking about it in Redstar just today. They're experimenting with a new power system, but in my opinion it's poorly conceived. Now they have to reboot the whole Station, one leg at a time. It'll take all night, possibly longer."

Thomas felt a wave of relief at the fortunate coincidence. At least the power outage would provide some cover to meet Ignatius.

"Terrible timing," Eno said.

"Why so?"

"I need to charge my new eye, and now I'll have to get back to the Infirmary in the dark."

"What makes you think Dr. Jax has power?"

"He has his own backup for emergencies," Eno said, climbing out of bed.

"You're going now? You just got here."

"I'm in no mood to sleep. Besides, I'm sure you could use the solitude."

"What do you mean by that?"

Eno paused at the door. "I can see that you've been extremely conflicted about something lately. Which is not like you. Whatever's on your mind, you should stop thinking about it."

"Stop *thinking* about it? That's strange advice, coming from you."

"Not at all. After living together all these years, I can honestly say that you're one of the most simple-minded people I've ever met. And I mean that in the best sense of the word. Your mind is clear and straight-forward, uncluttered by the kind of complicated thinking that can often sabotage us Cerebrals. It's a great strength, believe me, and you should rely on it."

With that, Eno left. Thomas couldn't decide whether his advice was an insult or a compliment, but either way, he had to admit something else. A sense of dread had been building since he first met Ignatius and heard his father's plan. The responsibility for fulfilling it felt like an impossibly heavy burden that would be with him the moment he agreed to take it on. In fact, he could already feel its weight. Beyond all the pros and cons, it was too much to bear.

Eno was right. It was time to stop thinking and make a decision.

Thomas breathed a huge sigh of relief.

His decision was made.

## CHAPTER 10

WITH ENO GONE AND the Station darkened by the power outage, Thomas had no trouble getting to the hatch where William was waiting. He drove farther from the Boys' Quarters than usual, until the tunnel gradually narrowed to a point where Thomas had to duck to avoid scraping his head. Finally, it came to a dead end and disappeared above them, as if it had suddenly turned skyward.

A ladder was bolted to the wall. William got out and pulled open a compartment next to it. Inside were a pair of hazard suits, the kind used by maintenance crews. One couldn't survive more than a few minutes in the outside temperature, let alone the radiation, without protective gear. Like every boy in the Station, he'd never set foot on Martian soil. So the suits could only mean one thing: They were going outside.

William handed him a suit and put one on himself. He then began to climb the ladder, which stretched more than twenty feet high. Thomas's heart beat rapidly at the prospect of leaving the confines of the Station. William opened a hatch and climbed out. Thomas eagerly followed.

They emerged into an outcropping of rocks that hid them from view. Behind it was a strange little hybrid aircraft, equal part car and rocket, covered with a dark rust that blended into the landscape. Unlike the sleek Ramjets, it was patched together from an older aircraft. William pulled open the cockpit and gestured for Thomas to climb into the rear before taking the pilot's seat himself. He turned on the ignition, and the engine sputtered to life.

"It's not the newest ship on the planet, but she's reliable as hell," William said.

With that, the rocket car lurched forward, shaking and rattling along the uneven Martian ground until it reached a speed of a hundred miles an hour, at which point it became airborne.

Thomas glanced back to the Station and could see it in its entirety for the first time in his life. The giant reptile looked pathetic, sprawled on the ground as if it had collapsed in exhaustion.

The rocket car wobbled as it went higher, straining to overcome the thin air, then leveled off at a few hundred feet, staying low to avoid detection. Ahead, Thomas could see the Mons. A jumble of stars appeared at the top, as if they were erupting from the mouth of the volcano.

William pointed to the ground, where a collection of aging rovers, satellites, and supply ships were scattered. "It's called the Graveyard, where the original exploratory missions from Earth landed twenty-five ago. That's where I got the parts for our aircraft."

In another nine minutes, they landed at the foot of the Olympus Mons. The rocket car rolled toward a set of hydraulic doors built into the mountain itself. They opened, allowing the aircraft to enter a huge cavern. William opened the cockpit, and Thomas heard a gurgling sound.

He looked out, speechless.

A waterfall cascaded down the wall and into an oval pool. Thomas had seen water running through the delivery tubes at the Station, but he'd never witnessed it flow freely. The sound was almost musical.

William stayed by the rocket car while Ignatius appeared from behind the waterfall.

"Thomas! Welcome to the Returner Compound. Our people have been anxiously awaiting your arrival."

"They know who I am?"

"Of course. You're famous here. In addition to being your father's son, word has spread of the help you gave our young escapees. Come inside and I'll give you a quick tour."

They walked past the waterfall, and Thomas reached out to let the water trickle over his fingers. They went through a second cavern, ringed with live trees, which Thomas had only seen in dioramas at the Artifacts Museum. Banks of lights hung above them, like artificial suns, illuminating fruits of various shapes and colors. They passed one filled with small yellow balls.

*Lemons*, Thomas guessed.

They continued into a third cavern filled with modest living structures, some built directly into the rock. Standing outside were small groups of people ranging in age from eighteen to eighty. Ignatius stepped forward to address the gathering.

"Thomas Knight, allow me to introduce you to the Returners."

The crowd clapped enthusiastically, and Thomas spotted Josef, who wore a sling on his arm. Lina stood by his side, beaming.

"We can never thank you enough," Josef said.

"We made you a small gift to show our appreciation," Lina said, sliding a thin gold chain over Thomas's head. Attached to the end was a small titanium disc. She kissed him on the cheek.

The Returners applauded once again, and Ignatius held up his hand.

"With any luck Thomas will return for another visit," Ignatius said. "But tonight, I'm afraid his time is precious."

A vehicle appeared from the cavern interior, and Ignatius gestured for Thomas to get in. He could still feel the imprint of Lina's kiss as they drove through a wide passageway. It was filled with a series of caverns dedicated to terra farming, water storage, and even recreation.

Ignatius pulled over and stopped. "What do you think of our little community so far?"

"Amazing," Thomas said.

"It's the work of many people, passionate about living a different sort of life."

"I can see that," Thomas started. "But I think I should tell you…"

"You've come to a decision then?"

"Yes." Thomas felt his throat catch, and he coughed nervously. "I'll do it," he blurted out, as if someone else had suddenly taken control of his voice.

Ignatius smiled, more from relief than joy. "May I ask why?"

Thomas hesitated. He honestly didn't know the answer. When he left the Boys' Quarters, he'd made up his mind to turn down the mission, but somewhere, somehow, *something* had changed it. Maybe it was Eno's advice to avoid the complicated thinking he warned him against.

Perhaps the decision hadn't come from his brain at all but some deeper part of his being. All he knew was that it felt right.

"There's no need to explain," Ignatius said. "But you should know I never had my doubts. You are, after all, your father's son."

"What happens now?" Thomas said.

"Now? We have work to do."

Ignatius started the vehicle and drove forward into a cavernous space, where several larger vehicles skirted back and forth, carrying workmen.

They got out, and Ignatius led Thomas into a room with a high wall at one end. Embedded in the wall was a glass-enclosed shelf holding Time Globes of various sizes. The rest of the wall was covered with sketches and blueprints, most of them on paper.

"This room is our Time Center," Ignatius said. "It contains a history of the research and development that went into time travel." He picked up a globe that was three times bigger than the one he'd held in the library. "An early prototype. But at eighty pounds, not very practical."

He led Thomas to a door that opened into a much larger space where several transports of various shapes were stored. "This is our garage. Are you familiar with the term?"

"A library for cars?"

"You could say that, yes," Ignatius smiled. "Though in this case, Time Transports." He pointed to one about twenty feet high and covered with rectangular mirrors, several of which were seared with burn marks. "That's the one I used for my first-time travel journey."

"Will I be traveling in one like that?"

"No, yours is much bigger, as it will need to carry a large group of children. Come."

Ignatius led Thomas down several flights of stairs into a cave at least twice the size of the others. An oval extension had been carved out of the volcanic rock in the ceiling. Directly underneath was a cylindrical ship, almost a hundred feet tall, surrounded by scaffolding. Tapered at the top, it had two short stabilizer wings pointed at the ground.

"Do you recognize this?" Ignatius said, leading Thomas to the ship.

Thomas had seen it in photographs at the Artifacts Museum. "An original Earth shuttle? I didn't think any still existed."

"They don't. This was rebuilt from the wreckage of the one you, your mother, and I traveled on. We've spent years retrofitting it for your mission." Ignatius drew his hand over its surface. "What better way to return to Earth than in the ship that brought you here?"

Up to now, the prospect of going to Earth had seemed to Thomas like a strange fantasy. But seeing the actual transport that would take him there suddenly made it real. Several workers moved about on top of the scaffolding, attaching large sections of mirror to the shuttle's surface. A few panels were already in place, making the shuttle's nose shimmer in the lights.

"What are the mirrors for?" Thomas said.

"They conduct negative energy, to propel the ship through a wormhole."

As Ignatius spoke, a pair of men appeared, carrying another object Thomas recognized from a diorama in the Artifacts Museum.

"A suspension chamber?"

"Also an original. But updated, of course."

"So, I'll be asleep during time travel?"

"Technically, no. But you'll experience a state of unconsciousness that could last anywhere from a few seconds to several hours."

Thomas watched as another pair of men appeared with a second suspension chamber. The obvious question flashed into his mind. "Is someone going with me?"

"Yes. You'll have a Navigator, who'll also serve as a Protector. I've been training him for some time now, but it's finally time for you to meet."

Footsteps echoed on the stairs. Thomas turned to see the profile of a man even taller than William standing at the entrance. "That's him?"

"No. That's Luke, his driver."

Luke stepped aside to reveal a much smaller figure. Thomas thought that his eyes were playing tricks on him. The figure appeared to be a small boy, who stepped into the light.

It was Eno.

## CHAPTER 11

Even with the shocking revelations of the past few days, nothing could have prepared Thomas for this. But before he could begin to make sense of it, Eno was standing in front of him. Ignatius put a hand on each of their shoulders.

"The secrecy regarding your participation in the mission was dictated by concerns for your safety. But now that Thomas has signed on, it's critical that you start working as a team. I wanted you both to see the transport for the first time together, as you could very well be sharing it for the better part of your lives."

With that, Ignatius headed back up the stairs.

Thomas and Eno stood facing each other for an awkward moment.

"After you," Thomas finally said.

"No, you're the mission leader. You should go first."

Thomas was immediately struck by Eno's attitude, which was respectful and even humble. It was as if he were meeting his counterpart all over again, only now he had a different identity. In a way, that's exactly what was happening. Almost everything he knew about Eno would have to be reexamined in light of his new role in Thomas's life.

Thomas climbed into the shuttle, followed by Eno. A thin set of stairs ran along the interior with a cable that served as a guardrail. On the first level, the passenger compartment held individual travel pods on each side. Thomas made a silent count.

"Twenty sleep chambers?" he said.

"Enough for us and seventeen orphans, with one to spare. Nine females and eight males, ages four to sixteen."

"I think Ignatius mentioned that," Thomas said, pretending he knew as much about the mission as Eno, though it was clear his cellmate was way ahead of him.

"When Ignatius first went over the mission objective with me, I asked all the pertinent questions. Apparently, the orphans were led by a very capable sixteen-year-old girl."

"Did you happen to get her name?"

Eno looked puzzled. "No. Do you think it's important?"

Thomas smiled.

"Ah, you were making a joke."

They continued to the top level, where the stairs ended at a semi-circular room that faced a control panel of some sort.

"This is the navigation board," Eno said. "I've been training on an identical simulator."

"For how long?"

"Nearly two years."

"Wow," Thomas said. "And you never even hinted about what was going on."

"I was under strict orders from Ignatius. Sorry."

"No, I understand," Thomas said, though he couldn't help feeling embarrassed that he'd been fooled for so long.

"So, the whole business about your being with the Redstar group?"

"I am a member, and we do meet on the first Friday of the month, but only for an hour or so. The rest of the time..."

"Training?"

"Correct."

"And the power outage at the Station?"

"Sabotage by the Returners to give us cover for tonight."

Thomas shook his head in amazement. "Just out of curiosity, how did you get involved with all this in the first place?"

"A year or so ago, Doctor Jax engaged me in a discussion about genetic engineering. Apparently he'd read my Seven-Class Annual about the rise of organ replacements on the Station."

"You mean eyes?"

"Eyes, lungs, and a recent spike in hearts. Dr. Jax explained that at the rate things were going, we'd effectively devolve into machines during our lifetime. When I expressed concern, he told me that the Station leadership didn't believe there was a profound difference between man and machine, and if that's what it took to achieve a Type Two Civilization, so be it."

"Unbelievable," Thomas said, shaking his head.

"Yes. Needless to say, I was as shocked as you. And when he saw my reaction, he told me there was someone who had an idea about how to subvert the Station's ambition. A few months later, he took me to meet Ignatius, who revealed your father's plan and your potential role in it. He explained how I might participate by becoming your Navigator and Protector."

Thomas nodded. He had no doubt that Eno would make a great Navigator, but the choice of his fragile counterpart as Protector left him baffled.

"I wouldn't blame you for being disappointed," Eno said. "A Navigator is one thing, but I'm hardly the ideal candidate to provide you with physical security ."

"I'm sure Ignatius had his reasons."

"As it turns out, he did. Unbeknownst to me, I was born for the job. You might even say created. One of Ignatius's responsibilities in the early days of the Station was oversight of the Birthing Lab. He identified me as a potential Navigator and made sure my DNA equation had an excess of loyalty genes. Whatever else I might lack, you need never doubt my allegiance. If it comes to it, I won't hesitate to give up my life for yours."

Thomas was stunned. Every aspect of the mission, including the very nature of Eno's existence, had been planned for many years.

Still, something bothered him.

"But if you were born for the job, why did you have to be recruited?"

"While I'm genetically designed, I'm not a robot. Ignatius believed it was crucial I undertake the mission of my own free will."

"And you agreed, even though it meant traveling to Earth?"

"I won't lie. As you well know, Earth has never held the fascination for me it does for you. Mars is my birthplace, and the Station my home. But I believe everyone should have the freedom to decide. And no one should be hunted down and killed for their choice."

Thomas suddenly felt terrible for doubting Eno's worthiness. But before he could apologize, William was on the scaffold, gesturing for them to come down.

Thomas and Eno climbed out of the shuttle to find Ignatius waiting.

"I'm afraid we have much more to accomplish, and the night is short. Eno, you'll need to go with Luke. Thomas, come with me."

Ignatius led Thomas into the next cave. Unlike the others, its ceiling was flat. A table in the center held four silver cases of various sizes and shapes.

As Ignatius turned on the overhead lights, Thomas inspected the gold chain Josef and Lina had given him. A tiny crystal twinkled at the bottom.

"Hold it to the light."

Thomas did, and an image of the Returner community appeared, with Josef and Lina standing at the front, waving. It was a holograph.

"Now turn it over."

Another holograph appeared, clearly made from a photograph taken in Colorado. Thomas's mother and father stood on a mountainside. Behind them, in the deep background, was a ragtag group of children. The seventeen orphans of Earth. Thomas held it up for a closer look, but the image was too small to make out their faces. But with their colorful clothing and variety of skin complexions, they looked like a different species than the children on Mars.

"With any luck," Ignatius said, "you'll be the one to save them. And in doing so, save Earth itself. But to that end, we have to ensure your own survival. I want to familiarize you with a few items that should help."

Ignatius picked up the first case and opened it to reveal six thin bars of metal.

"Gold?" Thomas said.

"Worthless here, I know, but on Earth it's used for currency."

"I thought that Earth money was made from paper?"

"It quickly became obsolete after the start of the superfloods, which brings us to the subject of fish. What do you know about them?"

"Aquatic creatures. There were thousands of species before the extinctions."

"Indeed. But the one you need to be most concerned with is the megalodon. A prehistoric shark, dormant in the lower depths of the oceans until the floods awakened them. Or at least that's the theory. One took my leg."

A look of horror crossed Thomas's face, but Ignatius smiled.

"It wasn't as bad as it sounds. I was drowning at the time, so it was a small sacrifice for my survival. But hopefully this should protect you from a similar fate." Ignatius picked up a triangular case and removed a black metal tube about ten inches long and four inches wide. Underneath was a trigger mechanism. "After centuries at the bottom of the oceans, the megalodon's sense of hearing became extremely sensitive. This device is called a Sonic Inducer. It emits a deafening underwater charge and is the only known defense against them."

Ignatius picked up a third, much smaller case.

"In the event you're forced to stay under water for more than a few minutes, this will prove indispensable."

Thomas opened the case to find a white cylinder with a small rubber mouthpiece.

"It's called a Porta Gill, and it allows you to breathe by converting the oxygen dissolved in the water. It was one of many devices invented to survive the floods, and while it won't provide long-term survival, it's quite effective in an emergency."

The final case was the smallest yet. Ignatius held it up dramatically.

"Last, but not least, I give you the Tetrascope."

The object vaguely resembled Thomas's father's folding knife. But instead of being red, it was cobalt blue with four black buttons along the side. Pressing the first, a sharp finger of metal protruded from the Tetrascope's tip.

Ignatius held it up to the light where it shimmered. "The blade is made from diamonds and will cut almost anything. And for those occasions when it won't, we have this."

Ignatius pressed the next button and a three-inch laser appeared. "It can be extended to two feet, though it diminishes in intensity as it gets longer. Go ahead, give it a try."

Thomas turned the laser toward the wall, where it bored a hole through the surface and into the permafrost, reducing the ice to steam.

"You'll inevitably confront hostile parties on Earth. At which point, you'll require the next function. Aim the Tetrascope upward."

Thomas turned off the laser and pushed the last button. A barb attached to a nearly invisible wire shot into the air and buried itself in the ceiling.

"Hold on tightly and push again."

Instantly, Thomas began to rise as Ignatius looked up at him.

"The barb's made from neodymium, the strongest magnet known to man, so it works with metal as well. Push the button again, and it will release."

Thomas did as instructed and dropped to the ground.

"There's one last feature, which could be the most important of all."

Ignatius took a few steps back and touched another button on the Tetrascope. The device emitted a high-pitched beep.

It's a Discovery Beam, which can alert you to a human presence by picking up the electrical charge of a heartbeat. It's good up to a half-mile, even through a mountain of snow or ice. This should help lead you to the children, and perhaps even your father."

"My father?" Thomas said, puzzled.

"Depending on when you arrive, there's a chance he might still be alive, monitoring the Biosphere to replenish the oxygen supply."

"How long do you think he could survive?"

"His goal was a full year, in order to give you a reasonable window of time to land. That's why you need to arrive before the end of 2071."

Ignatius handed over the Tetrascope. The pulsing beat made him feel like his father's heart was beating in his hand. It was as if they were making their first contact across time and space.

"Now that you're familiar with these tools, we can get on with the most fundamental aspect of your survival."

"What's that?" Thomas said.

"Self-defense."

# CHAPTER 12

IGNATIUS LED THOMAS TO a cave so dark he couldn't see his own feet. When his eyes adjusted, he noticed that the ground was covered in padding that extended onto the walls and ceiling.

"I'll leave you now," Ignatius said and exited.

Three figures in pale-green robes entered from the opposite door. The first was a man with muscles bulging from every part of his body. The second was smaller with a wiry build. The last was no bigger than Thomas, and he was surprised to discover it was a woman, probably in her twenties.

"My name is Marta," she said. "Diego, Eric, and I have been chosen to train you. We'll begin with a demonstration."

Diego and Eric dropped their robes, revealing formfitting uniforms. They turned to face each other, arms outward and bent at the elbows, palms sideways. The two men began to circle each other as Marta narrated their actions.

"The arms and hands are in what we call the floating position. They're prepared to attack any one of three major targets: neck, wrist, or ankle. If none are available, the aim is to engage one of two minor targets behind the knees or elbows."

As Diego and Eric made stabbing gestures toward the various targets, Eric lunged for the bigger man's ankle. With a swift move, he pulled back, sending Diego airborne. He bounced off the ceiling and landed with a thud.

Thomas looked at Marta in amazement. The height at which the bigger man traveled defied physics. "How did he do that?"

"Q-Rings," Marta said.

Diego and Eric held out their hands. Each wore a pair of silver rings on their middle fingers. A twist where the metal was joined made the rings form the letter "Q."

"Over the course of his work in time travel," Marta explained, "Ignatius developed a metal that had a minor effect on gravity. Unfortunately, it liquified in the presence of a wormhole but turned out to be effective for other applications. As you've just seen, the rings exert an energy that can help propel heavier aggressors. In the process, they also deliver a slight electric charge that causes a momentary distraction. In combination, the two things can not only disable an attacker but reduce the motivation to continue the aggression."

Marta withdrew a felt bag from her pocket and opened it, revealing a pair of similar rings. "Put one on the middle finger of each hand. When you grip your opponent, do it tightly, so that the rings embed themselves in the flesh."

Thomas slid the rings onto his fingers.

Marta removed her robe, revealing the same uniform as Diego and Eric. "Assume position," she said, holding out her arms.

Thomas imitated her stance. Marta grabbed him by the arm and whipped him across the room. Thomas bounced off the wall, stunned. Marta advanced as if she were prepared to throw him again, and he jumped to his feet. She stabbed at his wrist, which he avoided by thrusting his arms over his shoulders. But that left his knees vulnerable, and Marta attacked, tossing him so high that his kneecaps touched the ceiling. He landed on his back, breathless.

Slowly, Thomas got to his feet and resumed position. She reached out to take his hand, but Thomas lunged for her legs, pushing the surface of the Q-Rings into the soft flesh behind her calves. With that, he flipped her upward. To his disappointment, she barely left the ground.

"Keep in mind, it's not an issue of strength, like lifting a heavy weight. It's more like tossing a feather. Let the rings do their work."

Thomas leapt to his feet and grabbed Marta by the ankles. He lifted her as lightly as possible, and to his surprise, she flew toward the ceiling. Diego and Eric nodded with approval as Marta landed on her back. She quickly bounced to her feet.

"Good start. With a few hours work, you should get the hang of it."

✦✦

THOMAS HAD NO IDEA how much time had gone by when he finally shuffled out of the training room. Ignatius was waiting, and Thomas slid into his vehicle, wincing in pain.

"Are you all right?" Ignatius asked.

"I'll be fine once I get back to my cell and rest."

"I'm afraid we're going to have to put that on hold for a bit. There's been a change of plans, so we won't be taking you back until early morning."

"Is something wrong?"

"Since the escape attempt, there's been chatter from the governor's office about the search for Josef's friend Zev, who's currently missing. There's no indication they even know his identity, but they've suddenly gone silent, so we can't be certain. We've sent in some men to try and bring the boy out, but I have to be honest: There's a chance they might already have him."

"What can we do?"

"I'm afraid our choices are limited. If we don't bring you back to your cell by the morning count, they'll discover you're gone and assume you were party to the escape."

"Meaning I won't ever be able to return."

"Correct. The alternative is to return you to your room and find Zev before they do."

"And what if—"

"If they attempt to take you into custody, we'd mobilize our forces to retrieve you."

"How would you do that?"

"We'd have to make an assault on the Station."

"But wouldn't that be—"

"Tantamount to a declaration of war? Yes. Unfortunate as that would be, we've been preparing for such an eventuality for years."

Thomas couldn't believe this was happening. He'd decided to accept the mission only a few hours ago and already his decision might set off a war on the Station. But it was too late to change his mind, even if he wanted to.

"We'll continue to monitor the Station throughout the night," Ignatius said. "If nothing changes, you and Eno will be returned. In the meantime, we'll put all our resources into finding Zev. He's the only person who can directly implicate you."

At 5:30 a.m., Thomas found himself being driven through the tunnels on his way back to the Boys' Quarters. Every muscle on his body ached from the five-hour Q-Ring session, but his brain was working at high speed. He knew the next few hours would be critical, and he had to be constantly alert for any signs of trouble.

They pulled over and William opened the hatch.

Thomas shook Eno out of a deep sleep.

"Good luck, boys," William called out. "And don't worry, we won't fail you."

William pulled away as Thomas and Eno climbed up through the hatch. Thomas looked around to see that they were in the Boys' Quarters. "There's a hatch here?"

"They're everywhere," Eno said through a yawn.

"Like groundhog holes," Thomas said.

"Like what?"

"Groundhogs. Little creatures that dig up through the surface of Earth."

"Your arcane knowledge of the origin planet really is impressive."

They made their way to their cell and quietly entered.

"It's just after six," Eno said. "At least we have an hour to rest before class."

They collapsed into their sleep platforms. The only sound was the soft whir of the dust devil as it whipped around the planet's surface.

"I wonder what the sound of wind is like on Earth," Thomas said.

"Loud," Eno said. "And no doubt terrifying. Our thin atmosphere mutes most natural sound, even the asteroid collisions. It's one of my favorite things about Martian life."

Thomas disagreed. He was looking forward to the whine of high wind, the crackle of lightning, the roar of thunder. Anything but the never-ending silence on Mars.

After a short time, they heard the morning summons and joined the rest of the boys in the hallway headed for class. Eno turned to Thomas and shrugged, as if everything seemed fine. The class filed into the cafeteria, got their food, and took their seats. They had barely started to eat when a digital message scrolled across the wall screen:

ALL EIGHT-CLASS BOYS...PROCEED TO PLANETARIUM.

Thomas looked to Eno for his reaction.

"They know," Eno said, his voice quivering.

Thomas glanced at the doorway and could see several Professors, along with the Prefects, gathered, whispering among themselves. No way out.

The forty-eight boys began to gather at the exit. When Eno started forward, Thomas grabbed him by the arm and held him back. "We need to be last in line."

When all the boys were in the hallway, Professor raised his hand, and they began to move in unison, like a human centipede.

They filed into the Planetarium under the holograph of Mars positioned so that it occupied the center of the solar system. It cast an eerie red glow on the boys' faces. Balthazar, wearing the red uniform of the High Governor's office, appeared while his Commandos took up positions around the room. In addition to their handheld stun guns, they carried arm-length laser rifles.

"Early this morning we arrested an accomplice who was involved in the recent defection. The traitor admitted that a fifth boy collaborated in this traitorous act. I'm sorry to say that boy is a member of your own class."

A murmur swept through the room. Varik immediately looked at Thomas.

"Unfortunately, the accomplice refuses to name that boy. So I ask, in the name of our great society, for this person to do the honorable thing, and stand up to reveal himself."

No one moved.

"Very well then."

Balthazar nodded toward the side entrance, where Bron stood waiting. The Interrogator proceeded onto the stage, followed by a pair of Commandos who dragged in the shackled Zev.

"Point out the traitor," Bron said.

Zev hung his head in defiant refusal, blood dripping from the area of his missing ear. Bron grabbed him by his hair, snapping Zev's head back and forcing him to face the class.

"Point him out," Bron repeated.

Zev mumbled something inaudible, and the room hushed.

"What?" Bron asked, annoyed.

"I need my hand," Zev said.

Bron nodded to one of the Commandoes, who unshackled Zev's right arm. He stumbled forward, almost falling, as his eyes roamed across the boys.

"Where is he?" Bron commanded.

"He's over there," Zev said, pointing in the direction of Thomas and Eno.

Thomas could feel Eno's knees tremble against his as the Commandos pushed Zev toward them.

"Which one?" Bron said.

Zev pointed at Thomas.

"Him."

A pair of Commandos started toward Thomas. His first instinct was to resist, but to do so would be an admission of guilt. As the Commandoes were a few feet from Thomas, Zev shouted.

"No, I'm wrong."

The Commandos pulled up short, turning back to Bron for further instruction.

"It's him, over there," Zev said, turning to the other side of the theater and pointing at Poke. But before he could stand, Zev pointed in yet another direction. "No, it's him over there!"

The Commandos had barely altered course when Zev changed his mind yet again. "No, that's not him. It's him—and him—and him!"

"What do you think you're doing?" Bron demanded.

"If wanting to be free is traitorous, then we're all traitors!"

Bron struck Zev's good ear with his gloved hand, sending blood down his neck.

"Get him out of here!"

As the Commandos dragged Zev away, the enraged Balthazar turned to Professor. "Take them to the Birthing Lab. We'll get to the bottom of this once and for all."

A loud murmur erupted among the boys as they tried to figure out what was happening.

"Silence!" Professor shouted. "Form a line!"

Thomas whispered under his breath to Eno, "What's going on?"

Eno shook his head. "We're doomed."

# CHAPTER 13

The boys filed out of the Planetarium and into the hallway. The Commandos stationed at the door gripped their laser rifles and followed.

Thomas had visited the Birthing Lab only once but knew it was less than than nine-hundred steps, or about eight minutes, away. Eno's chest was heaving slightly, the first sign of his respiratory disorder.

"They're going to test for DNA, right?" Thomas whispered. "To see who helped Josef?"

"Yes. But that's the least of our problems. There's a basic DNA equation for each class. With slight variations, it's the same for every one of us."

"Except me?"

"The test will show you weren't genetically engineered. That you were born of biological parents."

A chill raced up Thomas's neck. A DNA test would prove that he was the child of legend—the child Balthazar had vowed to find and eliminate. And once they were in the Lab, there would be no escape.

Ahead of them, Professor approached the first connector, halfway to their destination.

Eno silently mouthed four words. "*WHAT. DO. WE. DO?*"

Thomas knew there was only one choice. "We'll have to make a run for it."

Eno looked back at the Commandos. His wheezing began to accelerate. "How are we going to get past them?"

"We're not. When everybody else makes the turn, we'll break off and circle back toward the hatch in the Boys' Quarters."

Professor came to an abrupt stop and turned to the boys. "There's to be no conversation, is that understood?"

The human centipede nodded its collective head.

Satisfied, Professor turned left into the connector. The centipede followed, its long body slowly disappearing down the hallway.

As they approached the turn, Thomas whispered a countdown. "Three. Two. One. Go!"

Thomas and Eno broke off from the end of the group and began to run.

Professor could no longer see them, but the pair of Commandos directly bringing up the rear reacted immediately.

"Stop!" one of them shouted.

The Commandos sprinted after Thomas and Eno while the centipede collapsed into an unruly crowd, animated by the sudden development.

Glancing back, Thomas saw Varik and the Moons spill out into the hallway. He made a right turn into the first connector, but Eno was now breathing heavily.

"I don't know if I can make it," Eno called.

An ear-splitting alarm pierced the hallway. Thomas looped an arm through Eno's and pulled him forward. As they turned the corner, blocking their way at the end of the connector stood three figures: Varik and the Moons.

"I knew it was you!" Varik shouted.

"Get out of the way!" Thomas yelled back.

"Simon, Bruno, get them!"

The Moons charged. Bruno was the fastest and came first, but Thomas easily sidestepped and tripped him, sending the huge boy skidding over the polished floor.

The slower Simon followed, and Thomas grabbed him by the neck. He felt the Q-Ring bury itself in his thick flesh as he lifted the Moon off his feet and hurled him toward Varik, who barely had time to dive out of the way.

Eno pointed in the other direction. "Thomas, behind you!"

Two Commandos were at the other end of the connector. To make matters worse, Bruno was back on his feet and charging. Thomas grabbed him by the wrist and tossed him toward the Commandos, sending them all to the floor in a pile of arms and legs.

Only Varik blocked their exit. Thomas held up his hands, exposing his Q-Rings, ready to take him on. "Come on then, arrest us. I'd like to see how high you can fly."

Varik took a step forward then glanced back at the Commandos still recovering from their collision with the airborne Moon.

He turned and ran.

Thomas led Eno toward the nearest connector. His detour bought them a few precious seconds, but as they came into the deserted Boys' Quarters, he staggered and fell.

Thomas picked him up and helped him forward.

As they passed the Magnum Screen, Thomas looked back to see that the two Commandos had stopped and were kneeling into firing position.

Thomas grabbed Eno and pushed him to the floor, using the momentum to slide them both toward the hatch. Once there, he rolled off Eno and lifted the hatch up as a shield against the laser fire. The Commandos continued to fire as Thomas pushed Eno into the opening then dropped through himself, pulling the overhead hatch closed.

Landing in the tunnel, Thomas flicked on his wrist pod light and helped Eno to his feet. Together, they started down the tunnel. Navigating the slippery permafrost was difficult on foot, and Thomas's light was only strong enough to see a few feet ahead, making visibility difficult.

"Maybe they won't follow us," Eno said.

A moment later, they heard the hatch clank open and saw a pair of legs descending in the darkness.

Thomas helped Eno forward, but after only a few steps he clutched his chest. "I can't do it," he said, gasping for air. "Go ahead without me."

"No way. I can't navigate the shuttle without you."

They stumbled a few more steps before a harsh light blinded them. A man in a white hazard suit appeared out of the darkness in front of them and pointed a weapon in their direction.

"Get down!" the man yelled, preparing to fire.

They dropped to the ground as a laser beam streaked over their heads. The Commandos returned fire from behind, sending hunks of permafrost to the floor. The man in the hazard suit stepped over them and kept firing as one of the Commandos fell to the floor.

The other Commando pulled a cannister from his ammo belt and tossed it at Thomas and Eno. It landed at their feet and caused a yellow flash with enough light for them to see William.

"Knockout gas," William shouted, tossing them a pair of oxygen masks. Using the smoke as cover, he led the boys toward the bottom of a rock ladder, where a pair of hazard suits were waiting. "Get these on, fast."

The smoke in the tunnel began to settle, and the Commandos reappeared, firing. William returned their fire as Thomas pushed Eno up the ladder to the open hatch. A laser hissed beneath him, and William slumped to his knees, his white hazard suit soaked with blood.

"William," Thomas said, alarmed.

"Go! Luke's waiting!"

Thomas froze. After seeing how Bron had treated Zev, he could only imagine what the Interrogator might do to William. Several more shots tore into the wall, sending shards of permafrost onto William's prone body.

"Thomas!" William screamed. "Go! Now!"

Reluctantly, Thomas crawled up the ladder and outside, where Luke was already tucking Eno into the back seat of the rocket car.

"William's hurt," Thomas said. "We have to help him."

"He can take care of himself," Luke said, shoving Thomas inside and jumping in after him.

In seconds they were rattling over the hard Martian surface in a cloud of red dust. Eno stared straight ahead, paralyzed with fear.

"Don't worry," Thomas said. "We'll be all right once we get to the Returner Compound."

"I wish that were true. Now that they know about you, there's only one place we're safe."

"Where's that?" Thomas said, puzzled.

"Earth."

# CHAPTER 14

THE ROCKET CAR LEVELED off at cruising altitude. A rumble echoed from the Station, and Thomas looked back to see the Defense Dome open.

With a low growl, the Mastership rose up like a phantom, hidden in the blackness of space. The only way Thomas could determine its position was by the squadron of Ramjets that surrounded it.

The rocket car increased speed, but within seconds, the Station fleet caught up. The Mastership appeared directly above them, suddenly reflecting the rocket car, making it look like a toy by comparison.

Thomas looked up to see Balthazar standing in the cockpit with Bron behind him. As the ship descended over the rocket car, Thomas could see his dark eyes locked onto he and Eno.

"They're going to attack!" Eno said.

"No, they're not," Luke said. "They want us alive."

"What are they doing then?" Thomas asked.

"Following us, to see where we're going."

"We're just going to let them?" Eno asked.

"We can't stop them, so we'll do the next best thing and give them a scare."

Luke abruptly slowed the rocket car, forcing the Mastership to slide ahead. He squeezed the steering mechanism and a burst of laser fire shot from the front of the car. It bounced harmlessly off the Mastership's tail section.

"We can't penetrate its exterior," Luke said, "but since Balthazar's on board, they can't take the chance. They're required by code to evade."

"How do you know?" Thomas asked.

"Because I used to fly it."

Sure enough, the Mastership began to retreat back into the protected center of the Ramjet formation, which gathered below it like a shield.

"Hold on," Luke said.

As Thomas and Eno grabbed their seats, Luke rolled the rocket car onto its side and over the deep canyons of the Valles. They dropped into the darkness of the gorge, out of sight. Luke tucked the rocket car against the walls of solidified lava and flew sideways. Eno, whose eyes had shot open when they went into a roll, quickly shut them again.

After ten minutes, the gorge opened up, and Luke turned the rocket car upright and then out of the Valles. As they banked toward the Mons, the Station fleet was nowhere to be seen.

"Where did they go?" Thomas asked.

"They're flying at a higher altitude, which bought us enough time to land."

The rocket car landed and skidded to a stop in front of the Returner Compound.

The doors opened, and Thomas leapt out to find Ignatius waiting. "Are you boys all right?"

"We're fine," Thomas said. "But William was hit…"

Ignatius put a hand on his shoulder. "Thomas, the only thing you can do for William now is complete your mission. Like the rest of us, he's counting on you."

The image of the Returner community filled Thomas's mind. He could picture Josef and Lina, their faces filled with hope.

"We didn't hear about Zev until it was too late," Ignatius said, "but I knew Eno would understand the significance of the DNA test."

Eno didn't acknowledge the compliment. His eyes were fixed on the roof of the cave, where the Ramjet squadron rumbled overhead, becoming louder by the second.

"Come along now, we haven't much time."

Ignatius led the boys into the next cave, where a backpack now rested on a table. "Thomas, it's time for you to take permanent possession of this. But always remember, the most important things your father gave you aren't inside. You have his inner compass, his nerve, and above all his instincts. Trust them." Ignatius retrieved a second backpack, sheathed in silver metallic casing. "Eno, this is yours."

Eno slung the backpack over his shoulders as Ignatius hurried to a safe mounted in the wall and removed the Time Globe case.

"I took the liberty of programming the globe. You only need to activate it."

Eno clutched the case to his chest as Ignatius put a hand on his shoulder.

"Eno, I couldn't have asked for a more brilliant student of time mechanics. I have no doubt that you'll be invaluable to Thomas and the mission."

The enormity of what was happening suddenly hit Thomas. They were headed for Earth—but also leaving the Station, never to return. He could see the sadness in Eno's face.

Suddenly a missile rocked the ground above, jolting Thomas back to the moment. He and Eno hurried after Ignatius into the Shuttle Cave.

Ignatius leaned closer to Thomas, so that they were eye to eye. "Don't forget, while you're a native of Earth, you return as an alien. There are many more things I wanted to tell you about, but now you must discover them for yourself. It will take time and patience."

Another missile landed, sending huge hunks of rock crashing to the floor.

"Always remember one thing, Thomas—you're our future!"

An even stronger missile shook the cave, punctuating his farewell.

"Good luck, boys!"

As they started down the stairs, a missile landed directly above, sending Eno tumbling. The Time Globe case dropped, and Thomas dove across him to snatch it up. With his free hand, he pulled Eno to his feet.

The shuttle hatch was already open. The boys climbed inside and hurried to the cockpit. Eno punched several buttons on the control board.

"What are you doing?" Thomas asked.

"Activating the mirrors on the outside of the shuttle. The quark attractors will start to pull us into the wormhole any second now."

Thomas felt a hum of energy vibrate through the shuttle. Eno reached up and threw open a panel above the cockpit. Inside was a network of metal rods pulsing with electricity and a hollow at the center.

Eno held out his hands. "Time Globe."

Thomas handed over the globe, which Eno inserted into the hollow. He hit another switch, and the globe began to turn. A constellation of lights made a patchwork of tiny dots across their faces. The digital timer began the countdown.

"We have sixty seconds to secure ourselves," Eno said.

Strands of white-hot light crackled around the shuttle as the boys removed their backpacks and slid into opposite suspension chambers.

Thomas flipped up his hazard helmet. He pulled the restraining straps across his chest and checked the timer—thirty seconds. Thomas glanced over at Eno. "I just want you to know, I'm glad you're coming with me."

But Eno's eyes were shut, his body curled into a tight mass, his head hidden by his arms. He gave no sign of hearing a word.

The timer reached zero.

The shuttle began to spin. The powerful wormhole tore at the cave walls, creating an artificial sandstorm. The cave itself began to vibrate, but as it reached a crescendo, the noise morphed into a strange hum, as if the cosmos itself were preparing to deliver them to some unknown realm.

And then it abruptly stopped.

"What happened?" Thomas shouted.

But the question was drowned out by a thunderous boom, and the world went black.

# EARTH

## CHAPTER 15

Thomas struggled to open his eyelids, which felt as if they were held down by lead weights. At least he didn't feel any of the vertigo Ignatius had warned him about. Other than a slight tingling at the tip of his nose, he felt remarkably good.

He heard a buzzing sound and turned on the light to see a swarm of multicolored particles floating around the cabin. They gathered around his face, hovering near his ears. And then he heard something amazing. It was the distant echo of Ignatius's voice, repeating the last words spoken to him before he got on the shuttle.

*You're our future.*

Message delivered. The particles began to disappear, snapping and popping as they went. Within seconds, they were completely gone.

Thomas glanced out the portal but could see only darkness. Eno was asleep, and he remembered Ignatius saying it might be a while before regaining consciousness after a landing. In the meantime, Thomas needed to check the perimeter to assess their situation.

He undid his harness, lifted himself out of his chamber, and fell toward the navigation cockpit. Grabbing one of the shoulder straps, he swung in the air before dropping to the ceiling. The shuttle was not only lying upside down but at a steep angle.

By working his way along the stabilizing handles, he managed to reach the stairs. At the top, he punched in the lock code and the hatch popped open. He removed his hazard suit and tossed it back inside the shuttle.

Thomas climbed outside to see that the shuttle was lying against a hillside. He was immediately struck by the colors, which were bold and bright, mimicking the ones he'd seen in his box of crayons. The sky was *cornflower*, the ground *chestnut*, and the sun a brilliant *canary*. He looked up to see that he was surrounded by towering trees. This was a forest, he thought, and the color was exactly like the crayon named for it: *forest green*. It seemed as if the Earth were dipped in fresh paint.

The air was cool and damp, but most of all fresh, not remotely like the Station's. It made his chest so buoyant that for a moment he thought he might levitate. A pair of squirrels raced across his eye line, chasing each other, and Thomas knelt down to watch them. When they disappeared into the forest, he lifted a handful of dirt from the ground. It fell through his fingers, stranding a small insect on his palm. As it crawled onto a fallen leaf, a flutter echoed from above, and a bird dropped out of the treetops and flew toward him. It landed on a branch directly overhead, only a few feet away. It had a bold blue back and a thatch of black feathers on top of its head. Thomas had never seen a bird before and couldn't quite believe his luck.

A smile broke out on his face.

There could be no doubt about it.

At long last, he was on Earth.

Thomas got up and slowly made his way downhill until he lost sight of the shuttle. He paused, wondering whether he should venture farther, when he heard a strange sound from somewhere below him. Piercing and guttural, it came in short bursts. He ducked behind one of the giant trees and peeked out to see a small black dog, much larger than the stuffed version in his mother's room but clearly the same species. Thomas had no idea how to address the animal and didn't know whether the dog would understand him.

"Hello. My name is Thomas."

A voice immediately shot back. "Nice to meet you, Thomas."

He looked up to see a girl appear behind the dog. She was roughly his age, with light brown skin as smooth as liquid and a mass of black hair that seemed to spring in every direction as if it were electrified. Her eyes seemed to glow when she smiled. Thomas couldn't help but stare at her clothes, starting at her black canvas shoes with white rubber soles. Above them were a pair of faded blue pants and a thick gray shirt with a hood of some sort. On her long neck, she wore a bright yellow cloth tied with a simple knot.

"His name is Charlie. We were setting up for lunch when we saw this flash of blue light. Did you happen to see it?"

"No," Thomas said, knowing that she must be referring to the blue shift that accompanied their landing. But since he was inside the shuttle and didn't see it, he wasn't lying.

"I'm Elly," she said. "Elly McAllister. Actually, the name's Elpis, but nobody actually calls me that except for my father when he wants to pretend he's annoyed."

Thomas had never heard a voice like hers. It had a kind of propulsive energy, as if it could keep going forever.

She thrust out her hand as if expecting Thomas to do the same. Thomas put out his hand and she took it, then gave it a quick up and down motion.

"What are you doing out here, hiking?" Elly said. "I hardly ever see anybody in this part of the woods. You know you're well off the trail?"

Thomas nodded as casually as possible, hoping his response would cover both questions.

Elly looked him over, and it made him wonder if she found his Station uniform suspicious. "Are you alone?"

"No, I'm with a friend, but he's back up there somewhere." Thomas gestured in the general direction of the shuttle.

"Are you lost? I know boys hate to admit it, but it's not like I'm going to announce it to the universe."

"No," Thomas said, which was at least partially true.

"I don't mean to be nosy, but where are you from?"

This was the one question for which Thomas was not only well prepared but could answer with complete honesty. "Colorado."

"You hiked all the way from Colorado? Wow. I rarely see real trekkers out here. Most of the people you run across are day trippers from the city."

Thomas was tempted to ask which city, and how far it was from Colorado, or anything else that might establish his location, but a question like that might generate questions in return, and he wanted to stick to the truth as long as possible. "It's been a hectic morning, and I've sort of lost track of time," Thomas said. "I'm not even sure what day it is."

Elly glanced at her timepiece, a large black model that dwarfed her wrist.

"It's one forty-eight p.m., Wednesday, July second."

"And the state?"

Elly laughed. "Did you just ask me what state this was?"

"I'm sorry, I meant where we are now."

"Muir Woods, Marin Country, California."

"California," Thomas repeated, recalling the stretch of vertical land that ran along the western edge of his father's map. "And the city you referred to?"

"San Francisco? Just over the bridge."

Thomas tried to hold back his excitement. "There's a bridge, over water?"

"Uh, yeah, the Golden Gate." Without taking her eyes off him, Elly used her thumb to gesture over her shoulder. "Big orange contraption a few miles thataway."

"I must've gotten turned around," Thomas said, hoping that would justify his confusion.

"Sure, happens to the best. I was about to have lunch," Elly said, nodding toward her backpack. "I've got plenty if you want to join me. You can invite your friend."

"Actually, he's unconscious at the moment."

"Unconscious?"

Thomas quickly corrected himself. "I mean sleeping."

"Well, hard to blame him if you've been hiking from Colorado. But you're smart to avoid the heat. This is the time of day when it starts to warm up."

Elly pulled her hooded shirt over her head, revealing a white shirt with short sleeves. Her arms, unlike those of the Station girls, were firm and athletic. If anything, she was like a younger version of Marta, his Q-rings instructor.

"I prefer the winter myself, when the place isn't overrun with tourists. Unfortunately, summer's the only time I can do any real field work."

Thomas knew about summer and winter, since Mars had the same seasons as Earth, but didn't understand what *tourists* were. He guessed they must be a species of insects.

"So, what about lunch?" Elly said.

Charlie barked, as if to second the invitation.

"I just uttered the magic word," Elly said, as she turned and started down the hillside. "He'll put up with all my craziness as long as we eat on time. C'mon, I have a reserved tree with a canopy in case it rains, which it's supposed to do later on if you trust the weather bimbo."

"Rain?" Thomas asked, unable to hide his excitement at the prospect.

"Yeah, even if it doesn't pour, you can still get soggy out here. The fog rolls in every afternoon around four. You can set your watch…or whatever you're wearing there…to it." Elly glanced at his wrist pod before asking, "I assume you like PB and J?"

"Yeah," Thomas said, unsure of what he'd agreed to.

Elly led Thomas to a spot under the trees where a water-repellant blanket was already spread out. She dropped to her knees and pulled three glass jars out of her backpack. Each contained several small yellow objects that crawled around inside. Thomas lifted one up to examine it more closely.

"Is this the PB and J?"

Elly laughed. "Has anyone ever told you that you have a dry sense of humor? No, these are my specimens. I'm an amateur naturalist, and I'm doing field work on banana slugs."

"*Banana slugs*," Thomas repeated. Two more words he'd never heard.

"I know, not the most exciting creatures. But they're our largest land mollusk, so that's something at least. Still, I'd still rather be in New Zealand looking for a tuatara. Unfortunately, my father, who's a naturalist, too, says I need to start small, in my own backyard, and work my way up the species ladder."

"So, you live in the city?" Thomas asked, fairly sure this was the one question he might pose that wouldn't seem ridiculous.

"Yeah, in the Sunset District, not far from the university where my father teaches. He normally has summers off, and we get to travel somewhere exotic to do field study. We were supposed to go to New Zealand this year, but he got slammed with administrative stuff and had to postpone, so I wound up back here in Muir Woods. Not that I'm complaining, mind you, this place is like a second home for me."

"Your father allows you to come out here alone?"

"Sure. I've got my cell phone, portable GPS, and Swiss Army knife." Elly pulled out a device similar to Thomas's father's and used it to cut open a plastic bag that contained a stack of white food sliced about a half-inch thick. "The rangers all know me by name, and I have pepper spray if I run into a crazy person. As long as I'm home before dark, dad's copacetic." She removed two more jars, one of which was filled with a pale brown substance. The other contained a purple gelatinous substance. "Hope you don't mind blueberry—it's my favorite."

"No," said Thomas, anxious to try a new flavor.

He watched closely as Elly took four of the white squares out of the plastic bag and spread the brown paste over their surfaces. She put two of the slices on a paper plate and handed it to Thomas. "I'll let you do your own jelly. I know it's a personal thing."

Thomas watched carefully as Elly slathered a huge amount onto her slice and then handed him the jelly, along with the knife.

"Don't worry," she said. "It's organic. I get it at the farmer's market."

Again, Thomas nodded as if he knew what she meant. Elly finished making her sandwich and took a bite. Thomas copied her. "Amazing," he said, before his tongue stuck to the roof of his mouth.

"I've got water—or lemonade, if you prefer?"

"I'll take the lemonade," Thomas said, recalling the lemon flavor of Ignatius's tea.

"Careful. It's my own mix—hundred proof, all natural, no sugar added." Elly pulled out a pair of metal containers, each with a plastic cup attached, and poured the yellow liquid.

He took a gulp, and his entire face contracted. The lemon was far more potent than Ignatius's tea.

"I warned you, I like it strong."

Elly watched him carefully as he took another sip and slowly ate. "So, Thomas, I'm not usually this blunt—well, actually I am—but what's the deal here?"

"The deal?"

"First off, there's that big flash of blue light, which you claim you didn't see, even though you came walking out of the woods a minute later. Second, Colorado to California has to be five hundred miles, give or take. You're not really dressed for that kind of trek, and to be perfectly honest, I don't know *what* you're dressed for. Then there's that gizmo on your wrist."

Thomas glanced down at his wrist pod. With its elevated heptagonal prism and pulsing green face, it looked nothing like Elly's timepiece.

"At first, I thought it might be some hi-tech wilderness gadget that, not being a gadget person, I'm unfamiliar with. But that plus your outfit plus the fact that you're obviously unfamiliar with PB and J, not to mention San Francisco, is a little strange. It's none of my business, live and let live, that's the naturalist motto, but I'm out of here by five sharp and I wouldn't want the rangers to find you, cause they have no sense of humor when it comes to kids being here after hours, so if you're in some sort of trouble, I'm probably your best shot at help."

Thomas knew he needed to respond, but Elly seemed too smart for any lie he could concoct. He remembered Ignatius's advice about relying on his instincts. "Can I trust that whatever I tell you will stay between us?"

"Of course. Unless you're planning to steal redwood, start a forest fire, or do anything to violate the health of any animal, in which case I'd have to kill you."

"Kill me?"

"Joke," Elly said. "But I'd definitely turn you in."

"I'm not here to do any harm to the land or any living thing, I promise you. But I do have to ask you a strange question."

"Ask away."

Thomas took a deep breath. "What year is it?"

"Seriously?" Elly said, half smiling.

Thomas nodded, and she could see that he was.

"2023."

Thomas winced, unable to hide his disappointment.

"Not the answer you were looking for?"

"No."

"Listen, Thomas, what do you say we play twenty questions?"

Thomas looked at Elly with a blank expression.

"Yeah, I didn't think you'd be familiar. It's a game where I ask you a series of questions and you answer with a simple yes or no, unless you need to clarify."

"All right."

"Have you escaped from somewhere?"

Thomas paused to consider this. "I guess you could say that."

"That would be a 'yes,' yes?"

Thomas nodded.

"A foster home?"

Another phrase he clearly didn't recognize.

"You don't know what that is?"

"No."

"Was the place you escaped from a juvenile facility or mental health ward?

Thomas shook his head tentatively.

"Are the authorities looking for you?"

Thomas hesitated, worried that the truthful answer might give Elly the wrong impression. But he saw no reason to lie.

"Yes. But fortunately, they're unable to…"

Thomas stopped short of saying "time travel."

"Can't what?"

"I can't say."

"Can you say where you escaped *from*?"

"Yes. I mean no. I can't say."

Elly looked at him with genuine concern on her face. She let out a big sigh. "I'm kind of running out of questions here, and believe me, that never happens."

Thomas had the urge to confess his entire story, but at that instant a sharp crackling noise startled them both.

Charlie jumped to his feet and barked in the direction of the sound.

Elly looked up hill. "Someone's up there."

A shaft of bright light lit up the woods, and Thomas realized it was the sun bouncing off the shuttle mirrors. Eno stumbled out of the light, as if he had come directly from the sky. He was still wearing his hazard suit and helmet, and looked very much like an alien.

He paused at the sight of Elly, then wobbled once and fell face first onto the ground.

Elly turned to Thomas, her expression changing from concern to seriousness. "All right, Thomas. Game's over. What the heck is going on?"

## CHAPTER 16

THOMAS RACED UP THE hillside with Elly and Charlie right behind. He dragged Eno's limp body to the nearest tree and propped him against the trunk in a sitting position. He pulled back his helmet to see that his replacement eye was rolling around, as if trying to get its bearings. It focused on the trees above, and his good eye followed.

"Eno, are you all right?" Thomas said.

"Dizzy. Very, very dizzy."

"It's the vertigo Ignatius warned us about."

"There's something else," Eno said, and let out an explosive sneeze.

"It's probably the sword ferns," Elly said to Thomas. "Some people are really allergic."

Eno brought his eyes down from the trees to see who was speaking.

"This is Elly," Thomas said. "And Charlie, the dog."

Charlie padded over to inspect Eno, who instinctively slid back as he approached.

"It's all right," Thomas said. "He won't hurt you."

"Not unless I tell him to," Elly said. "And I will, unless I get some answers."

Thomas could no longer avoid the truth, or at least part of it. "I'm sorry, you're right," Thomas said. "What do you want to know?"

"Let's start with the basics," Elly said. "Who are you and what are you doing here?"

"Thomas, no!" Eno said, suddenly aware of what was happening.

They heard the noise of an engine approaching in the distance.

Elly glared at Thomas. "That would be one of the rangers I told you about, probably Mike Bender. He'll see my blanket then check in on me to see what's going on. You want me to bring him up here so you can tell him instead?"

"He won't believe us," Thomas said. "And I'm not sure you will either."

"What makes you think that?"

The sound of the truck's engine rumbled to a stop.

"Because we've come from another planet."

"What?"

"I know how that must sound, but I can prove it."

A deep voice echoed through the trees. "Elly, you around?"

Elly whispered to Thomas. "Don't move."

She took off down the hill, with Charlie at her side, kicking up a trail of debris.

Eno started to wheeze. "We should make a run for it."

"You're in no shape for that. Besides, where would we go?"

"I don't know, but what if she turns us in?"

"I don't think she will," Thomas said. "Ignatius said I had to trust my instincts, and there's no time like the present."

"May I remind you, we don't know exactly when or where that is."

"I do. Elly told me, and I trust her."

Thomas sprinted over to another tree, where he could see Elly approach a man in a brown uniform with a silver badge on his chest. He wore a strange hat and had a piece of equipment strapped to his waist, in all probability a primitive weapon. Thomas could hear them.

"Ranger Mike, what's up?" Elly said.

"I saw this flash of blue light a little while ago and came over to check it out. Then I noticed your stuff and thought I heard you talking to somebody."

"Right," Elly said. "I ran into a friend up the hill, but he just left. Is everything all right?"

"We got a report from one of the local weather choppers, said they saw something kicking off a lot of light. Have you seen anything suspicious?"

"Now that you mention it, I think I saw something over by the West Gate."

"The West Gate, huh? I'll head over there and check it out."

"Good luck," Elly waved.

Ranger Mike got back into his truck and drove off. Once he was out of sight, Elly and Charlie ran back up toward Thomas, who'd rejoined Eno.

"Thanks," said Thomas.

"You're not out of the woods yet, forgive the pun. I saved your butts with Ranger Mike, but unless you come clean, I'll get him to come back."

"Could you clarify the meaning of 'come clean'?" Eno asked.

"The truth, the whole truth, nothing but the truth," Elly said.

Thomas glanced at Eno, then back at Elly. "Follow us."

He helped Eno to his feet and led them back up the hill into the thicker part of the woods. He stopped next to a pair of massive boulders and pointed farther uphill. "Over there."

Elly took a few tentative steps forward to see the nose of the shuttle. Thomas watched her as she took in the sight of the whole ship.

She muttered a single word. "Whoa."

"You're welcome to inspect it," Thomas said.

Elly ran her hands along the surface of the shuttle, then began to circle it, momentarily disappearing from sight.

Eno turned to Thomas. "How did you find her?"

"She found me, or I should say, Charlie did when I came out to get our bearings."

"And?"

"It's 2023. We missed our destination by almost fifty years."

Eno's face drooped with disappointment. "The globe must've gotten damaged when I dropped it back at the cave. This is all my fault."

"It wasn't anybody's fault. We were under attack, remember?"

Elly reappeared at the shuttle hatch. "Under attack?"

Thomas nodded. "The authorities tried to prevent us from leaving."

"Leaving from where?"

Thomas looked at Eno, reluctant to utter the one word that might undo all the progress he'd made with Elly. But he also realized that any version of the truth would sooner or later bring him to the same place. "Mars."

Thomas waited for the word to sink in. Elly was silent.

"The blue light you saw was our arrival," Thomas added.

"I doubt she's familiar with the phenomenon of red shift," Eno said.

"You mean wavelengths of light from the stars? I take AP Physics."

"Then you know that the light is red on the way out, blue on the way back," Eno said. "Needless to say, we couldn't see it because it preceded us."

"I see," Elly said. "So, you're saying you're…Martians?"

"Well, yes and no," Eno said, glancing at Thomas.

"Eno and I both grew up there," Thomas said. "But I was born on Earth. In Colorado. We're trying to get back."

Elly nodded thoughtfully. "Okay, so you're trying to get home. That leaves the question of how you got to Mars in the first place, or back here, for that matter. I'm sure you're aware that the technology doesn't really exist for that kind of trip."

"It does in the future," Thomas said.

Elly looked to Eno, who nodded in agreement.

"The future? So, in addition to being Martians, you're also time travelers?"

"Yes," Thomas said.

He waited for the shock to register. But if anything, the information seemed to make Elly calmer.

"Actually, that's the only thing that makes sense."

"Then you believe us?"

"No. I just said that it fits your story. It's very well thought-out."

"It's not a story," Eno said, offended.

"Or a very elaborate hoax," Elly countered.

"If it is," Eno said, "then where do you think we got the shuttle?"

"I heard they're filming a new sci-fi movie in the valley. It's probably a prop, and you guys are extras or something. In any case, the burden of proof is on you."

Thomas and Eno had no idea what Elly was talking about. It was clear they'd reached an impasse. "I don't know what else we can do to make you believe us," Thomas said.

"I do," Eno said. "I'll use the Arrometer."

"The what?" Thomas said.

"Ignatius anticipated we might encounter this problem, so he added one to my kit. Given our last-minute leave-taking, I assume he never got the chance to mention it. Give me a minute."

Eno climbed into the shuttle while Thomas stayed with Elly. She looked him over as if this new information required her to reexamine him.

"I take it Ignatius is your mission control?"

"Yes. He was my father's friend and colleague on Earth."

"When was that, if you don't mind my asking?"

"In the years before…"

Thomas suddenly realized that any discussion of the years leading up to the Final Evacuation would only make matters more confusing, but he was saved from further explanation when Eno reappeared at the hatch and lowered himself down. He was holding a small metal cube attached to a thin handle. On the handle was a digital read-out with a single switch.

"The Arrometer was an early prototype of the Time Globe," Eno explained. "It proved useless for travel, but Ignatius thought it might come in handy on our mission."

Elly eyed the device warily. "What exactly does it do?"

"It can manipulate a small temporal field short distances, though the most I've been able to squeeze out of it is about a minute and a half."

Elly looked skeptical. "So, you're going to send us back in time?"

"If you can stop talking for a moment, yes. But you'll need to move closer. It only has a range of about three feet."

Thomas gave Elly a reassuring nod, and she reluctantly stepped forward, standing shoulder to shoulder with him.

"Tell me the exact time," Eno said to Elly.

Elly glanced at her watch. "Twelve twenty-three, eighteen seconds."

"Now take off your wrist pod and put it on the ground."

Elly laid her watch at her feet. Eno upheld the Arrometer, and Elly felt a small ripple of air brush against her eyebrows. "How long does it take?

"It's done," Eno said. "Check your time piece."

Elly started to reach for her watch—and realized it was back on her wrist. "Whoa!" she said, taking a step back.

"What time is it?" Eno asked.

Elly glanced at her watch in disbelief. "Twelve twenty-one exactly."

Eno nodded, as if he expected no less. "Two minutes eighteen seconds earlier, when your timepiece was still on your wrist."

Eno turned to Thomas, impressed with his own handiwork. "I broke the two-minute mark. It must be the extra gravity here."

Elly rolled her wrist over and jiggled the band to make sure it hadn't been tampered with. Finally, she looked up. "How do I know that wasn't some sort of trick?"

"I think I can answer that," Thomas said. "Where's the shuttle?"

Elly looked up to see that it was no longer in front of them.

"Where did it go?"

"It's still back up the hill," Thomas said. "But two minutes and eighteen seconds ago, we were down here."

Sure enough, Elly looked around to see that they were standing next to the fallen tree where they'd had their initial conversation.

Elly looked completely bewildered. And genuinely impressed.

For the first time since landing, Eno's face relaxed into its normal state of superiority. "Will any further proof be required?"

# CHAPTER 17

Thomas, Elly, and Charlie followed Eno back up the hill.

"I need to check on the Time Globe," Eno said, as he climbed inside the shuttle. Thomas glanced at Elly, who still regarded the futuristic ship suspiciously.

"Would you like to inspect the interior?"

"Is that all right?"

"Why not?" Thomas said.

He jumped up on the side of the shuttle and offered Elly his hand.

She turned to Charlie. "If I'm not out in two minutes, go get Ranger Mike."

He let out a single bark in response, and Thomas pulled Elly into the shuttle interior. She took one look at the cabin and froze.

"What do you think?" Thomas said.

"Awesome."

"Meaning?" Thomas said.

"Astonishing, incredible, unbelievable."

"It's a twenty-first-century Earth model," Thomas said. "Originally built around 2070 but reconstructed in the last few years. C'mon, I'll show you the cockpit."

Elly followed Thomas along the stairs. Eno was hunched over a foldout table with his silver backpack next to him. He strapped a pair of magnifiers over his eyes, and after removing the globe's outer shell, he separated it into halves.

"What exactly is the Time Globe?" Elly asked.

"A cosmic map," Thomas said. "It controls our destination in space-time."

"The good news is that none of the internals seem damaged," Eno said.

"So, you can take off again?" Elly said.

"Time-jump," Eno corrected her. "But unfortunately, no."

Eno grimaced. His eyes, magnified several times, made him look like an insect.

"When the globe fell, a small piece of metal dislodged from the beta sphere. Even the smallest irregularity can alter space-time by decades, which no doubt is the reason we're here."

"Can you fix it?" Thomas asked.

"If I can make a patch," Eno said, turning to Elly. "Is there an alloy factory nearby?"

Elly looked confused.

"A place where they fabricate metals," Thomas translated.

"The closest we've got is a hardware store," Elly said. "There's one just a few blocks from my house actually, in the city."

"We can't leave the shuttle," Eno said.

"As long as we bring the Time Globe with us, no one can use the shuttle," Thomas said.

"But you can't leave it here in the open," Elly said. "The rangers are already out looking for whatever caused that reflection."

"It must be the mirrors," Thomas said. "We'll have to take them off."

"You can do that?" Elly asked.

"Of course," Eno nodded, as if it were obvious. "Each one has a separate release switch."

"How many are there?"

"Twenty-four," Eno said.

"But we only need to remove the ones facing the sun," Thomas said.

"Okay," Elly said. "It'll go a lot quicker with three of us."

✦✦

THOMAS AND ELLY WENT to work carefully removing the individual mirrors, while Eno remained at the command console, releasing the magnetic clamps and overseeing the operation. Thomas straddled the curved surface of the shuttle and handed down the delicate two-by-five-foot rectangles to Elly one at a time.

"Wow," Elly said, "they're surprisingly light."

Eno's disembodied voice echoed from the shuttle. "They're made from dielectric crystals."

"Ah," Elly said, smiling. "That explains it."

Thomas could see that she wasn't serious and smiled back.

"Is he always like this?" Elly said.

"Pretty much. His bio rank is four, which means he's the fourth smartest kid out of the eight hundred on the Station, and the other three are girls."

"Can't keep us down," Elly said.

Slowly, they carried the dozen mirrors down the hill to the nearest flat ground and laid them on Elly's all-weather blanket and covered it with dirt. By the time they were finished, Thomas and Elly were drenched with sweat.

"You must be roasting in those uniforms," Elly said to Thomas.

"We never had a chance to pack. Besides, this is all we wear anyway."

"Well, there's more than one way to cool down. C'mon."

Elly led Thomas to a small stream and untied the yellow cloth around her neck. Dipping it into the water, she ran it over her face and neck before handing it to Thomas. He did the same, letting the cold liquid drip into his mouth. Unlike the Station's water, which had a distinct chemical taste, it was delicious.

Elly walked to the nearest tree and tied the cloth around a large branch. "There. My bandana will mark the spot when you return. It's the modern equivalent of breadcrumbs."

"I'm not sure I…"

"It's a famous story about a couple kids trying to find their way out of a forest. They leave a trail of the stuff to get home."

"Ah," Thomas said.

"Now that the mirrors are hidden," Elly said, "can I ask what they're for?"

"They help attract the negative energy it takes to connect us to a wormhole."

"Wormhole," Elly nodded. "Should've guessed."

Eno appeared from the shuttle carrying his silver metallic backpack, which contained the Time Globe. "She still doesn't quite believe us," he said.

"You have to admit," Elly said, "it's a lot to swallow in one gulp. But my father always says a scientist's first duty is to go with the facts. So, until somebody comes up with a better explanation, I'm willing to roll with it."

Elly checked her watch. "We should get going if you want to make it to the city and back before dark."

"I need to grab my stuff," Thomas said.

"You're not bringing any weapons, are you?"

"Only if you count the Sonic Inducer, in case we encounter any megalodons."

"Megalodons?"

"A species of prehistoric predator active in your future," Eno said.

"I can pretty much guarantee we won't run into any in the city."

Thomas disappeared back into the shuttle and hid the Sonic Inducer under his suspension pod. But he decided the Tetrascope was more a tool than a weapon and slid it into his pocket. He hurried back to the hatch and jumped to the ground.

Elly picked up her backpack and slung it over her shoulder.

"Listen, if anybody asks any questions, let me do the talking, all right?"

"I doubt there's anything we could do to prevent you," Eno said.

✦✦

CHARLIE TOOK OFF DOWN the hill as Elly led the boys toward the park exit, while staying off the largest trails to avoid human contact. After twenty minutes, the giant redwoods thinned and the two-lane road outside the park came into view. A few minutes later, they came out of the trees and had a clear view of the bay, forcing Thomas and Eno to come to an abrupt stop.

"Something wrong?"

Thomas and Eno were speechless, eyes wide with awe. After a moment, Elly got it.

"Oh, the bay. No bodies of water on Mars, right?"

The boys nodded in unison, though Thomas's expression quickly morphed into a smile, while Eno regarded the water as if it were about to attack him.

Thomas pointed toward the massive orange bridge that arched over the water to the city. "What's that bridge?"

"That's the Golden Gate, the one I told you about. It's a major landmark of San Francisco, which is right behind it."

"What's the tall structure with the triangular roof?" Thomas said.

"The Transamerica building, another landmark."

"Is that where you live?" Eno asked.

"No," Elly chuckled. "It's an office building. I live near the beach."

"Near the ocean?" Thomas asked, excited by the possibility.

"Not far," Elly said, leading them across the street.

"So, we're basically surrounded by water?" Eno said, clearly anxious.

"Pretty much," Elly said.

"I assume we're taking the bridge into the city?" Eno asked.

"No, too slow with rush hour traffic. We'll take the ferry," Elly said, pointing to the large dock jutting into the water, where a huge boat was sitting.

"We're going to travel on the surface of the water?" Eno said, horrified.

"Yep," Elly said. "I guess you've never been on a boat, huh?"

"We've never even seen one," Thomas said.

"Well, I think you'll love it. Unless of course you get seasick."

As they reached the ferry, Eno's pace slowed and his breathing quickened.

"Don't worry," Elly said. "It's perfectly safe. The physics are foolproof."

Eno seemed slightly comforted by the mention of science, and Thomas threw an arm around his shoulder to usher him forward.

"C'mon," Elly said. "The best seats are outside, on the upper deck. We'll hit the café for some donuts on the way. It's Charlie's favorite part of the trip."

After a stop at the café, they settled into the front row with Charlie on Elly's lap. A loud horn sounded, causing Eno to jump, and the ferry slowly began to move. Eno closed his eyes and took a deep breath as Thomas gazed out at the shimmering water and devoured his donut.

Within minutes, the ferry was at full speed. Thomas marveled at how it skimmed so smoothly over the water. The bay was filled with boats of all shapes and sizes. As they passed by, Elly announced their names, from the smallest to largest, rowboats and dinghies, tugboats and sailboats and luxury yachts, even a pair of tankers on the other side of the bridge.

Eno turned a pale shade of green and stood up. "Excuse me, I think I might…"

"There's a bathroom right before the café," Elly said.

Eno staggered away, slightly unsteady on the moving boat.

"He's always had a weak stomach," Thomas said.

"He doesn't seem very healthy in general."

"He's been that way since he was little," Thomas said, licking the remainder of donut crumbs from his fingers. "He has a replacement eye and weak lungs. But a good heart. I know he can come off as a little…off, but that's because he's so brilliant. He's one of only ten kids out of eight hundred chosen for the Redstar Group. Last year, he won the top award for his research project."

"In what?"

"I don't really know. He doesn't talk about it and I probably wouldn't be able to understand it anyway."

"How long have you two been together?"

"Since we were six, when we're all assigned a counterpart until the age of sixteen. Eno's mine. And then he was chosen to be my Navigator."

"Some Navigator. He managed to land you in the wrong time *and* place."

Thomas tried not to laugh. Elly was not only direct but funny.

"Where are you headed, if you don't mind my asking?"

"Colorado, 2071. But any time after the Final Evacuation would be…." Thomas stopped short, suddenly realizing what he had said, but it was too late to get the words back in his mouth.

"Evacuation? What happened?"

Thomas hesitated.

"Hey, cat's out of the bag. The least you can do is give me a heads up."

Thomas glanced around the deck. "Eno would be really upset if I told you."

"I promise not to mention it, cross my heart."

Elly drew an imaginary vertical and horizontal line across her chest in what Thomas assumed to be a secrecy ritual of some sort.

"Okay," Thomas said. "There's a polar meltdown just after the middle of the century."

"Shut up," Elly said, then realized that Thomas might take her literally. "Sorry, that's just an expression. Keep going."

"The oceans converge with the smaller bodies of water to flood the planet. I escaped with my mother when I was an infant, but my father stayed behind."

"That's awful, I'm sorry. But at least you had your mother."

"I never knew her. I never even knew I had one. She died before I turned one."

"Mine, too. I'm adopted."

"What does that mean?"

"Another person accepted legal responsibility for raising me. My adoptive father found me in the Planetarium at the university where he teaches when I was just a few months old. There was a letter in my cradle with my name on it. It explained how my mother had died shortly after I was born and that my birth father couldn't take care of me. But despite everything, I still had a great father growing up. Losing both parents must be awful."

"I never knew what I was missing."

"But still, you must've felt some *absence* in your life."

"I felt different, that's for sure. But I didn't really know why. Nobody has biological parents on the Station. Everyone's genetically designed, like Eno."

"Well, that explains a lot."

Thomas laughed as Eno reappeared behind them. "Did I miss something?"

"I was just asking Elly the meaning of 'cat's out of the bag.'"

"No need to learn the local dialect," Eno said. "We'll be gone by nightfall."

## CHAPTER 18

The ferry docked, and Elly led the boys through an open area bordered by a building filled with shops and restaurants, some of which spilled into outdoor seating for patrons. Despite the fact that it was late afternoon, it was crowded with people, many of them passengers from the ferry. Thomas's head swiveled from side to side, trying to take it all in, and even Eno seemed fascinated. As they approached the building, a girl rolled by on a flat board with four small wheels next to two boys straddling small metal devices with a pair of much larger wheels.

"What are those? Thomas said.

"The girl's on a skateboard; the boys are on bicycles."

"They're common means of transportation?" Eno said.

"Depends where you are. They're a good way to get around in the city, particularly with the traffic, but kids everywhere grow up riding them just for fun."

Thomas was distracted by a man and a woman swinging a small child between them.

"That's what we call a nuclear family," Elly said.

"One male, one female, and one child?" Eno asked.

"Actually, you can mix and match. It can be two men, which is the San Francisco version, or two women, or even a single parent, like I have. All you need is love, as they say."

"Love?" Eno said. "How does that work?"

"To be honest, it's kind of a mystery. And a much longer conversation. Here we go."

Elly led them through the open archway at the center of the building. It was filled with people, some waiting in lines, others eating food they carried in their hands.

"So, people can just get whatever they want and walk around eating?" Thomas said, amazed by the idea.

"That's about it," Elly said. "We can stop and grab something if you want."

"We should keep moving," Eno said. "We need to leave as soon as possible."

"Eno's right," Thomas said, obviously disappointed.

They passed through the opposite archway to a busy four-lane street. Hundreds of cars flew by in each direction, broken only by the occasional truck or trolley.

"Wow," Thomas said. "I didn't realize there'd be so many different kinds of cars."

"Too many, if you ask me." Elly said.

As they waited for the light, a young couple drove by in a turquoise car with the top down. The girl's hair flew behind her like a flag as Thomas craned his head to watch them go.

"You probably don't have convertibles on your planet, huh?"

"The temperature's sixty below," Thomas said. "And then there's the radiation."

"But you can't live your entire life indoors?"

"Actually, we do," Thomas said.

"That's the saddest thing I've ever heard, other than the fact you don't have dogs," Elly said, glancing down at Charlie. The light changed and she waved them across the street along with a small pod of moving pedestrians. "This is the Embarcadero. The Financial District is that bunch of skyscrapers over there. But we're heading the other way, through Chinatown."

"Are we walking?" Eno said.

"No, it's too steep and too far. We'll take the cable car."

"What's that?" Thomas said.

"The rectangular thing over there," she said, pointing to the cable car that was turning around in order to go up the hill.

Thomas's eyes lit up. "Is it a train?"

"No," Elly said. "They don't have engines, for one thing."

"Then what's their power source?" Eno said.

"Electricity. They're connected to those cables in the street, see?"

Eno shook his head. "They can't possibly be safe, can they?"

"Well, I've been taking them to the ferry for three summers now and never had a problem."

Elly ushered them onto the back of the cabin, already filled with a group of teenagers, talking and laughing. They slid into the last row, and Eno grabbed the safety pole while Thomas studied the kids. He noticed that several had dark complexions.

"I take it you don't have people of color on Mars?" Elly said.

"Only a few of the original settlers, all much older." Thomas said. "Eno's eye doctor is dark brown, and the woman who runs the Artifacts Museum has yellowish skin, like her," Thomas said, nodding to a girl who was singing out loud.

"That would be Asian." Elly said. "Specifically, Chinese. So, you have no kids of color?"

"Variant skin coloration is considered part of the genetic chaos on Earth," Eno said. "Our founders chose to pick a uniform template going forward."

"And that just happened to be white?" Elly said, with a hint of sarcasm. "Have to say, it's a novel solution to the diversity problem. You just stop making people of color."

"I'm sorry," Thomas said. "For the record, I think your skin is beautiful."

"Thanks. I owe it all my mother, who apparently was Jamaican."

"Is there a name for it?" Thomas said.

"My skin color? Chestnut, caramel, coffee, take your pick. There's like twenty different shades of brown. What would you call it?"

"It reminds me of the color of some crayons."

"Which ones?" Elly said, suddenly curious.

"*Almond* comes to mind, but I don't even know what that is."

"It's a nut. Nutritious but bland. What else?"

"Desert sand, golden beige. My favorite is Tiger's Eye."

"Hey, I like that one. From here on, if anybody asks, I'll go with that."

Eno's body was rocked by a powerful sneeze.

"After we hit the hardware store, we'll find a pharmacy and get you something for those allergies. You don't want it to turn into an infection."

"I'm not taking anything I can't analyze," Eno said, his voice thick with congestion.

THEY TOOK THE CABLE car to the end of the line, and Elly walked the boys to a store called Ed's Hardware where they found a wall of bins that held a variety of thin metal rods called nails.

"Is this what you're looking for?" Elly said.

Eno picked one up and examined it. "It should do."

Thomas removed the globe, while Eno held the nail by the shaft and delicately tried to insert it into its surface. It was too small. He did the same with several other nails until one fit.

"Looks like we have a winner," Elly said.

"I still have to cut and mold it. We'll need access to a metal shop."

"There's one at my school, but we'll need to wait until tonight, when nobody's around and it's only patrolled by one security guard."

"Will we have to break into the shop?" Thomas said.

"Possibly," Elly said. "Is that a problem?"

"I doubt it," Eno said. "Thomas has broken into virtually every facility back on Mars."

"Then this should be small potatoes for him. Worse case, the guard will call the cops, in which case we'll just have to wing it," Elly said. "As in improvise."

"Thomas is also an expert at that, particularly in the face of imminent death."

"Trust me, nobody's going to kill two white boys."

Elly paid for the nail, and they went outside where the sun was setting.

"We have time, so we might as well head back to my place and chill."

Elly thrust her hand into the air. A yellow car seemingly appeared from nowhere and screeched to a stop. Elly opened the rear door and gestured toward them.

"Taxicab. Jump in."

✦✦

THE TAXI MADE ITS way out of the commercial zone and soon arrived at a residential neighborhood of small houses. It pulled in front of a two-story blue dwelling.

"Here we are," Elly said, checking her watch. "It's almost seven o'clock. My father doesn't get home until seven-thirty, and then we eat dinner. After dinner, I'll say I'm meeting friends for a movie. You have movies, right?"

Thomas and Eno gave her a blank look.

"A story with actors?"

"We live in a post-narrative society with no need for stories," Eno said.

"Sounds like fun," Elly said. "Anyway, I'm not supposed to have boys in the house when dad's not here, so you'll have to spend the night in the Maple Motel."

"Where is that?" Thomas asked.

Elly threw open a wooden gate leading to the yard and pointed to a large tree. Tucked into the upper branches was a miniature house with a rope ladder. Thomas followed Elly, but Eno stopped abruptly before passing the chicken coops.

"They're harmless," Elly said. "On our planet, it's the humans you have to worry about."

Eno didn't budge, still not convinced.

"They're basically pets," Elly said, "though we are addicted to the eggs, which is one of our most popular foods, especially for breakfast."

"Too bad we won't be here to try them," Eno said with obvious relief.

Elly pointed to an area enclosed by a fence. "That's my vegetable garden."

"What are those big round things on the ground?" Thomas asked.

"Melons. Care to try one?"

"Can we?" Thomas said.

Elly picked one up and tucked it under her arm, then led the boys toward the rope ladder hanging from the tree house.

"After you guys."

Thomas put the backpacks over one shoulder and climbed the ladder. Eno went next, followed by Elly, who somehow managed to climb with one arm, then swung into the tree house and rolled the melon onto a table.

"This is all yours?" Thomas asked.

"It used to be the headquarters of the Weed Warriors, a club I formed to destroy invasive plant species in the city. But we ran into trouble with the law and had to disband."

"The place is small, but what it lacks in size it makes up for with a great view." Elly threw open the curtains and pointed to the sliver of blue shimmering in the distance.

"Pacific Ocean, sixty million square miles of water. Never gets old," Elly said.

"Wow," Thomas muttered in awe. "How far away is it?"

"About a twenty minute walk. If you wind up staying overnight, I can show it to you."

"Too bad we'll have to miss it," Eno said.

"What do you say we slice that melon? I'll go get my Swiss Army knife."

"I might have something better," Thomas said, reaching into his pocket for the Tetrascope. He held it up and hit a button, revealing the diamond blade.

"Whoa," Elly said. "I guess that's the expensive model."

Thomas handed her the Tetrascope, and she cut the melon into slices. Eno looked at the orange fruit suspiciously while Thomas took a huge bite.

"Delicious," he said.

"It's all yours," Elly said. "I should get inside. My room's over there." She pointed to a small wooden balcony on the second floor. "I'll come get you after dinner. I'll bring along some leftovers in case you're hungry."

Eno was about to protest, but Thomas spoke up first. "That would be great, thanks."

Elly retrieved a small harness, which was attached to a cable at the top of the tree house. It hung over the yard and extended all the way to her balcony.

"What's that?" Thomas asked.

"It's called a zip line. My dad made it, but it's my design."

She sat on the short metal bar at the bottom of the harness and pushed off. Thomas watched as she deftly flew across the yard and onto the small balcony outside her room. With a quick wave, she disappeared.

Thomas shook his head and turned to Eno. "Pretty awesome, huh?"

"The ocean, the melon, or the zip line?"

Thomas smiled. "The girl."

# CHAPTER 19

WHILE ENO NAPPED, THOMAS made some entries on his wrist pod, though he couldn't help being distracted by the sun setting over the ocean. It produced a stunning array of colors—pink, blue, orange, and everything in between. Occasionally he was hit by a wave of disbelief that he was actually on Earth and kept glancing up to the sky to confirm that there was only one moon.

It made him smile every time.

Thomas lifted the chain that Lina had given him back at the Returner Compound and dangled the holographic crystal of her and Josef in front of the window.

"*I'm on my way,*" he thought. "*Our mission has begun.*"

As lights began to appear in the neighborhood, Eno stirred. "What time is it?"

"Eight-twenty-four," Thomas said.

Eno yawned. "What have you been doing?"

"Adding words to my vocabulary list while they're fresh in my mind. I've got *awesome, butts, cable car, chicken, convertible, donut, fun, pets, movies, skateboard, and zip line.*"

"How do you know any of those will be relevant in 2071?"

"I don't. But if we're here longer than expected, they could come in handy."

"Suit yourself, but I should warn you there are over seven thousand languages currently in use on this planet, which is one more reason our founders wanted to distance themselves from the civilization. It reeks of chaos. No one eats the same food or even dresses alike, let alone has the same skin color. And did you notice the long hair on the girls? That can't be very sanitary."

"I actually like it," Thomas said. "Maybe everything not being the same isn't such a bad idea. As for my list, it could only help to understand the language."

"Perhaps. But if you insist on knowing the definition of every single word that comes out of Elly's mouth, we'll be stuck here forever."

"We're stuck until we get the globe fixed, so I might as well put the time to good use."

"Suit yourself. Personally, I have more important things to do."

Eno grabbed his backpack and pulled up a single red antenna imbedded in the side.

"What are you doing?" Thomas said.

"Sending Ignatius a signal we've landed. Once I connect, he can track our movement on the space-time continuum."

"So, he'll know where we are?"

"That's the theory," Eno said. "Not that it's ever been done." He removed the black rectangular case and punched in the digital code to open it.

"What's in there?"

"Globe repair instruments, communication apparatus, biochemical analysis kit. In a pinch, I can construct basic weaponry. But first things first."

Eno removed several metal tubes and connected them to form an octagon, then attached a ball-shaped device to the end. He hit a small switch, sending the ball spinning at hyper speed. In a matter of seconds, it was crackling with a small halo of energy.

"There. Now all we need to do is let it run for a little while."

"What does it do?

"Scrambles energy. It's similar to the concept of time-travel, though in this case it sends messages instead of people."

Out of the corner of his eye, Thomas noticed the lights in the house across the street surge, so that they were burning much brighter.

"Are you sure it won't cause any damage?"

"It shouldn't. The amount of energy is extremely small, less than a millionth of what's produced by the Time Globe."

Thomas noticed that the lights in several other houses began to glow vividly. Within moments, the entire neighborhood was lit up as brightly as the power station back on Mars.

Suddenly, there was a loud bang, and the lights went dark. In less than half a minute, a high-pitched siren began to sound.

"What's that?" Eno said.

"Unless it's Ignatius responding, my guess is it's the local authorities."

Elly suddenly appeared out of the darkness on her zip line, wearing a backpack.

"Seems like we just had a power outage in the neighborhood."

"I'm sorry," Thomas said. "Eno was sending a message to Ignatius."

A cacophony of horns echoed in the distance.

"Well, he also sent one to the Taraval Police Station, Engine Company Forty-Five, and the Department of Water and Power. From the sound of it, they're all on their way."

"What should we do?" Thomas said.

"Get out of here," Elly said. "Now."

Elly led the boys through the back gate into the alley as a crowd of neighbors poured onto the street. They walked for about ten minutes when Elly stopped at a red light. She pointed across the street to a block filled with white stucco buildings trimmed in navy blue and gold.

"That's my school."

"What's your level?" Eno asked.

"It's a little complicated. I'm in the gifted program, so I started a year early. Technically, I'm a sophomore but a junior in Chinese and math and a senior in physics and biology."

"Does being in the gifted program give you special privileges?" Thomas said.

"Just extended hours at the library, which is useless unless you plan to sleep there. But I've got some books in my bag, so if anybody asks, we're returning them, and you guys are watching my back, got it?"

"Watching your back?" Eno repeated.

"Girls under sixteen aren't allowed alone on campus at night unless they're chaperoned."

"How old are you?" Eno said.

"I just turned fifteen a few weeks ago. What about you guys?"

"Since our entire class came into existence the same day," Eno said, "we all turn sixteen simultaneously," Eno said.

"June first," Thomas added.

"Wow, that must be one heck of a party."

"Party?" Thomas said.

"Cake, candles, wishes?"

"I worked through most of the 'C' words back on Mars, so I know about cake and candles. But wishes…"

"Something you'd desperately like to have or do or be."

"That sounds pretty good," Thomas said.

"Only if they're fulfilled, I would think," Eno said. "Anyway, our birth dates correspond to the academic calendar, so we change ages at the conclusion of every school year. No cake, candles, or wishes involved."

The light changed from red to yellow.

"Okay, guys, here we go."

Elly led them across the street, and they entered the school grounds down a passageway to a courtyard with a handful of outdoor tables. She gestured toward a pair of guards.

"Just our luck. The guards are changing shifts."

"Why is that a problem?" Eno asked.

"We're standing in the exit."

The guards began to walk in their direction. Elly waved the boys toward a nearby building, and they ducked through a side door.

They passed through a row of tall lockers, each of which contained a blue-and-gold helmet. Underneath were shirts with large numbers on the front. Thomas noticed the depiction of a large bird that took up almost the entire wall.

"The eagle," Elly said, "is our school mascot."

"Where are we?" whispered Eno.

"The boys' locker room. It's where they get dressed for sports."

Eno pulled down one of the helmets and inspected it. "We could use a few of these."

"For what?" Elly asked.

"After we insert the patch, we'll need to test the globe. It might give off a small amount of random energy."

Elly pulled down another pair of helmets and handed one to Thomas, tucking the other under her arm. They headed to the door on the opposite side of the locker room and went through a side exit that deposited them in front of a building with a sign that read "Science."

Elly nodded toward a window at ground level.

Thomas knelt by the window and pushed. "It's locked. Do you have anything adhesive?"

"I've got some gum," Elly said, pulling out a strip and popping it into her mouth. After a few chews, she removed it and held it out to Thomas.

Thomas flattened the gum against the window next to the handle, then removed his Tetrascope. Using the diamond blade, he traced a circle around the gum and pulled the section of window away. He reached inside, unfastened the latch, and crawled into the dark basement.

Eno handed Thomas his backpack through the window and lowered himself down. Thomas reached up and helped Elly. As he did, her hair brushed against his face, and he felt a strange tingle on his cheeks.

Eno held up his wrist light to reveal that the room was filled with several worktables. Scattered on top were a variety of tools.

"That saw over there should work," he said, gesturing toward a table.

Thomas pointed to a table covered with a strange contraption consisting of a network of thin metal strips about three feet high and twice as long. It curved up and down in dramatic fashion. A tiny open car, similar to the one William drove in the Station tunnels, sat at the bottom.

"What's that?" Thomas said.

"Roller coaster," Elly said. "It's the freshman class project."

Eno retrieved the nail from the hardware store and held it up to the saw as Elly stepped on the switch pedal. Holding it by the shaft, Eno lowered it over the blade. Within seconds, the tiny head dropped into his hand. "Perfect cut, if I do say so myself. Now for the attachment."

They moved to the welding table. Eno pulled up a chair and removed the Time Globe from his backpack.

"This might take some time. There can't be any extraneous metal on the globe's surface. The difference of a few yoctometers can cause a variation of years."

Elly turned to Thomas. "While Eno's working, we should check on the guards."

Thomas nodded and followed her up to the third floor. They looked out the nearest window to see that the guard was sleeping in his chair on a green field divided by white stripes.

"What's that?" Thomas asked.

"The football field. It's our most popular sport, though not for girls."

"So, your games are segregated, like ours?"

"Boys pretty much rule, at least in high school. It's still the dark ages here and absolute rock bottom in high school."

"You don't like school?"

"I like the learning part, but prefer doing it on my own. I have a tendency to get distracted, and lately my teachers say I seem to be on another planet."

"Me too. Or at least I always wanted to be."

Thomas noticed that she was staring into his eyes.

"Is something wrong?"

"I just noticed, you have eagle eyes," Elly smiled.

"What?"

"They're amber, like our mascot's. They're almost gold."

Thomas nodded. "The girls in Nursery always used to point that out."

"I'm not surprised."

"They don't help me see any better, so I'm not sure what good they are."

Elly smiled. "After you're on Earth awhile, I'm sure you'll figure it out."

Suddenly, there was a noise from the other end of the hallway.

"You hear that?" Elly whispered, then motioned for Thomas to follow her.

They crept toward the classroom where they'd seen the light. Peering through the door window, they saw a woman in her early thirties.

Ellie kept her voice to a whisper. "That's Miss Coventry. She teaches advanced biology. Wonder what she's doing here so late."

Another figure appeared, wearing one of the shirts Thomas had seen in the locker room. The number one was written on both the back and front.

"Is that another teacher?" Thomas asked.

"Sort of. He's the assistant coach of the football team."

They watched as the teacher and the coach embraced.

"What are they doing?"

"Uh, let's just say she's tutoring him in biology."

Suddenly a loud hum emanated from the basement, followed by a vibration.

"We better get back downstairs," Thomas said.

They hurried down to the basement, where Eno was hunched over the Time Globe. He was wearing a football helmet twice the size of his head. "I did the test. The power comes from a quark-gluon plasma bubble, and I need to make sure it interacts properly with the globe."

"How will you know?" Elly asked.

The light shafts began to ricochet wildly around the room.

"Because that happens," Eno said. "I think we're done here."

Eno turned off the globe, but Elly could feel the room continue to vibrate.

"Is this the 'small amount of random energy' you were talking about?" Elly said.

"The plasma bubble is hard to quantify. But it should dissipate soon."

The window above them exploded, accompanied by a terrified scream.

Elly turned to Thomas and Eno. "We'd better boogie."

Elly put her football helmet on her head, and the boys did the same. They went to the window, climbed out, and ran. The guard's flashlight beam strafed the area as they reached the exit and made it back to the street. They walked briskly to the traffic light. Elly slowed when she saw two uniformed men on the other side of the street.

"Police. Act normal."

"How do we manage that?" Eno asked.

"Taking off these helmets would help," Elly said, removing hers.

Thomas and Eno did the same as the traffic light changed to green, then slowly walked past the two police officers to Elly's block. Reaching the house, they dropped their backpacks and sat on the front steps, relieved.

"Well, that was an adventure," Elly said.

"And we learned something valuable about globe testing," said Eno.

"Yeah," Thomas said. "Never try it again."

Elly broke into laughter and Thomas joined in. The more they tried to stop, the harder they laughed, until a voice suddenly echoed from above.

"Elly, is that you?"

She looked up to see her father standing at his bedroom window. In the darkness, Thomas could only make out a thick gray beard.

"Sorry, Dad. Hope I didn't wake you. I was just saying goodnight to my friends."

"It's quite all right. Forgive me for not coming down, but I have a class early in the morning so I'm already in bed."

"No problem. I'll be in soon."

"Good night."

The bedroom window closed. But almost immediately, it reopened. "Oh, Elly? Almost forgot, your friend Ranger Mike from Muir Woods called. He wanted me to tell you that you can sleep in tomorrow. The park is closed until further notice."

"Why is that?"

"They found the sourcelight he told you about. It was a piece of space junk."

# CHAPTER 20

The news about the shuttle hit Eno particularly hard. He had what Thomas thought was one of his bronchial episodes, but Elly said it was something called a panic attack. She made him breathe into one of the brown paper bags she used for school lunches. After he stabilized, she insisted they spend the night in the tree house, providing them with pillows and blankets. After she left, Eno passed out, and Thomas turned his mind to the problem at hand. He could depend on Eno to fix the broken Time Globe but finding a substitute shuttle would be up to Thomas. Considering the incredible variety of vehicles on Earth, there had to be something that might work. With that on his mind, he drifted off and opened his eyes as the morning sun flooded the tree house. He was surprised to see that Eno was already awake, staring into space.

"Eno," Thomas said. "How you feeling?"

Eno didn't look at him. "How do I feel? Let's see, we're trapped on Earth, in the wrong space-time, with no transport. Could it get any worse?"

A piercing shriek came from the yard. Thomas looked out the window to see Elly in the yard, holding one of the chickens.

"Sorry about the rooster. I tried to beat him to the punch, but his internal clock is better than mine. Dad just left for work, and I told him I let some friends crash in the tree house, so come on in. I'm making breakfast."

"Be right there," Thomas said.

"Under no circumstances am I eating an egg," Eno said, pulling the blanket over his head.

Thomas climbed down the tree ladder and followed Elly into the house. Charlie wagged his tail as he entered the kitchen.

"I know how disappointed you must be," Elly said. "But somebody sure is happy you didn't leave. Where's your partner?"

"Let's just say he's having a hard time adjusting."

"That's what I figured. Pull up a seat."

Thomas sat at the counter as the front door opened, and an older woman with skin slightly darker than Elly's arrived, carrying a bag of groceries.

"Morning, Rosario. This is my friend, Thomas."

Rosario gave him a wave and began to unpack the bag.

"Rosario's part of the family. She's been with us ever since I can remember. We'd be lost without her. She taught me how to cook, among other things."

"Do you make all your meals?" Thomas said.

"Yeah, I do. Except for Sunday, when we go out to eat at a friend of my dad's place in Chinatown."

Rosario said something to Elly in a strange dialect. Elly spoke back, using the same language, as Rosario laughed and left the room.

"Spanish," Elly said, as she took out several eggs and began breaking them into a bowl. Thomas watched with fascination. It hadn't occurred to him that the eggs needed to be broken.

"Has there been any more news on the shuttle?" he said.

"Nonstop. It's the story of the day, even nationally. Front page of the Chronicle."

Elly handed Thomas a copy of the day's newspaper. He looked at it with a mixture of confusion and wonder. "You get one of these every day?"

"On the doorstep," Elly said. "It's a method of communication that's going out of style, but Dad believes it's important to support local journalism. Not to mention the Giants."

"Giants?

"Our city's baseball team. He's sort of addicted."

Thomas glanced at the large paper document.

"For those of us who want the cut-to-the-chase version of the news, there's this," she said, using the remote to turn on the small television on the counter. A line of military vehicles now blocked the entrance to Muir Woods, while several helicopters hovered above.

A voice echoed from the doorway. "Oh, no. What are they doing?"

Thomas and Elly turned to see Eno, shaking his head in despair.

"Airlifting it out," Elly said. "It's not like they can just leave it sitting there."

Eno crossed the kitchen and took a seat next to Thomas. "What will they do with it?"

"Probably stash it in some heavily fortified and super-secret warehouse in the middle of nowhere, New Mexico. If you're even considering trying to retrieve it, move directly to Plan B. But first you need to eat. That always helps."

Elly slid the eggs onto a hot frying pan. They sizzled and popped.

"And since you'll obviously be here a while longer, you're gonna need a good cover story. I'm thinking you could be exchange students from Iceland."

"Ice…land?" Eno said. "That's actually a place?"

"Yeah, it's a small island in the North Atlantic Ocean. Most people couldn't point to it on a map, but they speak English there, as you do. And since nobody knows much about the place, it'll explain your general, well…weirdness."

"Weirdness?" Eno repeated, slightly offended.

"Nothing personal, but you're not familiar with the food, geography, or dialect. And then there's your wardrobe."

"What's wrong with our clothes?" Eno asked.

"Other than the fact that you're dressed in identical uniforms made from a substance that looks vaguely metallic?"

"Lurex mixed with Twaron, reinforced by glass fibers," Eno said.

"I rest my case."

"Iceland it is," Thomas said. "Anything else?"

"If we're going to be hanging out, I should probably know your last names. It'd be helpful for the sake of intros."

"Mine is Knight," Thomas said, "but Eno doesn't actually have one since we don't use them on Mars."

"What do you use?"

"A bio rank," Eno said. "Are you familiar with DNA sequences, nucleotide triplets?"

"Codons," Elly nodded.

"I'm the sixth child generated in my birth class, so my full name is Six-D-Eight X."

"Ah," Elly said. "Well we can't have you walking around with a moniker like that. Tell you what, I'll lend you our street name. Holloway Drive, though you can lose the 'drive.'"

"Very well," Eno said, though he didn't seem particularly enthusiastic.

"Okay then. Thomas Knight and Eno Holloway, this is what we call an omelet."

Elly slid the eggs onto a plate. Eno looked repulsed by the sight.

"I'm assuming you don't eat eggs on Mars?"

"No," Eno said. "Food is considered fuel, no more, no less."

Elly produced a tall rectangular box. "I've also got cereal."

Elly handed Eno the box, and while he read the contents, Thomas began eating.

"Incredible," Thomas said through a mouthful of omelet.

"I can't take all the credit, but I'll pass it along to the chickens," Elly said.

Thomas took the remote and turned up the volume on the TV. A military spokesman was being interviewed, saying that the shuttle was part of a military satellite system launched years ago and presumed lost. Its fall to Earth was an "isolated incident."

Thomas looked at Elly, surprised. "That's not true. Why would they say that?"

"It's the best lie they could come up with on short notice, which is usually what you get in situations like this. But in this case, I kind of understand. If they said the shuttle came from Mars, they'd immediately have to answer a whole lot of other questions, like where are the Martians who brought it here."

Eno put down the cereal. "This is a complete disaster."

"Not necessarily," Thomas said. "We've still got the Time Globe and the rest of our stuff. The only thing we lost, other than the shuttle, was the Sonic Inducer."

"My fault, sorry," Elly said. "But if it's any consolation, you can stay in the tree house until you figure something out. I told my father about you guys hiking from Colorado, meeting you in Muir Woods, etcetera, and he was totally agreeable to your staying."

"That's very generous," Eno said. "But we need to keep moving."

"Assuming we find something to move in," Thomas said.

"I agree," Elly said. "That is a major problem."

"I did some research last night," Eno said, "and discovered there are three retired American Space Shuttles, one of which is here in the state of California. Perhaps we can—"

"You heard Elly," Thomas said. "We need a Plan B. I did some research of my own, and I think I found something that could work."

"What's that?" Eno said.

"Elly, do you mind if I change the frequency?" Thomas said, gesturing to the TV.

"Knock yourself out," Elly said, handing him the remote.

"Thanks, but I won't need that," Thomas said.

He removed his wrist pod and propped it on the counter facing the TV.

"What are you doing?"

"Using your monitor to play back yesterday's trip. I set my wrist pod to record everything from the time we left the shuttle."

Thomas pressed a button on the pod and the bow of the ferry appeared on the TV screen, skimming across the bay toward the city.

"You're not thinking about using that boat?" asked Eno.

"No. The last thing we want is another transport that's too big to hide. We need something a lot smaller than a space shuttle, or we'll keep having the same problem."

Thomas continued scrolling as they left the ferry and entered the city.

"Here we go," said Thomas, stopping the playback as they approached the cable car.

Elly leaned in to see the frozen image on the TV. "A cable car?"

"You can't be serious," Eno said. "It's preposterous."

"Can't we even discuss it?" Thomas said.

"No. It's out of the question," he said, turning to Elly. "Trust me."

Thomas handed Elly the remote, with the cable car frozen on the screen.

"Maybe we should just take our minds off the subject while we eat breakfast. It looks like a nice day outside. Maybe you'd like to take a tour of the city."

Eno didn't respond. Thomas gave Elly a look of frustration.

"Eno," Elly said, "Thomas tells me you won a big award in your research group."

"Correct," Eno said curtly.

"What was it for, if you don't mind my asking?"

Eno didn't respond.

"Yeah," Thomas said. "We'd both like to hear about it."

"If you must know, I created a way to neutralize the DNA mutation that triggers a disease caused by exposure to Martian radiation."

"You mean like a form of cancer?"

"That's an antiquated term, but basically yes."

Elly glanced at Thomas, stunned by the revelation.

"I told you he was brilliant."

Eno shrugged modestly at Thomas's compliment.

"Well, I have only one thing to say, Eno," Elly said. "If you can cure a form of cancer on Mars, you could sure as heck figure out how to modify a cable car for time travel on Earth."

Thomas could see that Eno was softening, but still not quite agreeable.

"Look, I'm not trying to be difficult, but any transport we used would have to weigh a minimum of ten thousand pounds to withstand passage through a wormhole," Eno said.

"A cable car weighs fifteen thousand five hundred pounds. I checked," Thomas said.

"And of course it would need mirrors," Eno countered.

"We already have them. As soon as they move the shuttle, we could dig them up."

"How will we attach them? We can't do it with Elly's gum."

"We'll get some industrial strength adhesive and bolt them in place to be extra secure."

"The Time Globe requires a navigation chamber. We can't just hang it from the roof like an ornament."

"I figured you could make one here and then put it all together when we get the cable car. The best part is that there's forty of them, so we won't be depriving the city of transportation."

"How would we even get one?" Eno asked.

"They store them in a place called the Cable Car Barn. It's a museum during the day. Elly can show us where it is, right?" Thomas said.

They both turned to Elly, who'd been following the back and forth of their conversation like a ping pong game. She suddenly seemed hesitant. "Guys, while I think Thomas may be on to something here, we need to talk."

She led them into the den, which was filled with photos of Elly and her father.

"Thomas, when we met in Muir Woods, I had every reason to believe you were lying about who you were and what you were up to. Even after I saw the shuttle and Eno did his Arrometer thing, I wasn't completely convinced. But I decided to take a leap of faith, mainly because you didn't seem like the kind of person who would lie about something so important."

"I'm not," Thomas said.

"I know. And I feel the same way about Eno. But I still don't know what you're actually doing here on our planet. Which is fine as long as all you're asking me to do is help you get into the school metal shop. But now it sounds like you want me to help you steal a cable car?"

"Oh, no," Thomas said, with complete sincerity. "I just want to borrow it. I have every intention of bringing it back once we're finished."

"Be that as it may..." Elly said, giving Thomas an incredulous look.

Thomas suddenly realized what was bothering her.

"Oh, I see. You want to know the exact nature of our mission."

Eno quickly stood up. "Out of the question. Under no circumstance can we divulge—"

"Why not?" Thomas said. "Ignatius never said anything about keeping it a secret. And it's not like Elly will tell anybody. Look, she saved us from the park rangers, took us into her home, and helped us get the Time Globe fixed. The least we can do is tell her why we're here."

Eno sat back down.

Thomas turned back to Elly. "It's a long story, but I'll give you the short version. Before I left Earth with my mother, my father took a group of orphans under his protection. He stayed behind and sheltered them in a Biosphere he built in the mountains of Colorado with the idea that someone would someday need to rescue them. My mission, our mission...is to find the Biosphere and take the orphans to the year 2100 when the Earth is livable again."

Elly sat back, silent, contemplating what Thomas had just told her.

"We understand," Eno added, "that with the time travel component, the mechanics of the mission must be terribly confusing."

She shrugged. "Time travel to 2071, pick up kids, time travel to 2100, start over."

"Exactly," Thomas said.

"Surely you must have questions," Eno said.

"Just one," Elly said.

"What?" Thomas and Eno said in unison.

"How many orphans are there?"

"Seventeen," Thomas said. "Why?"

"Well," she said, "we need to make sure the cable car is big enough for all of them."

## CHAPTER 21

Thomas, Eno, and Elly got off the bus and walked toward the Cable Car Barn, a large red brick warehouse with a massive smokestack at one end.

As they reached the entrance, Thomas paused. "You sure you're okay with this Elly? Eno and I could do it alone, so you wouldn't have to be involved."

"If this was just about taking the you-know-what, I'd bail. But since you need it to save civilization as we know it, that rules the day. Besides, this feels like a three-person job."

"Thanks," Thomas said.

They went into the barn, which was crowded with school-age children touring the museum. Elly led them to an elevated gallery, where they could look down at a set of massive cogs that held the miles of steel cables that controlled the system.

"This is the Powerhouse. Those cables run underground and attach to the cars, which is how they move. There's a demonstration video over there," Elly said, pointing to a large screen on the opposite wall.

They joined a group of children watching a grip man work the hand brake that protruded from the floor at the middle of the car. By the time the demonstration ended, Thomas had disappeared. Elly and Eno saw him standing at the balcony overlooking an open garage where several cars were being repaired.

"I think I found our transport," Thomas said, pointing down.

"Number twelve?" Elly asked. "Does that have some sort of significance?"

"It's the number of the observation tower where I used to look out at the Earth," Thomas said. "How many mirrors do you think we'll need, Eno?"

"Eight. Three for each side and one each at the front and back."

"Sounds like a plan," Elly said, as she noticed a guard watching them. "A plan we should now take outside."

They'd barely gotten out of the Cable Car Barn when a voice stopped them.

"Elly, is that you?" A girl with long yellow hair was waving at them. She carried a pink shopping bag and was flanked by two other yellow-haired girls, all wearing very short shorts.

"Oh, no," Elly muttered under her breath.

"What's the matter?" Thomas asked.

"It's Jessica. She used to be one of the Weed Warriors, until she became a cool girl."

The three girls made a beeline toward Elly.

"What are you doing out?" Jessica asked.

"Just visiting the museum," Elly said, as if it were something she did on a weekly basis.

"Oh my God, why?" Jessica said, rolling her eyes in mock horror.

"My friends here are on a cultural exchange trip." Elly nodded toward Thomas and Eno. "It's their first visit to the country."

"Cool," Jessica said, looking Thomas over. "I'm Jessica. These are my besties, Erica and Veronica."

"This is Thomas and Eno," Elly said.

The girls all smiled at Thomas, ignoring Eno.

"Where you from?" Jessica asked.

"Iceland," Thomas said.

"I totally don't know where that is, but it sounds really cold."

"Yeah," Elly said. "You'd probably get hypothermia in those shorts."

"We were shopping for something warm for tomorrow night," Jessica said.

"Tomorrow night?" Elly asked.

"Fourth of July?"

"Oh, right." Elly turned to the boys and quickly translated. "Big American holiday."

"The seniors are throwing a massive rager on Stinson Beach. You should totally come," Jessica said, addressing Thomas directly. "I promise it'll be more fun than the museum."

"Sorry," Elly said, "but they have a flight home."

"Too bad."

"Totally," Elly said, though Thomas noticed that she didn't seem very disappointed. "Well, it was great running into you Jessica. But we should get going. We're late for the Exploratorium."

"Sounds like fun," Jessica said. "Later then."

She led her two friends across the street, giggling as they went.

"That was close," Elly said.

"Why?" Thomas asked, completely baffled by the encounter.

"She's the biggest gossip on the planet. The last thing we want is her telling everybody she met two guys from Iceland."

"So, why did you say it was great running into her?" Eno asked.

"Because she reminded me that tomorrow's the fourth. Since it's a holiday, the Cable Car Barn will be shut down, along with the rest of the city. By the time the sun goes down, everybody will be off watching the fireworks. It's a perfect cover for your jump."

Thomas nodded, though part of him was sorry they'd be missing the *rager,* as well as the *bonfire* and *fireworks*—whatever they were.

THOMAS, ENO, AND ELLY spent the rest of the day shopping for supplies. It was late afternoon by the time they got back to Elly's house.

"Anybody home?" Elly called out.

Rosario responded in Spanish from the kitchen.

"Thomas and Eno are with me. We're going downstairs."

Elly led the boys to a converted basement with a large couch and TV, where Thomas noted a framed poster of a man with a beard. "Is that your father?"

Elly laughed. "No. That's Charles Darwin, the father of evolution, and Charlie's namesake. You've never heard of him?"

"We don't really study Earth scientists," Eno said, "except those responsible for building the Station. The creators of synthetic nutrition, water conversion, and radiation protection."

Thomas put down his supplies and noticed a small glass globe filled with clear liquid sitting on the shelf. Inside was a tiny replica of a ship of some sort. "What's this?"

"A snow globe," Elly said. "Inside is a model of Darwin's ship, the Beagle." She shook it, setting off a flurry of waves. "It's the one he sailed on to the Galapagos Islands to develop the theory of natural selection."

Thomas looked to Eno, who shrugged as if he had no idea.

"Evolution?" Elly said. "How organisms, animals, change over time?"

"Mars is a dead planet," Thomas said. "We don't have organisms."

"And thankfully no animals," Eno said.

"All I can say is you don't know what you're missing," Elly said.

"We should get to work," Eno said.

"And I should get a status report on Muir Woods," Elly said, turning on the TV.

Thomas put the snow globe back on the shelf and pulled a glue gun and two large cans of adhesive out of his backpack while Eno removed a length of marine rope from his.

Elly checked her watch. "It's almost four, and we can't dig up the mirrors until dark, so we have a few hours to kill. There's a video game console under the TV if you're interested."

Eno inspected the TV, while Thomas wandered over to a circular object on the wall. It was divided into small triangular sections, each with a different number.

"What's this?"

"Dart board," Elly said. "It's a game. Want to give it a try?"

"You'll have to teach me how to play."

"It's simple," Elly said, finding some darts. "You throw these at the numbers and work your way around the board in order."

Elly handed Thomas a dart. He casually tossed it toward the board, where it landed in the smallest circle at the center.

"You hit the bulls-eye."

"Is that good?" Thomas asked.

"You can't do better," Elly said. "Sure you haven't played before?"

"He's Games Champion back on the Station," Eno said.

"My turn," Elly said. But as she aimed her dart, the doorbell rang. A man's muffled voice echoed from above. While she couldn't hear what he was saying, his tone sounded serious.

"Hold on. I'll be right back."

In the foyer, Rosario was closing the door, a business card in her hand.

"Who was that?" Elly asked.

"Some men want to speak with your father."

"Did they say what it was about?"

Rosario said something in Spanish and handed her the card. Elly took a quick look and ran up the stairs to her room. She looked out the window to see the two men, one tall and thin, the other short and heavy, get into their car.

A moment later, Thomas appeared in the doorway. "What's going on?"

"We just had a visit from a couple FBI agents. They're like the national police. Ranger Mike probably told them I was in Muir Woods yesterday. I guess they want to know if I saw anything."

"We're not getting you into any trouble, are we?" Thomas said.

"No. You didn't do anything illegal, so it's not like I'm harboring fugitives or anything."

Elly smiled. But Thomas could see it wasn't her normal smile.

"Are you sure?"

Elly sighed. "I'm sorry, I should've told you, but I have a rap sheet, which is a record the police keep once you've been arrested. Remember when I told you about how my club, the Weed Warriors, ran into a little trouble?"

"Yeah."

"Well, it was more than a little. I discovered some Algerian Ivy growing on a deserted piece of land out near the Presidio. It was killing everything, so we decided to dig it out. There were five of us: me, Jessica, and three other kids. We went in at night and collected ten huge trash bags full of the stuff. But an off-duty police officer happened to see us leave, and since it was after curfew, he called the police. Fortunately, we got off with a warning."

"That doesn't sound so bad."

"Yeah, we thought the whole thing would blow over, but the landowner pressed charges for property theft, and we got a three-day suspension at school. Since it was my idea in the first place, Jessica and her friends weren't allowed to associate with me anymore."

"Was your father upset?"

"Actually, he was pretty cool about it. I promised I wasn't going to get in any more trouble, and I didn't. Not until Earth Day, that is."

"Earth Day?"

"Every April we celebrate the planet, and there's a lot of protests against producers of fossil fuels. I heard about one at the corporate office of a big oil company, so I made some signs and decided to go."

Elly threw open the door to her closet and pulled out two cardboard signs stapled to flat sticks. One said MARS NOT FIT FOR HUMANS, and the other, THERE IS NO PLANET B.

Thomas couldn't contain a smile. "Well, you're right on both counts. Just the same, I wouldn't let Eno see these. He's a little sensitive on the subject."

"I can imagine."

"So, what happened at the protest?"

"I joined a peaceful demonstration. Or it was until some guy mouthed off to a police officer, and before I knew it, we were all being loaded into a police van. Since it was my second offense, and I was the only minor, I had to go to juvenile court."

"That doesn't sound good," Thomas said.

"It wasn't. The judge said she appreciated my civic passion, but if I was arrested one more time, she'd send me to juvey, which is short for juvenile hall."

"Is that like prison for kids?"

"Pretty much."

"But you haven't done anything else since then?"

"Well, no. Not until I met you and started planning the great cable car heist."

"You think the FBI knows about your trouble with the police?"

"They could easily find out. In fact, they probably have."

Thomas stood up. "Elly, you understand you can't help us anymore."

"That's what I thought you'd say. And that's why I didn't tell you. But you have to at least let me do *something*."

"You already have. And we really appreciate it. But I can't let you get sent to…juvey. What would your father say?"

"He'd quote Albert Einstein's line: 'You've got to color outside the lines once in a while if you want to make your life a masterpiece.'"

Thomas didn't know who Einstein was and had never heard the quote, but instantly saw its wisdom.

"At the very least let me go with you to get the mirrors back," Elly said. "They're your property, so you have a right to them. But I promise not to go inside the Cable Car Barn, so I won't be trespassing. After that, you'll be on your way, and I'll know I've done my part for the planet."

Elly held out her hand to shake. "Deal?"

"Deal."

Thomas took her hand and felt a powerful kind of connection, one that he didn't fully understand. He'd only known Elly for two days, but somehow it seemed much longer. The moment was broken by the sound of a car pulling up in front of the house.

Elly hurried to the window.

"Is it the FBI again?" Thomas asked.

"No," she said. "It's my father."

# CHAPTER 22

Elly led Thomas down the stairs. "Don't be nervous," she said, nervously.

"About what?" Thomas asked.

"This is actually the first time I've had a boy in…never mind…."

The front door opened and they stopped mid-flight as Elly's father appeared. Though he was smaller and heavier than Ignatius, Thomas guessed that Mr. McAllister was about the same age. And his eyes gave off the same good will.

"Hey, Dad. What are you doing home so early?"

"I let the staff off to beat the holiday traffic. Rosario said your friends were still here?"

"Right. Eno's downstairs playing video games, but this is Thomas."

"Nice to finally meet you, Thomas. Elly said you were hiking from Colorado. Is that where you're from?"

"No. Actually we're from Iceland."

"You don't say? I spent a few blissful months in your lovely country, once upon a time."

Elly looked puzzled. "You did?"

"Before you were born, honey. When I was in college I did a semester at the University of Reykjavík, studying sea birds. Where do you live, Thomas?"

Elly shot Thomas a nervous glance.

"Höfn," Thomas said. "It's a small town on the eastern coast."

"I never got out there, but I hear it's breathtaking."

"If you're familiar with our birds, you'll be interested to know we have a large population of puffins as well as kittiwakes. And our black pudding is famous all over the country."

"Is that so? I'd love to hear more about it. Are you staying for dinner?"

"No," Elly said, a bit too quickly. "I promised the boys I'd give them a tour of Chinatown and grab dinner down there."

"Not to be missed, I agree." Mr. McAllister said. "What about tomorrow then? One of my colleagues is hosting a dinner at her home over in Berkeley. Everyone's invited to stay for the fireworks."

"Actually, there's a party out at the beach, and I thought it would be a great opportunity for the guys to mix and mingle with some Earth kids."

Thomas gave Elly a glance, and she quickly corrected herself. "American kids, that is."

"Well I'm sure that will be a lot more fun than spending the holiday with a bunch of professors. Have a great time. And if you happen to get back this way Thomas, you can always stay with us, right Elly?"

Elly nodded enthusiastically. "Yeah, absolutely."

"Well, if you don't mind, I've got work to finish before the holiday. Happy Fourth."

Elly gave her father a quick kiss, and he headed to his office. Elly turned to face Thomas.

"Höfn, kittiwakes, black pudding? Where did all that come from?"

Thomas shrugged. "After you assigned me a nationality, I did a little research. Figured I'd better familiarize myself with my native country."

✦✦

ELLY LED THOMAS TOWARD the back door, still impressed by his interaction with her father. When they'd first met in Muir Woods, he seemed so lost and unsure of himself that she felt sorry for him.

But lately she was starting to see that he had a real talent for thinking on his feet. In that way, he was unlike any boy she'd ever known.

"Where are we going now?" Thomas smiled.

"We've got some work of our own to do," Elly said.

She took Thomas into the garage and locked the door behind them. She rummaged through some old camping supplies to find three moth-eaten sleeping bags. Wrapping them around some small gardening tools, they prepared for the excavation of the shuttle mirrors.

At five o'clock, Thomas, Eno, and Elly boarded the final ferry to Sausalito. After they got off, a taxi took them to a remote area past the park. Elly led the boys to a fire road. "We can wait here until the sun sets. The fog gets thicker then, and it'll give us extra cover."

Mention of the fog reminded Thomas of Josef using the dust devil on Mars to conceal his escape. It was hard to believe it had happened only days ago and that he was now on Earth, using a completely different weather system for concealment. He closed his eyes and inhaled the smell of the forest, which seemed even stronger than the morning they'd landed.

"Nothing like it, huh?" Elly said. "Between the redwoods and the animals, it's truly unique."

Eno looked alarmed. "We won't be meeting any of those animals, will we?"

"Unlikely, but it's good to stay alert. We don't want to scare them. It's their home, after all, not ours."

Elly pointed up to the sky. "Hey, look, we've got company."

Thomas turned to see a bird gliding out of the sky. It looked identical to the one he saw after he first left the shuttle. "Hey, it's the one I saw when I landed."

Elly smiled. "It's a Steller's Jay."

"You know this creature?" Eno said, slightly confused.

"Hard to say. They're all over Muir Woods."

The bird hopped onto a branch a bit closer to Thomas and looked right at him.

"It does seem like he recognizes you," Elly said. "Your luck could be changing."

"What do you mean?" Thomas said.

"They're supposed to be a symbol of good things to come."

"We can certainly use that," Eno said.

"Starting tonight," Elly said.

Twenty minutes later, the sun disappeared and the fog began to thicken so much so that Thomas tried to grab a handful. Unlike the dust devil, the wall of mist had an almost magical quality, swirling around them in the darkness, creating exotic patterns and shapes with an almost mystical effect as it worked its way through the trees. A boom rumbled in the distance.

Eno jumped. "What's that?"

"Thunder," Elly said. "Looks like we might have some rain."

"I hope so," Thomas said.

"I take it you don't get much of that back on Mars?" Elly said.

"Never," Eno said. "We have no magnetosphere."

"It's hard to picture," Thomas said. "The rain just falls from the sky?"

"Usually in small drops," Elly nodded. "But sometimes it rains so hard you can't see through it."

"What kind do you think this might be?" Eno said anxiously.

"Probably on the lighter side. What we call 'drizzle.'"

Elly held out her hand. "You can already feel the moisture in the air. Let's go."

She picked up her sleeping bag and led the boys into the forest. They hadn't gone more than a hundred yards when the rain began to tap out a soft patter on the trees. Thomas looked up and held out his hand in the way Elly did. To his amazement, the water puddled in his palm. He grinned. "This is really amazing."

"We take it for granted," Elly said, "but yeah, it really is."

They turned down a steep hillside shrouded in fog. Thomas glanced over to see Eno looking up at the giant redwoods nervously.

"Magnificent, aren't they?" Elly said.

"That's one word for them," Eno said. "Can you imagine if one fell on you?"

"It's the ones that have already fallen you have to worry about," Elly said as Eno pulled up short in front of a downed tree, then gingerly made his way over it.

Moving cautiously, they navigated several more as they made their way into the forest interior. They'd already lost track of time when Elly abruptly stopped and pointed to the treetops. "Check out those broken branches, that's where they lifted the shuttle out."

Thomas pulled out his Tetrascope and scanned the woods with its high-powered beam. Elly followed the light's path with her eyes, confused.

"I don't see my bandana."

Thomas aimed his light at the ground and moved it back and forth.

"Isn't that where we dug up the ground?"

While Thomas held his light steady, Elly used an old hoe to scrape off a few inches of surface soil. Almost immediately, a sliver of light bounced back at them from one of the mirrors.

"Nice call, Thomas."

They cleared the remaining dirt, then pulled out the mirrors and slid them inside the bags.

"Probably easiest to carry them like surfboards," Elly said. "Here, I'll show you."

Elly put a bag on top of her head, and Thomas followed suit. Eno needed help to balance his and tottered for a moment before finding his footing.

Then, with Elly leading the way, they started down the hillside.

They walked for about twenty minutes, taking only short breaks. Thomas saw a flash of light in the distance, a sign that they were getting close to the road. But when he turned to tell Elly, he suddenly noticed that Eno was no longer in sight.

"Where's Eno?" Elly said.

"I don't know. He was behind me a minute ago."

They put down their bags and hurried back up the hill until they saw him standing up on the hillside, his body frozen with fear.

"What's he doing?" Thomas said.

"Look over to the right," Elly said. "It's a baby deer."

The doe stood off to one side, clearly as frightened as Eno. But as Thomas took a step forward, it bolted into the darkness, and Eno dropped his mirror bag with a loud crash. A few moments later, a car engine rumbled to life somewhere down the hill.

"Rangers," Elly whispered urgently.

They ran up the hill as a pair of headlights streaked through the trees. When they reached Eno, they dropped to the ground and remained motionless until they heard the truck's engine go off.

"What's he doing?" Thomas said.

"Parking," Elly said.

"What now?" Thomas said.

"Get comfortable," Elly said. "We may be spending the night."

# CHAPTER 23

They made themselves as comfortable as possible on the wet forest floor, the boys flanking Elly. Despite the presence of the rangers, the night was quiet, and at some point Elly seemed to doze off. Her head fell against Thomas's cheek, and he noticed that her hair had a fragrance he couldn't identify. Whatever it was, he liked it even more than lemon. Directly above, the clouds slowly crept over the treetops, half-shielding the moon, which gave the sky an orange tint. The quiet was finally broken by the distant sound of an engine from somewhere high above.

"Helicopter," Elly whispered. "Don't move."

The boys stiffened as it began to descend, then leveled off just above the treetops. A high-powered searchlight strafed the ground, only a few feet away. It banked around and strafed the ground a second time and third time, before finally moving on. Minutes later, they heard the ranger's truck start up and drive away. They were free to go.

It was almost midnight when they got back to Elly's, and Thomas quickly fell asleep in the tree house. For the first time in memory, he didn't have his nightly dream about Earth. Instead, he dreamt of his escape from the Station, and the moment the Mastership began to bomb the Returner Compound. He woke up hoping Ignatius had survived the attack.

At eight o'clock, Elly called to say the coast was clear. Despite the late night, Thomas felt energized. The trek to the forest had been an adventure, the kind he'd always hoped to have on Earth. Not only did he get to experience rainfall but see an animal in its natural habitat. Eno didn't move a muscle, broken from the ordeal.

Thomas entered the kitchen to find Elly whipping up a cream-colored mixture in a large glass bowl. Charlie gave him his customary greeting.

"My dad left early, so I thought we'd get the day started. How're you doing?"

"Good," Thomas said, "though we have a minor mirror issue. Two of Eno's are cracked. But I should be able to patch them up."

"If it's not one thing, it's another, huh?" Elly said.

Thomas laughed. It was a good way to sum up the mission so far.

"In honor of your last day, I'm making pancakes," Elly said. "But I should warn you, they involve eggs. How do you want to break it to Eno?"

"I'll explain it later. Maybe in a few years."

Elly laughed as Eno shuffled into the kitchen. "Explain what?"

"The secret ingredient that makes pancakes so amazing," Thomas said.

"No need," Eno said. "I'll take your word for it."

"Grab a seat guys. The counter gets crowded when the batter lands."

The boys sat at the counter and watched with fascination as Elly ladled the batter onto the pan, where it congealed into neat circles. Charlie planted himself under Elly and looked up in anticipation.

"Does Charlie like pancakes?" Thomas asked.

"His favorite food, ever since he was a puppy."

"They smell incredible," Thomas said.

Eno scrunched up his nose at the sight.

"I'm not sure your sidekick agrees."

"Is that what I am, the sidekick?" Eno said.

"After your run-in with Bambi, you've actually earned the right to be called a second banana."

Thomas could see by the half-smile on Elly's face that she was teasing. "If Eno's a second banana, what am I?"

"Well, Charlie would definitely consider you a top dog."

Eno frowned at Elly. "And what does that make you?"

"I'd be your third wheel, unfortunately," Elly said, sliding the pancakes onto their plates. She opened a bottle of amber liquid and poured it over them.

"It smells a little like the forest last night," Thomas said, "only sweeter."

"Good nose," Elly said. "It's basically essence of tree, better known as maple syrup."

"Whoever thought of such a thing?" Thomas said.

"Whoever, indeed," Eno mumbled.

Thomas cut a forkful of pancakes and put it in his mouth. "Are you allowed to eat these at every meal?"

"Where food's concerned, it's a matter of personal taste, no pun intended. After you finish breakfast, you probably want to take a shower."

Thomas and Eno gave her a blank look, and Elly mimed the experience.

"Washing with running water…from overhead?"

"On Mars, water is rationed to two liters a day," Thomas said.

"We prefer a chemical scrub," Eno said. "It's far more efficient."

"Well, I can't offer you anything chemical, but you're welcome to give the shower a try," Elly said. "Just as soon you're finished eating."

"That might take a while longer," Thomas said, putting another forkful into his mouth.

✦✦

Twenty minutes later, Elly led Thomas to the bathroom. She pulled back the shower curtain as if revealing a magic trick and waved her hand dramatically.

"I give you…the shower."

"The levers control the water?" Thomas said.

"And, just as importantly, the temperature. Red for hot, blue for cold."

Elly turned on the shower and tested it with her hand. Thomas looked on in utter amazement as water shot out of the shower head. "What next?"

"Simple. Take off your clothes and get in."

Thomas began to remove his shirt.

"Uh, not until I leave," Elly said. "There's soap for your body on the dish right there. You rub it between your hands until it foams up."

"How long do you stay in?"

"For conservation purposes, I never go over three minutes. It's easy to let you mind wander and lose track of time. In fact, some people do their best thinking in the shower."

Elly handed Thomas a bottle of pale purple liquid and a towel. "Here's some shampoo for your hair. You might want to go easy. It's got a vague floral scent, lavender. You may not like it. I just buy whatever's on sale and live with it until I run out."

Elly handed over the items and left. Thomas removed his clothes and set the timer on his wrist pod. He stepped into the shower and under the water. He was surprised at how good the hot water felt as it hit his body, and he tilted his face toward the shower head, so he could feel its full effect. It was unlike anything he'd ever experienced; soothing and invigorating all at once.

Thomas poured some shampoo into his hair. As he worked it into a lather, he recognized it as the smell of Elly's hair from last night and felt grateful for all the things she had taught him about life on Earth. Meeting her had been a stroke of extraordinary luck. Or maybe it wasn't luck at all. He remembered what Ignatius had told him about the tide of time and its unique force. Perhaps, he thought, it had landed him in Muir Woods for the sole purpose of meeting Elly.

As he watched the lather slide over his chest and down his legs, he noticed a small puddle of red dust gathered at the drain. He couldn't help thinking that he was expelling the last traces of Mars's oxidized soil from his body. Cleansed of the past, he was finally ready to make direct contact with his new world.

Minutes later, Thomas entered the kitchen to find Eno hunched over an old garbage can lid with Thomas's Tetrascope laser. Elly sat at the table, writing on a pad of yellow paper.

"How was the shower?" she asked.

"Fantastic. I was really tempted to break the three-minute mark."

"Yeah, showers are like that. Once you're wet, there's no going back."

"Mind if I have another pancake?" Thomas said.

"Not at all," Elly said. "Might as well finish them off."

He took the rest of the pancakes and covered them in syrup. "You two seem busy."

Eno didn't look up. "I'm constructing a navigation chamber for the Time Globe, and Elly was kind enough to let me have this wonderful refuse component."

"I'm drawing up a master plan for tonight," Elly said. "Ideally, we should be at the Cable Car Barn no later than nine, when the fireworks begin. That should provide enough distraction for the break-in, not to mention your time-jump."

She slid the yellow pad over to reveal a rough sketch of the Cable Car Barn, complete with street signs and a map of the surrounding blocks.

"You'll enter through the side door here. I'll position myself directly across the street on the second-floor fire escape to keep watch."

"That's hardly necessary," Eno said. "Once you get us to the barn, you're free to leave."

"And miss the big launch?" Elly said.

"We'll simply disappear, that's all." Eno said.

"In a blaze of red shift," Elly added. "Not exactly an everyday event in these parts. I'll probably never see another one in my lifetime."

"Are you sure it won't draw some unwanted attention ?" Thomas said. "Like the blue shift when we landed?"

"Don't worry. Everybody will just assume it's part of the fireworks."

The word was barely out of her mouth when the doorbell rang, and they all froze.

"Rosario?" Thomas asked through a bite of pancakes.

"No, she's got a key." Elly said, as she got up and hurried to the den.

Thomas and Eno followed. She pulled back the shades to reveal two men in suits standing at the front door. One was tall. The other was shorter and carried a clipboard.

"It's those annoying FBI guys," Elly said. "Stay put. I'll get rid of them."

Elly went to the front door, and Thomas moved to the window for a closer look. He couldn't help noticing that the agents' car was the same industrial green as the hallways in the Boys' Quarters on the Station. When Elly opened the door, he could hear every word.

The taller one did the talking. "Miss McAllister? Hi. My name is Ed Collins, and this is my partner, Jim Rollins. We're agents with the local office of the FBI. We hope we're not interrupting, but we wanted to ask you a few questions."

"About what?" Elly said.

"We're investigating the recent incident in Muir Woods."

"Incident?"

"The fallen space junk? It's been all over the news."

"Oh, right," Elly said, as if she barely remembered it. "My dad mentioned it."

"One of the rangers, Mike Bender, said you were in the park when it happened. Only a few hundred feet away, from what he tells us. I assume you must've heard it come down?"

"Actually I didn't. I had headphones on and was listening to a book about Leafcutter Ants. Really fascinating, by the way. I was totally lost in it."

"So, you didn't see anything out of the ordinary?"

"Well, now that you mention it…"

Agent Rollins slid the clipboard out from under his arm, ready to write.

"I came across an incredibly large banana slug. Biggest one I've ever seen. I was in the woods gathering specimens," she added for clarification.

Agent Collins glanced at his partner to see his reaction.

"And what about your friend?"

Elly gave him a baffled look. "My friend?"

"Ranger Bender reported that someone was with you?"

"Oh, you must mean the foreign exchange student from Iceland. Yeah, he was hiking and got lost. He asked for directions, and we chatted for a few minutes, but that was it."

"Do you know where we might find him?"

"No. I offered to show him the city, but he was leaving the country that afternoon."

"I don't suppose you got his contact information?"

"No, sorry," Elly said.

"On the off chance he manages to contact you, would you take my card and get in touch?"

"Sure thing."

He held out his card, but Elly didn't take it.

"I already have one, thanks. Have a great day."

But before she could close the door, Agent Rollins finally spoke.

"One more thing Miss McAllister," he said, pulling a clear evidence bag from his jacket. "Does this belong to you, by any chance?"

Inside the bag was Elly's yellow bandana, the one she used to mark the spot where the mirrors were buried. She thought about denying it was hers, but quickly realized it might be traced back to her through DNA.

"Hmnn, it might be. Why?"

"It was found near the spot where the space junk you didn't see or hear came down."

"There were footprints in the area as well," Agent Collins said. He glanced down at Elly's feet as if to make his suspicion clear.

"That's where I found the giganto slug, and I put the bandana there to mark the spot. Guess I won't be able to go back now, huh?"

"Sorry about that," the agent said. "So, the footprints are yours?"

"Probably."

"And the exchange student? Was he with you at the time?"

"I don't know. He might've been but I really can't remember. Why?"

"We thought that might account for the second set of footprints," Agent Collins said. "The larger ones. Unless they belong to the third set, which were nearby."

"The third set," Elly repeated, trying to buy time to decide on the best response.

"I assume somebody was with the exchange student. Perhaps another exchange student?"

Elly scrunched up her face as if searching her memory. "Actually, he did have a friend come to think of it. Of course, the footprints could belong to anybody. The park gets thousands of visitors every day. They're not supposed to wander off the trails, but they all do. That's how I met the boys in the first place. Like I said…"

"Right," Agent Rollins said. "They were lost."

Agent Collins nodded slowly, as if he were considering another question, then reconsidered. "I guess that's all. For now. Thanks for your time, Miss McAllister."

The two agents turned from the door and started for the street.

"Uh, can I have my bandana back? It's a personal fave."

Agent Rollins turned. "Sorry, it's official evidence in the investigation, so we need to hold onto it. But we'll send it to you as soon as we're finished."

"We have your address," Agent Collins smiled, as if to remind her. "We were able to get it from the police department. Apparently you're well known to them."

"Thanks for your cooperation," Agent Rollins said, accenting the final word.

Elly shut the door, and Thomas watched from the den as the agents got back in their car.

Elly joined him at the window. "You hear any of that?"

"The whole thing," Thomas said. "You all right?"

"Totally," she said, though Thomas thought her voice had lost its usual confidence. "With any luck, I put them off the scent. Worse case, they'll head to Iceland to find you."

"Actually, I think they have something else in mind," Thomas said. He nodded toward the end of the street, where the agents had pulled into a cul-de-sac and parked. "It looks like they're watching the house."

"Don't worry, I have an escape route through the basement and out the back gate. I use it all the time, and it's foolproof."

# CHAPTER 24

AT THIRTEEN MINUTES AFTER eleven, Elly checked the window one last time. The FBI agents were still stationed at the end of the block. Thomas and Eno were standing by the doorway, waiting.

"They're still there," Elly said. "So here's the plan. I'll go out the front door and walk past their car. The moment you see it follow me go out the basement, climb the fence, walk to the next corner, and grab a cab to Ghirardelli Square on Fisherman's Wharf. I'll be waiting outside."

"How do you plan to lose them?" Thomas asked.

"I'll head to the Mongolian Barbeque on Jones, so they'll think I'm going to lunch and wait outside. But there's a rear exit, so I should be able to shake them. If they somehow follow me to the wharf, the place will be mobbed with tourists, so they'll be easy to lose."

"Why not simply stay here until we leave tonight?" Eno asked.

"Too risky," Thomas said. "We'll be carrying the Time Globe and mirrors."

"Yeah," Elly said. "We need them to think we're not coming back, so we might as well find someplace where we can kill the day."

"Kill the day?" Eno mused. "Now there's an interesting phrase."

"Fill the time between now and the fireworks," Elly clarified, just to be safe.

"What about the thing your friend invited us to?" Thomas said. "I think it was called a rager?"

"Huh," Elly shrugged. "I guess that would work. But we'll have to make a pit stop first."

"For what?"

"A makeover. The less you guys stand out the better."

"Whatever you think is best," Thomas said.

"Okay, I'm off."

Thomas watched as Elly left the house, carrying her backpack. She passed the FBI car and crossed the street. As she did, the car started and followed her.

"Let's go," Thomas said.

The boys went out the back door, and Thomas helped Eno over the fence. They followed Elly's instructions and hailed a cab on the next block. In a little over fourteen minutes, they arrived at the chocolate shop to find Elly waiting.

"How did it go?" Thomas asked.

"Mission accomplished," Elly said. "Come on."

Elly led the boys a few blocks away from Ghiradelli Square to a rundown storefront. "This is called a thrift shop. All the clothes are used, so we'll shoot for something circa 2018 to make it look like you've been here for years."

They entered to find a girl in her twenties behind the counter. She had bright blue hair, purple glasses, and was reading a graphic novel. On the cover was a girl with lime green hair and wings where her arms would normally be.

"Excuse me," Elly said. "We're looking for some stuff for my friends."

The counter girl looked at the boys for several seconds.

"We just got a shipment from the Bay Area Boy's Club that burned down last winter. I haven't had time to go through it yet, but my boss said he got everything that didn't smell like smoke. It's in the back. You're welcome to have a look."

"Thanks," Elly said as the girl went back to reading.

Elly and the boys found the boxes and began to pull clothes out while Elly sorted them into shirts, pants, and shoes. "Yell if anything jumps out at you."

Thomas held up a pair of patent leather loafers and looked at them suspiciously. "Maybe you should choose for us," he said.

Elly grabbed a pair of khaki cargo shorts and held them up to Thomas's waist, then fished a navy blue polo shirt and pair of dirty white skateboard sneakers out of the pile.

"Here, try these on behind the curtain over there."

While Thomas disappeared to try on the outfit, Elly turned to Eno.

"I'd prefer a single color," he said. "And no short pants."

"That's probably a good instinct."

Elly found a black shirt, a pair of black jeans, and high-top black sneakers.

Thomas emerged wearing his new outfit. "How do I look?"

"Like one of the locals. Check yourself out."

Elly took him by the shoulders and turned him toward a mirror. Thomas thought, for the first time since he and Eno had arrived, that he didn't look like an alien.

Elly handed him a faded gray sweatshirt. He put his arms through the sleeves, and Elly zipped it up. "It's called a hoodie. When it rains, or you need to go incognito, you pop the hood."

She flipped the hood over Thomas's head to demonstrate. But as she pulled the drawstrings, her eyes suddenly fluttered and then closed.

"Are you all right?" Thomas asked.

"Yeah, I'm just…"

Elly fell limp into his arms, and he gently lowered her onto the floor as Eno emerged from the dressing room in his black wardrobe.

"What's the matter with her?"

"I'm not sure," Thomas said. After a few seconds, Elly opened her eyes.

"Sorry about that. I get these mini-blackouts every now and then. No cause for alarm. They never last more than a few seconds and they seem to be harmless."

Elly sat up and took a deep breath.

"Have you seen a doctor?" Eno asked.

"Six. One internist, three neurologists, and a pair of psychiatrists. They've ruled out epilepsy, but think it might be some undiscovered genetic condition. Since we don't know anything about my real parents, it's anybody's guess."

"That's terrible," Thomas said.

"Hey," Elly shrugged. "What's life without a little mystery? C'mon, it's getting late. This is your last day, and we better make the most of it."

It was almost one o'clock by the time they got off the bus at Stinson Beach. They walked through the parking lot, and Thomas was immediately struck by the number of cars in every size, shape, and color. He was reminded of Eno's complaint about the variety of things on Earth. But to his way of thinking, it was one of the planet's best features. A small blue convertible with only two seats caught his eye. Sitting on its dashboard were a pair of miniature surfers. Their bellies hung over their shorts in comical fashion.

"Bobble head dolls," Elly explained.

"They look like the Moons," Thomas said, and for the first time, Eno actually laughed.

"Inside joke?" Elly said.

"Our school bullies," Eno said. "And close associates of Thomas's sworn enemy, Varik."

"Hard to believe you have a real enemy," Elly said.

"It's true," Thomas said. "Fortunately, I've seen the last of him."

"Why is that?" Elly said.

"He can't time travel," Eno said. "The technology developed by Ignatius is secret."

"Enough with Varik and Mars," Thomas said, glancing over the parking lot. "As long as we're her, we should take the opportunity to learn more about Earth."

"Well, as you can see," Elly said, "our current world is obsessed with cars, although in defense of my gender, it's mostly a boy thing."

"What do girls like?" Thomas asked.

"I'm probably not the best person to ask, but the standard answer is jewelry. Rings are very popular." Elly glanced at the Q-rings on Thomas's hand. "Like the ones you're wearing. They usually mean you have a relationship with a special person."

Thomas looked down at his hands. "These are for self-defense."

"So, you don't have a girl back on Mars?"

"To be honest, I don't even know any," Thomas said.

"Boys and girls are separated until the age of sixteen," Eno added. "Their neural networks are different, so we needn't constantly adjust our thinking to compensate for theirs."

"Ah," Elly said. "Then you should be right at home here on Earth."

As they came to the end of the parking lot, Thomas abruptly stopped. The crowd on the beach was enormous, as far as the eye could see, divided somewhat equally between boys and girls. He'd never seen so many people in one place, let alone in his age group.

"Here we are," Elly announced, kicking off her sneakers.

"Is it a requirement to remove your shoes?" Eno asked.

"Not as long you don't mind them getting filled with sand," Elly said.

Thomas removed his sneakers and wiggled his toes in the soft ground. The warm sand was a strange but pleasant sensation. As they started walking, Thomas pointed down the beach to a massive wooden pyramid.

"What's that?" Thomas said.

"It's for the bonfire. I take it you've never seen fire?"

"We've seen images," Thomas said, "but not the real thing."

"I wouldn't mention that if it happens to come up."

“Fire is hardly something to be proud of,” Eno said. “The burning of fossil fuels plays a critical part in the demise of your civilization.”

“That doesn’t exactly come as a shock,” Elly said. “But guilty as charged.”

They waded into the crowd of kids, most of whom sat under large umbrellas or laid on towels next to long oval boards. Elly spotted an unclaimed patch of sand halfway near the ocean and laid out their blanket. She removed a plastic tube of cream.

“What’s that?” Eno asked.

“Sunscreen. If you haven’t been exposed, you can get really burned.”

“I’d rather spontaneously combust than put any of that on my body,” Eno said.

“Suit yourself.”

“Is it all right if we go in the water?” Thomas asked.

“Sure,” Elly said. “Eno?”

“Are there creatures?” Eno said.

“Not unless you count crabs, jellyfish, and the rare shark.”

“Megalodons?” Eno said, shooting Thomas a nervous glance.

“No worry,” he said. “I don’t think they show up until sometime in 2051.”

Elly smiled. “I’ll put it on the calendar.”

As Eno plopped on the blanket, Thomas and Elly made their way toward the ocean. The sand gradually hardened, becoming dark and cool. Several people stood in the shallow water talking while a few laid on the oval boards and paddled farther out.

“You want a quick swimming lesson?”

“If you don’t mind.”

“The basic concept is simple. You hold your breath while your face is in the water, then breathe when it’s out. Paddle with your arms, kick with your feet. The trick is doing it all at the same time. It takes some practice, watch.”

Elly waded into the water up to her waist, then dove in and swam a few strokes, exaggerating the movements in slow motion. She then turned back to Thomas. "Got it?"

"I think so," Thomas nodded.

He put his head into the water and pushed off, taking several strokes. After a few moments he stood up, water sputtering out of his mouth.

"Not bad," Elly said. "Just remember to keep your mouth closed until you exhale. Let's swim parallel to the beach, so the water won't be over your head," Elly said.

Elly and Thomas began to swim. Remarkably, Thomas was able to keep up.

After a dozen strokes, Elly stopped. "You're a natural. You must be part fish." They continued to swim in short bursts for another twenty minutes, when Elly stopped and waved Thomas toward the shore. "I think you've got the hang of it. Let's take a break. I'll show you how to carve your initials in the sand."

Thomas looked slightly embarrassed. "Actually, I don't know how to write by hand. Everything on Mars is done digitally."

"Don't worry, it's easier than swimming," Elly said, grabbing the nearest seashell. She knelt in the wet sand and, using the shell's sharp edge, slowly carved a large T. "There, try to copy it."

Thomas knelt next to her and carefully made his own primitive version.

"Nice. Now let's try the next letter."

As Elly began to carve an H, a hunk of wet sand landed on the letter.

Thomas looked up and was startled to see a grinning Jessica. She wore a bright pink bathing suit and was flanked by her two friends, who wore matching suits in neon yellow and blood orange.

"Hey, there," Jessica said. "I see you changed your mind after all."

"Their flight got delayed," Elly said.

"I hope you're staying for the bonfire? That's when things really start to heat up."

"No," Elly quickly said. "They have to be out of here by sundown."

"Too bad. You may want to get a later flight."

"Not possible," Elly volunteered.

"I guess you'll never know what you missed," Jessica shrugged.

She brushed Thomas's shoulder with her hips as she continued down the beach with her girlfriends. After a few steps, she looked back and waved.

Elly jumped to her feet and began walking away from the water's edge. Thomas caught up with her, and noticed that her eyes seemed somehow darker.

"Is something wrong?"

"No," Elly snapped.

Thomas jumped in front of her and walked backward, trying to get her to make eye contact. But she kept looking away.

"You're walking backward, Thomas. The last thing you should be doing is trying to attract attention."

"I'm not. I'm just trying to get yours. I may be new to Earth, but I can tell you're unhappy. Is it something I did?"

Elly sighed. "Let's go over there, where we can have some privacy."

They walked toward a giant piece of driftwood and sat in the sand.

"There's something I haven't told you, about my Earth Day bust."

"You don't really owe me any..."

"No, I want you to know. After we left the courtroom that day, my father took me for dim sum at our favorite Chinese restaurant. I thought he was upset, since I promised I wouldn't get into any more trouble. But he just wanted me to understand that because I was so young my true destiny probably hadn't revealed itself yet, and I needed to stay open to it."

"I don't understand."

"I didn't either, though it was strange that he used the word 'revealed,' like it was going to arrive in a fortune cookie or something. I didn't think much about it after that, until the other day when you walked out of the trees in Muir Woods, and I suddenly had this weird feeling my destiny was about to be revealed. And when you told me what your mission was, I knew that was it. Unfortunately, there's a major problem."

"What's that?" Thomas said.

"I can't just leave my father and disappear into the future, you know?"

Thomas did. Even though he didn't actually know his own father, he could imagine what a terrible dilemma that would be for Elly, whose life was intertwined with her father's.

"Elly, for some reason we crossed paths, and I don't think it was an accident. Ignatius always said that time has its own tide and we have to trust where it takes us."

"Even when it takes me nowhere?"

Thomas didn't know what to say, so he reached out and put his hand on hers. She could feel the Q-Ring on his finger touch the back of her palm. The energy of the ring produced a strange sensation, and he wondered if it was just the power of the metal or something more.

"Even though you may not be able to come with us right now, I think time brought us together for a reason, and I don't believe we've seen the last of each other."

"I wish you could stay longer," she said.

"There's nothing I'd like more, believe me. But I can't."

He retrieved Lina's chain from his neck and held the titanium disc to the light. Thomas's father and mother came to life, along with a group of children in the deep background. "Those kids are the last hope for Earth. And right now, their fate rests with me."

"I know. You have an important mission to accomplish, and I want to do whatever I can to help. Is there anything else you'd like to do before we leave?"

"Actually, there is one thing."

"What's that?"

"Show me how to build a sandcastle?"

## CHAPTER 25

ELLY BUILT A SMALL demonstration model then asked Thomas to construct a sandcastle version of Olympus Mons with the Returner Compound inside. After he finished, Elly showed him the delicate art of using your fingers to carve out the tunnels that ran from the Station. It was almost five o'clock when they finished. Thomas stood back to examine the massive volcanic sandcastle and silently hoped that the real thing was still intact after his escape.

Elly jumped to her feet and brushed off the sand. "It's getting late. Race you back?"

Before Thomas could move, Elly was sprinting toward their blanket. Thomas almost caught up, and they arrived a few seconds apart to find Eno asleep face down, his back a bright shade of red.

"Eno?" she said. "I think you're going to regret the 'no sunscreen' decision."

Eno rolled over, wincing. "My only regret is having to spend all day in this torturous heat. Where did you two go anyway?"

"Fossil hunt," Elly said, unloading a pile of seashells from her pocket.

Suddenly, they saw everyone start to get up and head in the other direction.

"What's happening?" Thomas said.

"Looks like they're about to light it up," Elly said. "We should probably leave."

"Can't we just watch the beginning?" Thomas said.

"I guess," Elly said, reluctantly.

They gathered their backpacks and followed the crowd toward the giant wood pile. From the edge of the crowd, they could see a boy wearing one of the football jerseys from Elly's school light a driftwood torch. He touched it to the pyramid, and as it spread upward, everyone cheered. Thomas was mesmerized by the fast moving flames; even Eno was mesmerized. One of the boys passed out small cans of liquid from ice chests while another collected cash.

"Well, there you have it," Elly said. "Fire and beer, a classic American combo. Now, we really should hit the road. We don't want to miss the last bus."

They turned to go when a voice shot out of the crowd.

"Hey!"

They turned to see Jessica and her blondes, along with a few football players, one of whom dangled a muscular arm around her neck. He wore a jersey with the number nine on front and chopped off at the mid-section to reveal a set of well-developed abdominal muscles.

"You're not leaving already, are you?" Jessica said. "The party's just getting started."

"They have a flight to catch," Elly said.

"Where'd you find these dorks?" Number Nine said to Elly, whom he clearly recognized from school. "They in the gifted loser program, too?"

"He's the top dog," Eno said. "And I'm second banana."

The girls laughed, but Number Nine turned to Eno. "What are you, a wise-ass?"

"They're foreign exchange students," Elly said.

Jessica smirked. "From Iceland."

"Well they're in the USA now, and they can't leave until they pay the bonfire tax. Ten bucks a person, twenty for foreigners."

"That's ridiculous," Elly said. "C'mon, guys, we're out of here."

"Not so fast," Number Nine said.

Before they could take another step, they were outflanked by the other boys, who blocked them from leaving the beach. A boy with number one on his jersey broke through the crowd. Up close, Thomas recognized him as the one who lit the bonfire.

"They gotta pay up, one way or the other," he said, then reached out and grabbed Thomas's backpack from off his arm.

He unzipped the backpack and plunged his arm inside. "What do we got here? Oh how cute! A stuffed animal and a box of…crayons!"

"Maybe second banana got something better," one of the other boys said. He pulled Eno's backpack out of his hand and unzipped it. The expression on his face changed. "Hey, this stuff looks expensive," he said, pulling out the Time Globe.

"Excuse me," Eno said, "but we need that back."

"Says who?" Number One said.

"I do," Thomas said.

Elly glanced at him, and could see that the expression on his face had changed as he rolled his thumbs over the Q-rings on his fingers.

"Well, what are you gonna do about it, top dog?" Number One asked.

Thomas snatched the globe out of his hand and gave it to Eno as Number One threw a haymaker at his head. Thomas ducked and grabbed his wrist as the boy yelled in pain and dropped the backpack. Eno and Elly stepped to the side as Thomas swung Number One into the air, away from the fire. He landed with a soft thud, face down, and came up with a face full of sand. Stunned, his friends backed away as Elly grabbed the crayons and stuffed animal along with the backpack.

She turned to Jessica, who still had her hand over her mouth in shock. "We're leaving now. Thank your friends for the hospitality."

Elly took the boys by their arms and marched off the beach.

They rode the bus back to the city in silence. The ugly confrontation was an unfortunate way to end their stay in San Francisco, Thomas thought, but he could now see what Ignatius meant when he warned him that he'd always be an alien on Earth. Eno didn't seem as affected, but Thomas guessed it was because he expected no better from the kids on Earth. To his mind, they were the same bullies as those at the Station. Strangely enough, Elly seemed to take what happened the hardest.

"Are you all right?" Thomas said.

Elly shook her head in dismay. "One of the abiding mysteries of life on this planet is how some people take such joy in trying to put strangers down."

"Not everyone though," Thomas assured her. "You're proof of that. Besides, we shouldn't let a bad ten minutes ruin a great day."

"Speak for yourself," Eno said.

Thomas and Elly exchanged a smile, and then started to laugh.

At 7:58 p.m., Thomas and Eno scaled the back fence as Elly opened the kitchen door and let them into the house.

"All clear. No sign of the FBI. You guys can get ready while I get dinner started."

As Thomas took a shower and Eno a nap, Elly made spaghetti and meatballs, which Thomas and Eno both thought was the best thing they'd eaten on Earth. When they were finished, Thomas went to the garage to finish the mirror repair, while Eno returned to the basement to put the final touches on the Navigation Chamber for the Time Globe. After Thomas finished with the mirrors, he reorganized his backpack, wrapping the train locomotive in the sports section of the newspaper Elly had given him. That done, he packed the extra clothes Elly bought for him and Eno at the thrift store, but held out the baseball hat with the initials SF. He decided to wear it for the time-jump to remind her how thankful he was for all she'd done for them on their first days on Earth.

Elly appeared in the doorway. "Hey, Thomas, I have something for you. It's what we call a 'selfie.'" She handed him a photo of her and Charlie, taken in Muir Woods, holding up the jar with the banana slug she'd found the day Thomas landed. It now seemed like weeks ago.

Thomas smiled. "I don't have a picture of me and Eno. But I have this." He took his Earth-shaped hunk of hematite out in his pocket. "I always kept it with me because it reminded me of Earth, but since it came from Mars, maybe it'll remind you of us."

"I'm sure it will Thomas. Thanks."

As she clutched it protectively in both hands, a car horn sounded outside.

"There's the cab," Elly said. "I'll meet you upstairs."

Eno was already at the door when Thomas arrived with the mirror bags. Elly appeared with a small duffel bag she'd filled with supplies for their trip.

"I packed up the spaghetti, along with some PB and J. I don't know what they'll be eating in 2071, but it's hard to imagine a future where either one goes out of style. I gave you some books on geography and wildlife, and my foraging manual, in case you run out of food. I also threw in the sleeping bags. You'll need them, unless you meet another girl with a tree house."

Thomas didn't know what to say, and the three of them fell into a strange silence, as if some sort of final countdown had suddenly begun.

Elly finally spoke. "I hate to say this, but I guess there's a good chance we'll never see each other again."

"That's true," Eno said.

"No, it's not," Thomas said. "I promised to bring the cable car back."

"Right," Elly said, though Thomas could tell she was skeptical. "You'll probably need some help getting it into the Cable Car Barn, so give me a call."

Elly pulled out a battered cell phone. "Here's my old phone. I deleted all the other numbers, so it's basically a hotline to me."

The taxi honked a second and third time.

"Time to go," Eno said.

The threesome piled into the back of the taxi, Elly between the boys. She asked the driver to take the route that ran along the bayfront for one last view of the city. As they drove, Elly pointed out the famous landmarks of Alcatraz Island, formerly a prison, and Coit Tower, a monument to the city's heroic firefighters. Eno looked away. The very sight of the bay reminded him of his stomach-turning ferry ride. Thomas did his best to focus on the sights so that he could store the memories but was distracted by Elly's reflection in the window. Her hair was pulled back in a way that accented her pale green eyes, which seemed to glisten in the sun setting over the water. In place of her customary bandana, she wore a matching pair of silver metal clips in the shape of butterflies—a birthday gift from her father. Thomas wished they could ride around the city all night, but when they turned and started up the steep hill where they took their first cable car ride, he knew his time in San Francisco was coming to an end.

As they pulled up to the Cable Car Barn, it was deserted, just as Elly had predicted.

"I'll be on that fire escape across the street," Elly said. "Keep your phone handy. If anybody shows up, I'll call and warn you. The fireworks should go off any time now."

Thomas nodded but made no move toward the door.

"I guess this is it," he said.

"Goodbye, Eno," Elly said. "I know you'd be mortified by a hug, but Thomas definitely gets one."

Elly threw her arms around him. Thomas had never experienced a *hug* and was unprepared for the feeling of warmth it generated all over his body. Elly held the embrace for a long moment, then hurried across the street. Thomas watched her go.

When she reached the bottom of the fire escape, he gathered the mirror bags and the duffel while Eno took the backpacks and deposited them in front of the barn. Using his diamond blade, he made a box-like cut around the handle on the thick metal door.

Eno reached inside and opened it as Thomas transferred their things inside. He closed the door but glanced back across the street one last time to see that Elly was already on the second-floor fire escape.

She waved. He waved back.

They hurried to cable car number twelve. Thomas removed a mirror as Eno began to drill holes into the panel that ran alongside the cabin. Thomas then used the glue gun to lay a line of adhesive around the edges of the first mirror and held it in position while Eno inserted the bolts.

"It's for the best, you know," Eno said.

"What?"

"Leaving. I think you were beginning to develop an adverse physical reaction to Elly."

"What do you mean?" Thomas said.

"I could see it in your face. It became flushed when she put her arms around you. I suspect it was brought on by an electrolyte disturbance."

Thomas couldn't really explain what he'd been feeling. All he knew was that it was something he wanted to experience again.

After another five minutes, Thomas pushed the last panel into place. He checked his wrist pod to see that it was almost nine o'clock. "How you doing on the Navigation Chamber?"

"Installation complete. All I have to do now is insert the Time Globe."

A red glow suddenly appeared outside the window, and Thomas felt a vibration in his pocket. He pulled out Elly's cell phone.

"Elly?"

"How close are you to jumping?"

"Minutes. Why?"

"A police car just pulled up outside the barn. You must've tripped an alarm when you entered. Hurry, and I'll try to distract them."

Thomas ran to the second floor and looked out the window. Two policemen were getting out of their car and about to approach the Car Barn. Then he saw Elly limping toward them, as if she'd hurt her leg. They met in the middle of the deserted street, where Elly was now talking fast and gesturing toward her knee.

Thomas shouted down to Eno. "Set the timer!"

Eno peeked out from the cable car and looked up to Thomas.

"We need to go, now!"

Eno ducked into the cable car as Thomas watched one of the policemen usher Elly toward the police car. A loud pop echoed in the sky, leaving a streak of white light in its wake. As the first fireworks exploded in a shower of color, Elly suddenly pulled away from the policeman and ran. They began to chase her.

Eno shouted from the cable car. "Thomas! Countdown has begun!"

Thomas sprinted to the wall and hit a switch that caused the hydraulic doors to swing open, allowing the cable car to exit the barn. Eno had his football helmet on and was tying his restraining ropes when Thomas jumped into the cabin and grabbed the brake mechanism.

Imitating the man he'd seen in the car barn demonstration, he released the brake and the cable car began to roll toward the open door.

"What are you doing?" Eno shouted. "We can't be moving while we launch!"

"We still have time," Thomas said.

"Thirty-eight seconds!" Eno said, as the car scraped through the doors with a shower of sparks, and started down the steep hill.

Above them, the fireworks were in full bloom, lighting the sky in red, white and blue.

As the cable car picked up speed. Thomas spotted the police chasing Elly, who ran parallel to the cable car tracks. He hopped onto the running board and shouted.

"Elly! Come closer! I'll drop you at the bottom of the hill!"

Elly glanced back at the police who were gaining on her and quickly veered toward the cable car. As the cable car rolled toward her, she held out her hand and Thomas took it. Then, with one quick move, he pulled her up and into the cabin.

He turned to Eno and shouted. "Shut down the globe!"

But between the football helmet and the noise, Eno couldn't hear a thing.

Thomas grabbed the brake and leaned back on the grip handle, his palms stinging as the metal tore his skin. The car lurched sideways, almost going off the tracks, throwing he and Elly to the floor. It started to spin, and Thomas glanced at the timer to see that it read four seconds.

As the spinning accelerated, Elly rolled onto Thomas, and he held her tight so she that she wouldn't be slammed against the side of the cable car, which was now whipping around so fast that the fireworks seemed to stretch around them in a halo of multicolored light.

But before Elly could realize what was happening, the lights vanished in a sea of black.

# THE FUTURE

## CHAPTER 26

THOMAS WAS THE FIRST to open his eyes. He saw the same swarm of multicolored particles he observed after his first jump and again heard the voice of Ignatius. It reminded him that time would not always take him directly to his destination. He turned to see Elly, sitting next to him, looking at the particles in a state of wonder. They gathered around her in excitement, as if to welcome her to the mission.

"What are they?" she said.

"I'm not sure. They seem to carry messages from Ignatius. Did you hear anything?"

"No."

"Maybe it's just my imagination."

"What are they called?"

"I'm not sure they have a name," Thomas said.

"Time flies," she christened them.

Elly looked around the cabin and took a deep breath. Thomas couldn't tell whether she was excited or horrified by what had happened.

"I'm sorry, Elly," he said.

"For what?"

"I shouldn't have pulled you in."

"Don't apologize. Hey, you saved me from getting arrested."

"Hopefully, we can get you back home *before* that happens."

"Speaking of which, where's your Navigator?"

Thomas nodded toward the other end of the cabin, where Eno was tucked into a fetal position, arms over his helmeted head.

"You think he's okay?" Elly said.

"We won't know until he starts complaining."

Elly laughed. "Where are we? Or I guess I should say, *when*?"

"I don't know. The one thing the Time Globe doesn't do is confirm whether we've reached the destination of a jump, so we have to figure that part out on our own."

Thomas got to his feet and helped Elly up, then pushed open the small window at the front of the platform. It revealed a predawn sky and a sliver of moon. The temperature was warm, the air thick with morning mist. As it drifted past them, the cable car appeared to be floating through the clouds.

"I can tell you one thing," Elly said. "It's not the Fourth of July anymore."

"How do you know?"

"The moon's a waning crescent. When we left San Francisco, it was waxing."

Thomas leaned out the window and surveyed the base of the car.

"Can you see anything?" Elly asked.

"Yeah, we're on some tracks."

"Maybe we're still in San Francisco," Elly said, a hint of hope in her voice.

"I don't think so. They don't look like cable car tracks. They're much narrower."

Elly glanced down to see that the wheels of the cable car were wider than the tracks they were sitting on. When she leaned out, the front of the car suddenly lurched downward like one end of a seesaw. Elly let out a shriek and grabbed Thomas by the arm.

"Don't move!" Elly said.

"Why not?"

"We're on a roller coaster," Elly said.

She pointed out the window. The mist had thinned to reveal an elaborate network of horizontal and vertical struts rising hundreds of feet off the ground.

Thomas scanned the massive structure, which looked like the skeleton of a giant snake. "Isn't this the thing we saw in your school shop?" he asked. "The roller coaster?"

"Yeah," Elly said." But that was only a model. This is the mother-of-all version."

"I looked it up," Thomas said. "I understand they're really popular."

"Yeah," Elly said, "for people who don't mind riding in open cars at death-defying speed. Did I mention that I'm not one of them?"

Eno opened his eyes and looked up at Thomas and Elly.

"Where are we?"

"On a roller coaster," Thomas said. "A big one."

Eno carefully rose and peered out the window. "Oh no. This is not good."

"Why would the Time Globe land us in such a dangerous spot?" Elly said.

"It generally seeks out the most remote location, and failing that, the highest," Eno said.

"How are we going to get down?" Elly said.

"We can use the restraining ropes," Thomas said. "That way, even if you lose your grip, you won't fall."

"I should disconnect the Globe," Eno said.

Eno removed the Time Globe and put it into his backpack while Thomas retrieved the Tetrascope and zipped it into the pocket of his cargo shorts. When they were finished, he tied the rope around each of their waists. "Everybody ready?"

Elly drew a nervous breath. "Let's call it willing and leave it at that."

Thomas opened the door and stepped onto the running board, which hung over the tracks in mid-air. He inched toward the front platform and stopped. Elly went next, and then Eno. When they were all on the platform, Thomas stepped onto the tracks and knelt down. He tied the free end of his waist rope to the rail, then climbed over the side onto one of the horizontal struts.

"Any time," he yelled up.

Elly slid over the side and gingerly rose to her feet.

"Not so bad, huh?" Thomas said.

"Yeah, piece of cake," Elly said. "Eno, your turn."

Eno stepped out onto the track and froze.

Thomas saw that he was beginning to breathe faster. "Just sit down."

Eno sat on the tracks. Thomas and Elly grabbed his ankles and slowly guided him down so that he stood between them on the strut. Thomas then climbed up, untied the rope at the top, climbed back down, and retied it. The process was slow and painstaking, but after about ten minutes, the layer of mist directly below them started to thin.

"Can you see the ground?" Elly asked.

Thomas looked down. "Hmm."

"Is that a good hmm or a bad one?"

"Not sure. I'd say we're pretty close to…the water."

Indeed, the entire structure appeared to be sitting in a lake.

"That would be consistent with conditions during the Final Evacuation," Eno said. "Our jump must have been accurate."

"Hate to break it to you," Elly said, "but unless somebody's hiding the Rocky Mountains, this isn't Colorado."

Elly nodded toward the horizon. Indeed, there wasn't a mountain in sight. But in the early morning light, the park was slowly beginning to reveal itself. Thomas pointed to a large neon sign at the opposite side of the park, with its words facing backward.

Thomas read them aloud. "D-N-A-L-S-I."

"ISLAND," Elly said, as if it were a contest for who could decipher it first.

Eno nodded. "And my name is right next to it."

Sure enough, the letters E-N-O were in front of the word "island."

"But the letters at the beginning and end are out of neon," Elly said.

"What do you suppose they are?" Thomas asked.

"C and Y. Which makes 'Coney Island.' It's an amusement park in New York."

"How do you know?" Eno asked.

"I've been here before. When I was nine, my father had a teacher's conference in Manhattan and brought me. We took the subway from the city."

Eno looked to Thomas for a definition. "Subway?"

"An underground train," Thomas said. "It's on my list of things to do on Earth."

"Under the circumstances, I think we'll have to rule that out," Elly said.

"We can rule out the entire location." Eno said. "If this is a superflood, the region is submerged for miles in every direction. We should go back up to the transport and try another jump."

"You mean to San Francisco?" Elly asked.

"That's not what I was thinking, no," Eno said.

"It's your call, Elly," Thomas said. "We can take you home if you like."

"That would be a waste of time, in every sense of the word," Elly said "You might remember, I complained about not being able to go on the mission, but here we are. Even if we're in the wrong place, we should at least find out what year it is."

"How far are we from the city of Manhattan?" Eno asked.

"If memory serves, almost an hour by subway. But I remember we took the ferry back across the river and got there in half that time."

"I don't see any ferries around," Thomas said.

"No," Elly said. "But without some sort of boat, we're dead in the water, pardon the expression."

"There must be something around here that floats," Thomas said.

Elly thought about it for a moment. "I remember a ride with a Viking ship, or at least a smaller replica of one. I think it was near the Ferris wheel, which is that big round contraption sticking out of the water over there."

"Yeah, I can see it," Thomas said.

Thomas took off his backpack and began to untie the rope around his waist.

"What are you doing?" Elly asked.

"Going to look for the boat."

"It's a long way for somebody who just learned how to swim."

"No problem. I can breathe under water if I need to stop and rest."

"How's that?" Elly said.

"I have a secret weapon called the Porta Gill."

Thomas retrieved the Porta Gill from his backpack and held it up.

"Wow, you really came prepared," Elly said.

He pulled off his shirt and sneakers, and laid them on the coaster struts.

"Back in a few minutes."

Thomas put the Porta Gill in his mouth and then jumped into the water and began to swim. In minutes, he was around the roller coaster and out of sight.

"I should've gone with him," said Elly. "It's not smart to swim alone."

The words were barely out of her mouth when the water rippled in front of them. A massive black fin, easily as tall as she and Eno, broke the surface. In the confines of the small park, it looked ridiculously out of scale, like a barracuda in a goldfish bowl.

"What's *that*?" Elly said.

"*That* is a megalodon," Eno said, his face tightening in horror. "You remember, the creature you assured us we wouldn't run into?"

Elly felt a wave of guilt about making Thomas leave his Sonic Inducer in the shuttle. She quickly dropped her backpack, untied her waist rope, and pulled off her sweatshirt.

"What are you…" Eno started to ask, but before he could finish, she dove into the murky water.

# CHAPTER 27

THOMAS SWAM TOWARD THE Ferris wheel, occasionally ducking under water for a few moments to rest. As he did, he caught glimpses of several signs announcing various attractions like "The Wonder Wheel," "The Thunderbolt," and "A Trip to the Moon," but nothing featuring a boat of any sort. As he passed something called "The Freak Out," he heard someone calling his name and lifted his head out of the water.

He swiveled around to see Elly swimming toward him and pulled the Porta Gill out of his mouth. "What are you doing?"

"We've got company!" she shouted.

Thomas immediately spotted the massive fin behind her. The nearest tower, with a sign announcing a ride called the "Kamikaze," was twenty yards away. It was outfitted with short vertical bars for climbing.

"You think we can make it over there?" Thomas said.

"At the rate he's moving, I doubt it," Elly said, as she caught up to Thomas.

"We'll have to lose him then."

"What do you mean?"

Thomas handed the Porta Gill to Elly. "Here. Use this."

"What about you?"

"We'll take turns. Come on!"

Elly bit on the mouthpiece, and they dove down into the submerged amusement park. Several ghostly rides distorted by the water shimmered around them. They swam toward a circular platform filled with replicas of miniature horses and saw the megalodon clearly for the first time. Coming through the dark water, it looked like some sort of mythic sea monster.

The shark was at least fifty feet long. It swam toward them, ready to attack, but was unable to fit its massive body into the narrow space between the horses. Undeterred, it began to glide around them in slow circles, as if to make it clear he had no intention of leaving.

Elly looked to Thomas, her eyes wide with fear, as the shark made a second pass. She took a deep breath from the Porta Gill then handed it back to him. He took a few quick breaths and gave it back, then pointed in the direction of the Kamikaze tower. She nodded, and as soon as the shark passed them, they kicked furiously toward it.

The huge beast spotted them and followed.

Attached to the tower was a long metal arm connected to a caged gondola designed to swing in a circular motion. Thomas threw open the gondola door, but as he did, the shark lunged forward, jaws open. He slammed the door shut, but the megalodon kept going, intent on smashing through into the flimsy metal partition. The cage was badly twisted, but held.

Thomas glanced at Elly. The fear in her eyes had been replaced by pain. She held one of her arms across her hand, blood oozing out between her fingers. One of the shark's teeth had grazed her arm between the shoulder and elbow.

The megalodon began to look for another opening.

They were safe in the gondola but also trapped.

Thomas handed Elly the Porta Gill and held up a finger, as if to say he had an idea. Elly gave him a look of complete bewilderment, as Thomas threw himself across the cage so he was face to face with the megalodon.

The shark responded by slamming its giant nose against the cage, sending the gondola swinging backward. Elly could barely contain the blood that flowed from her arm, puzzled that Thomas would taunt the angry beast. It struck again, driving the gondola closer to the water's surface. And when the megalodon hit the gondola a third time, he drove it up and out of the water, putting it several feet above the surface, out of its reach. The frustrated megalodon swam beneath them like a submarine, its huge tailfin brushing against their feet.

Thomas doubled over, coughing water, gasping for air. He glanced at the blood running down Elly's forearm.

"Are you all right?" Thomas said.

"Blood and sharks." Elly winced. "Bad combination."

"We've got to get you out of here," he said, glancing around the gondola.

The door they used to enter was now above them, and Thomas climbed up and pushed it open. He scrambled out and then pulled Elly after him. They made their way onto the tower and stood high above the shark, which still circled beneath them, trying to decide its next move.

Thomas held Elly's arm and inspected the six-inch gash.

"In the Station Infirmary, they cauterize wounds like this with a laser," Thomas said. "There's one on my Tetrascope that should work. But it'll hurt."

"It hurts now, and it's not going to heal itself."

Thomas pulled the Tetrascope from the pocket in his shorts and activated the laser. He adjusted it to the lowest possible strength, then held Elly's arm firmly in the other hand.

Elly closed her eyes as Thomas quickly ran the beam along the gash. The smell of burning flesh wafted into the air. Elly gritted her teeth, stifling tears.

"Sorry," Thomas said.

"I'm the one who should be apologizing. If I hadn't made you leave your sonic thing behind, we wouldn't be in this mess."

"But if you weren't here, we wouldn't know about the boat."

"What boat?"

Thomas pointed to another ride about twenty yards away. A strange looking boat hung in midair over yet another tower. A banner on the platform read, "SEA VIKING."

"Isn't that the ride you were talking about?" Thomas said.

"Yeah. But you're not suggesting we get back in the water are you?"

"Of course not. I'll go. You stay here."

"Thomas, you can't."

"I'll be fine," he said, holding up the laser. "I have this."

"You think it's going to stop that thing?"

"No, but it should buy me enough time to get to the tower."

"I guess I can't talk you out of this, huh?"

"Not a chance."

Thomas knew Elly wouldn't even be here if he hadn't pulled her into the cable car, so he couldn't let any harm come to her until he got her home.

"Aim for the nose," Elly said.

"What?"

"The membrane's thin. It's a shark's Achilles' heel."

"How do you know that?"

"I'm a naturalist, remember?"

Thomas put the Porta Gill in his mouth and waited until the shark was far enough away, then dove over the side. He sliced into the water with barely a ripple, kicking as fast as he could toward the Sea Viking. There was no sign of the megalodon.

And then it appeared out of the murky water, where it had been waiting all along. Thomas knew he couldn't outswim the beast. His only chance was to make a stand. The nearest ride was called the "Little Air Force," featuring a squadron of metal jets, each about four feet long, hanging by chains from a circular bar. He quickly reached the jets, swiveled, and grabbed the tail end of one with one hand. With the other, he gripped the Tetrascope. When the megalodon was within striking distance, Thomas switched the laser to its full length and aimed the beam at the shark's nose. Stung, it threw its huge head to the side, then disappeared back into the shadowy water.

Thomas knew the beast would be back, and in a few moments he could see it coming. He put the Tetrascope back into his pocket, then gripped the tail section of the airplane with both hands, so that his legs dangled below it like bait.

The megalodon, sensing that he was finally about to have a meal, opened its jaws. Thomas gave a strong kick, pushing the plane forward and jamming the metal cockpit into the beast's open mouth. From her perch on the Kamikaze tower, Elly saw the megalodon thrash to the surface, and spit out the plane angrily. As it swam off, Thomas climbed onto the tower, which held the Sea Viking. Elly slumped in relief.

Thomas waved and shouted. "How's your arm?"

"Throbbing a little. But I packed some aspirin in the duffel."

"Good, we'll be back before you know it."

Elly gave Thomas a thumbs up.

Thomas turned back toward the Sea Viking. He remembered that the Vikings were ancient Earth warriors who conquered the world in long ships. The boat was over twenty feet long, and adorned with colorful shields welded to each side along with a pair of metal oars. Long chains were attached to the front and back, which allowed the boat to swing in the air.

Thomas used his laser to cut the chains, and the Viking ship dropped into the water. He jumped inside and cut away the metal oars, then used one to paddle toward Elly. Once there, he helped lower her into the boat. With her good arm, she grabbed the other oar.

"We'll move faster if we both paddle."

"Are you sure?"

"I'm no expert," Elly said, "but I've been on a few canoe trips with my dad, so I know the basics. You take one side and I'll take the other. That way we can stay in a straight line."

Thomas nodded, and together they began to cut through the water.

# CHAPTER 28

They picked up Eno twenty minutes later and were gliding underneath the Coney Island sign, headed toward the East River. Thomas glanced back to see the cable car perched at the top of the roller coaster like a bird on a wire. It looked as if a light breeze could send it plummeting over the edge, but the air was eerily calm.

They entered the first of many submerged neighborhoods and had to navigate carefully in order to avoid the many telephone lines slithering in the water like snakes. Elly suggested that they must've been severed by boats during the early stage of the evacuation.

There were no signs of people.

By mid-morning, with the sun burning bright in a cloudless sky, they got their first view of the New York City skyline. Elly was astonished at the sight of the once towering skyscrapers now eight stories under water.

"There it is," Elly said. "New York City. Or the top two thirds of it anyway."

"Answer a question for me," Eno said. "Why didn't your scientists see these superfloods coming?"

"Our scientists aren't the problem," Elly said. "They warn us constantly, but people are in denial, and, believe it or not, some still think global warming is a hoax."

Eno shook his head in disbelief while Thomas was distracted by a large green statue standing near the surface of the water, a few miles south.

"What's that over there?" Thomas said.

"The Statue of Liberty. It's so depressing."

"Why?" Eno asked. "It's just a statue."

"It's more than that," Elly snapped. "It's a symbol of freedom for—"

Eno cut her off. "Much as I appreciate the history lesson, we have a long way to go, and I'd rather not be out here at night. If there's one megalodon, there's bound to be more."

Elly went quiet. The sight of Lady Liberty being threatened by drowning was jarring. But for Thomas and Eno, a flooded Earth was what they expected from everything they'd ever been told. The closer they rowed toward the city, the stronger the tide grew, slowing their progress. By noon, the sun climbed directly overhead and they were dripping with sweat. If anything, they seemed to be in roughly the same place as they were hours ago.

"Maybe we should take a break," Thomas said, putting down his oar.

Elly pulled some spare bandanas from her backpack and soaked them in the water. She tied one around her neck and passed the others to Thomas and Eno.

"How far do you think we have to go?" Thomas asked.

"At the rate we're going," Elly said, "we'll be rowing the rest of the day."

"That's because we're taking the longest route possible," Eno said.

"You're the Navigator," Thomas said.

Eno checked his wrist pod. "I suggest we row in a diagonal direction toward the lower part of the city. According to my calculations, it's two point four miles shorter."

They picked up their oars and began to row. Within minutes, the water started to ripple as if it were flowing over small rocks. The current quickly became even stronger, first splashing into the boat and finally bringing them to a standstill.

Without warning, a gust of wind lifted Elly's oar out of her hands. Thomas managed to grab it, but the brief pause was enough to turn the boat downstream. It traveled a good distance before

Thomas, using his paddle as a rudder, managed to maneuver them to a spot where the tide wasn't so strong.

"Sorry, guys," Elly said. "I'd say we just lost an hour."

"Accidents happen," Thomas said.

"Why is the water so much stronger in the middle?" Eno asked.

"Because that's where the river is," Elly said. "It's moving faster than the floodwater and forging its own path. Unless we find a bridge, we have to take the long way around."

"There's a bridge here?" Eno said.

"Yeah, a few," Elly said.

"Let's see if we can find one," Thomas said.

They began to row again. After an hour or so, they came around a small bend in the river. Elly pointed a few miles ahead toward the top of a curved stone structure rising out of the water. "Look, it's a bridge tower."

"How do you know?" Eno asked.

"You can see the same tower on the other side. It's a suspension bridge, like the Golden Gate. The towers hold the cables, which hold the roadway, which unfortunately is now under water. It could be the Brooklyn Bridge."

"What makes you say that?" Thomas said.

"My father and I walked across it on our trip after lunch in Chinatown."

Thomas and Eno looked at each other, a bit puzzled.

"Yeah," she shrugged, "they have one of those, too."

"It'll be dark soon," Thomas said. "I suggest we spend the night here and cross tomorrow when the wind dies down."

"You mean sleep in the boat?" Eno said, as if he hadn't heard correctly.

"Why not?" Elly said. "We have sleeping bags, and enough food for the night. In an emergency, we could eat it fast and you could use your Arrometer so we could eat it again."

Thomas laughed, but Eno was clearly not amused.

"The Arrometer is not a toy," he said.

Elly smiled. "In times like this, we need to keep our sense of humor. Or in your case, find one."

Thomas paddled closer, until they could see the limestone tower with its two tall archways. As they pulled under the first arch, Thomas tossed one of the boat chains over a suspension cable. Sheltered from the wind and tide, with the city directly opposite, it was a perfect spot for a mooring. Exhausted, they put down their oars and leaned back against the boat.

In a short time, the sun began to drop toward the horizon. The river started moving faster, and the wind whipped it into small whitecaps. The temperature quickly fell, and a chill invaded the air.

"I don't know about anybody else," Thomas said, "but all that rowing made me hungry."

"Me too," Elly said. "What about you Eno?"

"No, you two go ahead and eat. I'm going to search for signs of life."

Elly pulled out the spaghetti she'd packed and dished it into small Tupperware bowls. She and Thomas ate slowly, relishing every bite, while Eno scanned the partially sunken skyline with binoculars. By the time they finished eating, the sun was going down behind the skyline, creating patches of golden light on the skyscraper windows.

Thomas rinsed the bowls in the river, while Elly dried them.

"Eno, you sure you don't want something to eat?" Elly said.

"Not at the moment," he said. "I think I may have spotted some human activity."

"Where?" Thomas said.

"In the building thirty-eight degrees west. It's difficult to tell with the glare, but I think I saw some movement four floors above the water line."

Elly sat up as Thomas took the binoculars and checked the building. He could make out a few people moving back and forth behind the windows.

"Yeah, I can see them," Thomas said.

"Who do you think they are?" Elly said.

"Scientists, most likely," Eno said.

"During the superfloods, they were always first to arrive and last to leave," Thomas said.

Thomas handed the binoculars to Elly.

"Yeah," she said. "Those are people all right."

"You don't seem particularly excited," Eno said.

"If this is a superflood, I'm actually witnessing the beginning of the end of the world."

"Hardly," Eno said. "The universe is actually doing fine. What you're witnessing is merely the end of your civilization."

"Thanks, Eno," she said. "That makes me feel much better."

"It must be terrible to see all of this," Thomas said.

"When I was a little girl, my father used to tell me what might happen to the world if people didn't start doing things differently. It seemed like a dark fairy tale then. But now it seems like a full on horror movie."

"Why don't we all try and get some sleep," Thomas said. "It's been a long day."

"Sounds like a plan," Eno said.

Thomas passed out the sleeping bags, and Eno quickly crawled into his at the front of the boat. He zipped it over his head, disappearing from sight, while Thomas and Elly laid out their bags at the rear.

"I'll take the first watch," Elly said. "I'm not really sleepy."

"Are you sure you're all right?" Thomas asked.

"Yeah," Elly shrugged. "It's just a lot to think about, you know?"

Thomas nodded, as Elly stared at the skyline, unable to pull her eyes away.

"So, what happens after this?" she said.

"Do you mean—"

Elly turned to face Thomas. "You know what I mean."

Thomas was reluctant to answer, but thought she deserved to know.

"The floods get bigger and bigger, until everybody finally realizes Earth won't be livable for much longer and the only hope for survival is to move off planet to a Station on Mars."

"The one you grew up on?"

Thomas nodded. "The plan was to build thousands of them, and ours was the first. It was supposed to be the capital of the new world. But the floods came sooner than anyone predicted, and by that time there was only one ready. Instead of being able to house millions on Mars, there was only room for ten thousand people. There were resource riots on Earth over food and fuel, but most people died in the floods or were killed trying to force their way onto the shuttles. The first one took off in 2061, and the Final Evacuation lasted until 2071, when I was born. My mother and I were on the last shuttle, along with Ignatius."

Elly was silent.

"I'm sorry. I probably told you more than you needed to hear, right?"

"Like my father says, it's always better to know the truth, even if it's not pleasant."

"Why don't you get some sleep?" Thomas said. "It might make you feel better."

Elly nodded and unzipped her sleeping bag. "If you see anything fishy, wake me up."

"Promise," Thomas smiled, imitating Elly's chest-crossing ritual.

✦✦

An hour later, the sun disappeared completely, and the sky became black. The few lights left in the city became sharper, like low-hanging stars over the water. The river, an even deeper shade of black, moved across the water like a liquid blur.

Thomas found himself mesmerized by the dark river, which sometimes played tricks on his vision. He fixated on a small disturbance a hundred or so yards upstream, and watched it for several minutes trying to decide whether it was simply one of the small waves that broke occasionally or something more menacing. Finally, he picked up the binoculars and tried to make out what seemed like a dark triangle moving in a slow circle. When a second triangle joined the first, there was no denying what it was.

He gently shook Elly, and her head popped out of her sleeping bag.

"Sharks?" she said, without prompting.

Thomas pointed upriver, handing her the binoculars.

"Two of them."

Eno's head appeared from his sleeping bag, "What's going on?"

"Our friend is back, and he brought his sidekick," Thomas said.

Without getting out of his sleeping bag, Eno calmly reached for his metallic backpack and removed the rectangular case he'd used to send the landing signal in the tree house.

"What are you gonna do, call home?" Elly said.

"No," Eno said. "I'm going to do something I should have done the moment we landed on this dreadful planet."

"What's that?" asked Thomas.

"Make a weapon."

## CHAPTER 29

Eno retrieved a ball of fine wire and begin to unroll it as Thomas and Elly watched.

"Anything we can we do to help?" Thomas asked.

"I'll need some cable from the bridge. About ten feet should do."

Elly fished one of the broken cables from the water with her oar, and Thomas used his diamond blade to cut away a ten-foot section.

"I'll also require a circular platform of some sort," Eno said.

"Will one of the Viking shields do?" Thomas asked.

"Perfectly."

Thomas cut one of the shields from the side of the boat with the laser.

"Now, anchor the cable to the shield and coil it. Start at the bottom and make it smaller as it rises, in a ratio of four to one, like a cone."

While Elly held the cable, Thomas used the laser to fuse it to the shield.

"You mind telling us what we're making?" Thomas asked.

"A resonant air-core transformer."

Elly nodded in recognition. "Otherwise known as a Tesla coil."

Eno looked up, surprised. "You're familiar with the concept?"

"Of course. But, full disclosure, I've never actually made one."

"What will it do?" Thomas asked.

"Send a million volts or so at anything that tries to attack us," Eno said.

He removed a small black metal square from the case and attached it by wire to what looked like a small battery. He then attached it to the cone of cable.

"What about a toroid?" Elly asked.

"This is it," Eno said, holding up a metal ball attached to a metal stem. "Now mount the coil on the front of the boat with the cone facing out."

"We'll need a swivel mechanism," Thomas said, "so it can be aimed."

Elly helped Thomas carve out a palm-sized circular disc from one of the other shields, and Eno carefully attached a wire to it.

"This is the trigger apparatus. All you need to do is touch your finger to the pad. But we should test it first. Elly, I suggest you tie down your hair. The static electricity will be intense."

Elly gathered her hair from her face and tied it behind her neck with a bandana. She moved to the rear of the boat with Eno while Thomas settled in the bow, behind the Tesla coil.

"Here goes," Thomas said, touching a finger to the pad. A bolt of electricity shot across the water, zapping the air with high-voltage current.

"Wow!" Elly said, impressed. "It really works."

"Of course it does," Eno said, as if there was never a question. "Keep an eye out for our friends and let me know if there's a status update." And with that, he pulled up his sleeping bag and zipped it back over his head.

For the next hour, Thomas and Elly sat behind the Tesla coil and kept silent watch on the two megalodons, who remained in their own orbit upriver.

"Strange," Thomas said. "It's almost like they're hunting something."

"At least it's not us," Elly said. "Were you surprised that Eno decided to make a weapon?"

"No, I'm surprised it took him this long. In addition to being Navigator, Ignatius made him my official Protector."

"Seems like it should be the other way around."

"Back at the Station, it was. But I guess Ignatius knew what he was doing. I wouldn't know how to make a Tesla coil to save my life."

Thomas yawned, as if the fatigue from the day was finally catching up to him.

"Hey," Elly said. "Why don't you get some sleep. I'll take this shift."

Thomas didn't respond.

"Unless you don't trust me," Elly said.

Thomas smiled. "You know I do. Here, take this, just in case." He handed her the Porta Gill and wrapped his sleeping bag around his shoulders. "Wake me if anything happens."

Elly smiled. "No need to worry about that."

Thomas closed his eyes and quickly nodded off.

With both boys sleeping, Elly couldn't help thinking about the bizarre nature of her situation. She was sitting in a 'borrowed' amusement park ride in the East River, thousands of miles from home, sometime in the future, with two boys she'd only met a couple days ago. But the strangest thing of all was the fact that it all felt perfectly natural, like this was exactly where she was *supposed* to be and what she was *meant* to be doing.

But then she thought about her father. If anything happened to her and she couldn't get home, it would be devastating to him. She glanced over at the sleeping Thomas and knew he'd do anything to prevent that from happening. He'd already come to her rescue twice, first with the police, then with the megalodon, proving it beyond a doubt. If Eno was his Protector, Thomas was hers. At that moment, he jolted upright, as if on cue.

"What is it?" Elly said.

"Over there," Thomas said.

She turned to see a huge fin surging toward them like a massive torpedo.

Thomas grabbed the trigger pad and slid behind the Tesla coil as the megalodon began to pick up speed. He waited until it was about ten yards from the boat and put his finger down.

A bolt of electricity shot out over the water, causing the shark to lunge downward under a cloud of sparks. Nothing moved for several minutes, but just when they were beginning to feel hopeful, they saw a fin reappear downstream.

"He's coming back," Elly said, nodding in the direction of a second megalodon. "And now it's a tag team."

The two sharks split off, as if planning to attack from opposite sides. Thomas waited until the closest one was in range and got off a shot, then swiveled around and fired at the second. Both shots produced a loud crackle on the river, sending up small clouds of spark-filled steam.

The two beasts slid under the water. After a few moments, they reappeared farther out. This time, instead of making another approach, they turned away.

"You did it, Thomas!" Elly shouted.

"I believe *we* did it," Eno said, popping out of his sleeping bag.

"Thanks, Eno," Thomas said.

Elly gave each of the boys a high-five as they watched the sharks swim back upstream, toward a small red light flashing in the distance.

"Do you see that light?" Thomas asked. "It wasn't there before, was it?"

"No," Elly said. "And there's two more."

A pair of yellow dots appeared below the red light, forming a triangle.

Elly grabbed the binoculars. "They're coming closer," she said.

"Can you tell what it is?" Thomas asked.

"Running lights," Elly said. "It's a sailboat, with no sails,"

The boat was about forty feet long, plunging in and out of the rough water, while the two megalodons were right behind, following in its wake.

"The red light's a distress signal," Elly said. "I think somebody's up on the mast."

Elly tried to train her flashlight on it, but the boat was bouncing so much it was impossible. Finally, the light landed on a pair of legs high above deck. They belonged to a small boy, no more than ten years old."

"It's a little kid," Elly said. "Alone!"

"That's why the megalodons were out there," Thomas said. "Waiting."

The boy was clinging to a lookout perch, holding the red light in his free hand.

"If we can get out there before the boat passes," Thomas shouted, "we can pull alongside and let the current take us right next to it!"

"And then what?" Eno asked.

"I'll pull him into our boat," Elly said. "Just like Thomas did with me back in San Francisco."

Thomas nodded. "I was thinking the same thing."

Thomas threw off the mooring chains and pushed the Sea Viking away from the tower. They began to row, fighting the rough water and heavy current. As they drew closer, Elly could make out the boy's face. He was no older than ten.

"We're almost there!" Elly shouted.

"Eno," Thomas shouted. "Man the Tesla coil!"

Eno crawled into position as the sailboat passed, with the megalodons in its wake. He fired a shot, hitting the tail of the first shark. It seemed to scare him off, while the second one circled around to the other side to avoid the same fate.

Thomas and Elly rowed toward the whitewater. The current carried the Sea Viking next to the sailboat, which was moving at the same speed. Elly stood up and waved frantically at the boy with open arms.

"Climb down! We'll catch you!"

The boy started down the mast. But a sudden wave hit the boat and it lurched sideways, forcing him to drop the distress light and send him overboard into the water.

"Thomas!" Elly screamed.

But Thomas was already on his feet. The distress light bobbed on the surface of the water as he dove into the water, now illuminated by the strobing red signal.

He spotted the boy, who was sinking, and off to one side, the first shark. It was now a race to see who could get to the boy first. Unfortunately, the current was so strong that it was pushing the boy back faster than Thomas could swim to get him.

Back in the Viking ship, Elly manned one of the oars, but suddenly remembered she'd forgotten to give Thomas the Porta Gill. Panic stricken, she pulled it out.

"Eno," she said. "Thomas forgot the Porta Gill! I have to get it to him!

"Don't even think about it," Eno said, grabbing the instrument out of her hand.

"Why not?"

"Because it's my job," he said. "Cover me with the Tesla."

And before she could react, Eno put the mouthpiece between his lips and jumped overboard, feet first.

Elly located the second shark and aimed the Tesla coil. She fired, lighting up the water with an explosion of electricity, forcing it to veer off into the murky darkness.

Under water, Thomas spotted the boy, suddenly illuminated by the flash of light from the the Tesla Coil. He noticed a churn behind him, and expected to see the shark, but it was Eno, the Porta Gill in his mouth, floating along with the current. Behind him was the shark.

Thomas waved at Eno to get out of the way, but Eno turned toward the megaladon and held his fist, as if ready to fight. Thomas couldn't imagine what Eno was thinking…until he saw the

Arrometer in his hand. The moment the shark came into range, Eno hit the switch and the beast vanished.

Thomas knew that Eno had bought them some time, but there was no way to know how much. Even worse, the boy was now even farther away from him.

Thomas kicked toward him, when he saw the second shark. It was swimming toward the boy, jaws open. Thomas pulled out his Tetrascope, ready to do battle, when he heard a low rumble from above the water. Moments later, a small cartridge pierced the surface. It drifted down between Thomas and the shark and produced a thunderous blast.

It was the last thing Thomas remembered.

# CHAPTER 30

THOMAS WOKE UP IN a small white room, the walls swaying. After a few moments, he realized the walls were actually sheets attached to the ceiling and moving in the morning breeze. He looked down to see that he was wearing a thin blue gown. His clothes were cleaned and neatly folded on a table next to his bed.

"Hello?" Thomas called out.

The sheets parted, revealing Elly, her arm freshly bandaged from shoulder to elbow. Eno stood behind her. Both were wearing clean clothes.

"How you doin'?" Elly asked.

Thomas shook his head. "A little groggy."

"The doctor gave you some sleep medication," Eno said.

"After he pumped all the water out of your lungs," Elly added.

"I guess I must've blacked out huh?"

"Actually, you were *knocked* out," Elly said. "They used one of those Sonic Inducers to ward off the shark."

"They who?" Thomas said, puzzled.

"The people on the other boat," Eno said. "The one belonging to the Science Alliance."

Thomas looked puzzled. "There was another boat?"

"Yeah," Elly said. "It showed up right after Eno used his Arrometer.

"Eight seconds afterward, to be precise."

"Afterward?" Thomas said, even more confused. "I thought the Arrometer pushed us *back* in time."

"It does both, actually," Eno said. "I heard the boat's engine and assumed it was some sort of rescue operation, so I thought it best to buy us some time until it arrived."

"It turned out to be a good bet," Elly smiled. "It saved your butt."

"What about the little boy?" Thomas said.

Eno looked to Elly, reluctant to explain.

"The good news is that he survived," Elly said. "But unfortunately the second shark, the one I thought I scared away, got to him just before the charge went off. He lost a leg."

Thomas looked stricken. "Oh, no."

"The doctor told us that the new prosthetics are so advanced you can barely tell the difference," she said. "He should be up and walking in no time."

Thomas nodded, but was clearly still disturbed by the news.

"Look," Elly said. "What you and Eno did by going in the water was incredibly brave. And there was no way you could've known the second shark was still lurking. If anyone's to blame it's me. If I was a better shot, that kid would still have his leg."

"No," Thomas said. "It's nobody's fault. Thanks to you guys, I'm still alive. And so is the boy."

Eno quickly changed the subject. "In case you're wondering, we're at the temporary headquarters of the Science Alliance, which from what I can gather is on the eleventh floor, just a couple floors above the flood line."

She pulled back a sheet, revealing a set of arched windows. In the distance, Thomas could see the water surrounding the nearby buildings.

"They came in to study the flood and help with the evacuation. The Alliance doctors set up a makeshift hospital for the sick and wounded."

"Did you tell them who we were?" Thomas said.

"They didn't ask," Eno said. "And we thought it best not to volunteer."

"Did you find out why the boy was on the boat alone?"

"Yeah," Elly said. "The flood came in so fast that a lot of people couldn't get out over land, so they had to go downriver. The megs were waiting for them. The Alliance set up a night patrol and they spotted the sailboat. But the boys' parents went overboard long before he did."

"Poor kid," Thomas said. "He lost both parents?"

"I'm afraid so," Elly said.

"It's not like one can't have a perfectly productive life without them," Eno said. "We're living proof of that."

"Hey, how about breakfast," Elly said, changing the subject again. "They have a cafeteria downstairs, and you can get pretty much anything you want."

"Okay," Thomas said. "But first I'd like to go upstairs to visit the boy."

They made their way to the elevators after Thomas got dressed. A group of doctors were waiting, and they decided to use the stairs, so they wouldn't have to explain who they were. When they got off at the tenth floor, they spotted a nurse.

"We're looking for the little boy who lost his leg," Elly said.

The nurse glanced up and down the deserted hallway. "Room 1012."

"Thanks."

They hurried to the room and peeked inside. The boy was under the covers, sleeping.

Elly expected to see him hooked up to a network of IVs, but there was only a small green light on his neck. It transmitted his vital signs to a futuristic monitor.

Thomas stood over the boy. There was something vaguely familiar about him, though he couldn't put a finger on what it was.

"We don't even know his name," Thomas said.

Eno picked up the boy's chart. "It's…" He stopped and turned to Thomas.

"What?" Elly asked.

"Ignatius."

Thomas glanced at the boy and then back at Eno.

"It can't be possible. Can it?"

✦✦

THE CAFETERIA WAS DESERTED except for a handful of scientists at a nearby table. Elly and Eno ate breakfast, but Thomas was too distracted to touch his food.

"I'm still not sure I understand why you think he's the same Ignatius as the one on Mars," Elly said.

"Our Ignatius lost his leg to a megalodon when he was a boy," Thomas said. "So if it's not him, then it's the most amazing coincidence in history."

Eno didn't seem as convinced. "And we just happened to be there the moment he went overboard?"

"I think that's the point," Thomas said. "Ignatius said the tide of time would overrule any setting we programmed on the globe. Destination meets destiny, remember?"

"So, you think we were meant to be here?" Elly said.

"Yeah," Thomas said. "I do."

"Wow," Elly said. "So, then you met me for a reason, too?"

"That was an accident," Eno said, "triggered by Time Globe damage."

Elly smiled to herself, secretly satisfied that her notion of being included in Thomas's destiny had been confirmed. Still, she had questions of her own.

"It makes sense," Elly said. "Saving Ignatius must've been important to the mission, right?"

"He made time travel possible, so without him we wouldn't be here," Thomas said. "There's also another possible reason we landed here."

"What's that?" Elly said.

"My father was head of the Science Alliance. Maybe he's here, too."

"Suppose we find him," Elly said. "Then what?"

"Simple," Eno said. "We tell him who we are and why we came."

"Wait a sec," Elly said. "You want Thomas to introduce himself as his father's unborn son, who has time traveled from Mars in the future?"

Eno thought about it for a moment. "I take your point."

"Just the same, it doesn't hurt to inquire discreetly," Elly said.

"Where do you think we should start looking?" Thomas said.

"Here comes your doctor," Elly said. "Why not ask him?"

Thomas looked up to see a middle-aged man in a blue medical uniform with the Science Alliance logo on the breast pocket.

"Hi, there. I came by to check on the patient, but he was gone."

"He was starving," Elly said. "Dr. Becker, this is Thomas."

"How are you feeling?"

"Fine, thanks to you."

"Actually, the person you should be thanking is whoever fired that sonic charge. Without that, we wouldn't be meeting."

"We'd also like to thank Dr. Knight for taking us in," Elly said. "Do you know where we can find him?"

"He's most likely in his office. He never leaves. I think he even sleeps up there."

THOMAS, ENO, AND ELLY got off the elevator on the ninth floor. The hallway wall was filled with maps and scientific graphs tracking the floods. A young woman was updating a large outline of the United States, using a blue marker to extend the flooded area from just north of New York City to just south of Washington, DC.

"Excuse me," Elly said. "Where would we find Dr. Knight?"

"Three doors up," she said, not looking away from her work.

When they arrived at Dr. Knight's office, Thomas hesitated. His palms were sweating, and his heartbeat quickened. He recalled the moment when Ignatius told him about the existence of his father and how it had seemed so difficult to believe. But the idea that he would actually meet him made him lightheaded.

Elly put a hand on his shoulder. "You're about to meet your father, Thomas. It's perfectly understandable for you to be nervous."

Thomas wiped his palms against his shirt, took a breath, and knocked.

"Come in," a voice called.

Thomas opened the door. A man with a tangle of white hair sat at his desk, his head bent over something he was writing.

"Dr. Knight?" Thomas said, his mouth suddenly dry.

"Yes?" he said, looking up. "What can I do for you, son?"

Thomas found himself speechless, and Elly quickly stepped forward.

"This is Thomas, Dr. Knight, the boy that was pulled out of the river last night. He's still in a little bit of shock."

"Well, that's certainly understandable," Dr. Knight said, getting to his feet. He looked Thomas up and down, confused. "I'm sorry. I thought your leg…"

"That was Ignatius," Elly said. "Thomas is the boy who dove into the river to try and save him."

Dr. Knight put out his hand. "That was an incredible act of courage."

Thomas shook his hand. "I can't take any credit."

"Indeed, you can, and you should. My son told me all about it."

"Your son?" Elly asked. She wasn't aware that Thomas had a brother.

"He was on the patrol boat. In fact, he's the one who fired the Sonic Inducer."

Footsteps sounded in the hallway, approaching the office.

Dr. Knight smiled. "Ah, there he is now."

They turned to see a boy in the doorway. He was the same height, weight, and age as Thomas. With his amber eyes, Thomas felt like he was looking at his double.

"Matt, I want you to meet the boy you helped rescue last night."

Matthew held out his hand. "Hey, how you feeling?"

"Alive," Thomas said, "thanks to you."

And with that, he shook hands with his father.

## CHAPTER 31

Matthew led Thomas to the elevator while Elly and Eno stayed a few steps behind in a state of astonishment. They could barely tell the difference between Thomas and his father, who walked and talked exactly the same. Even their hand gestures were identical. The only difference, especially from behind, was their hair. Thomas's buzz cut was a sharp contrast to Matthew's unruly mop, which frequently fell over his eyes.

"Amazing, huh?" Elly whispered. "They're like twins."

"You mean a zygote that splits into two embryos?"

"Yeah, just like that," Elly said.

Matthew suddenly turned and started walking backward in the same way that Thomas had done on Stinson Beach.

"You may have survived the megs," Matthew announced as if leading a tour, "but the real danger is *this* place. If you're not careful, you could die of boredom. Luckily, we've got the roof."

"What's on the roof?" Eno asked as they boarded the elevator.

"Tennis courts, gym, arcade, you name it. There's even an Olympic-sized pool. I can lend you guys bathing suits. Yours might be a little baggy, Eno, but Thomas and I look about the same size." Matthew stopped at the elevator and punched the up button with the side of his fist. They rose to the sixtieth floor, and the doors opened onto the roof. "We've got it all to ourselves. Nobody's been up here since the farewell dinner a week ago. The wives and kids all evacuated to Chicago."

"Your mom didn't mind you staying here?" Elly asked.

"Oh, for sure. But my dad convinced her it was a historic opportunity. We've had small floods the last few years, but he's been saying forever it was only a matter of time before the polar melts started to hook up and we get the big one."

"And no one believed him?" Eno asked.

"The scientists did, but the politicians keep telling everybody it's just a weird weather cycle. Like Dad says, bad news is bad for business."

Matthew led them toward a telescope near the rim of the roof. "Look, you can see where the Hudson and East Rivers meet up. That's where the roughest water is and where the megs like to hang out. It's probably where they got that kid's parents."

Elly looked through the telescope to see a collision of water forming into a small pyramid of white foam.

"The evacuation started a week ago, but a few stragglers still come down every night. Captain Clarkson, who runs the Alliance ship, organized a patrol and I volunteered for the night shift. He taught me how to shoot a Sonic Inducer."

"The next time you see him, could you thank him for us?" Thomas said.

"Will do," Matthew said.

"So, what's the plan going forward?" Elly asked.

"We're relocating to Chicago with the rest of the Alliance after we finish documenting the flood. Should take another couple weeks or so. Hopefully the worst will be over by then. What about you guys?"

"We don't actually have a hard plan," Thomas said, glancing at Elly.

"Where you from, anyway?"

Thomas turned to Elly a second time, more than happy to let her speak. "I'm from San Francisco," she said. "The boys were visiting from Iceland and I brought them to see New York. We were at Coney Island when the flood hit."

"Talk about bad timing," Matthew said.

"Tell me about it," Elly said.

"We're leaving in a few days but making a pit stop in Pittsburgh," Matthew said. "That's the nearest working airport, so you can get a flight home from there if you want."

"Thanks," Elly said. "I guess we should talk about it and make a decision."

"Sure, take your time, no hurry," Matthew said. "I'm sure you could stay with us as long as you want. Talk it over and let me know. I have to go down and see my dad about something. You're welcome to hang here, and I'll meet up with you when I'm finished?"

"Sounds good," Elly said.

"Anything else you need for now?"

"Actually, there is one thing," Thomas said. "We were wondering about the date. We've kind of lost track of time."

"I know the feeling," Matthew said, glancing at his watch. "It's July fifth."

"And the year?" Eno asked.

Matthew took his question as a joke, and laughed. "Still 2051."

THOMAS, ENO, AND ELLY gathered at one of the roof-top picnic tables. Eno put his head in his hands, unable to hide his disappointment.

"I don't understand how we could still be twenty years off. Maybe there's something wrong with the composition of the metal in the Time Globe patch."

"Or not," Thomas said. "I mean, we've witnessed the first superflood, crossed paths with Ignatius, and I've met my father."

"You couldn't really ask for more out of a single time-jump," Elly said.

Eno threw up his hands in frustration. "Even if you're right about our being here because of the *tide of time*, then it's accomplished its purpose and there's no real reason to stay. We need to drop Elly back in San Francisco and get on with our mission."

Thomas nodded half-heartedly. Secretly he was hoping to spend more time with his father, despite his age. But the main priority now was getting Elly home. "I guess you're right."

"There's one little problem," Elly said. "We don't have a boat. After the patrol boat picked me up, the Sea Viking floated down river. It's probably in Florida by now."

"I'll find Matthew and talk to him about getting another one," Thomas said. "But maybe you can check in on Ignatius while I do that. A few of my mother's children's books are in my backpack. Maybe you could bring him one?"

"Sure thing," Elly said. "Our stuff's in the recovery room, so I'll pick one out."

"If you don't mind," Eno said, "I think I'll stay here, assuming I can find a place to get out of this dreadful sunshine."

✦✦

THOMAS GOT OUT OF the elevator on the other side of the building from Dr. Knight's office. As he came down the long hallway, he heard a voice raised in anger. He turned the corner toward the office when he saw Matthew storm out of his father's office. Dr. Knight took a few steps after him and called his name, but Matthew ignored him and kept walking. Clearly, they were having a disagreement of some sort. Thomas waited for Dr. Knight to reenter his office and then jogged after Matthew, who disappeared into the next hallway.

Thomas followed, but the hall was now deserted. He saw a pair of double doors at the end of hallway and heard music playing from inside.

He opened the door and looked into a dimly lit room filled with leather booths. A long counter ran along the wall, lined with stools. Behind it was a shelf filled with colorful bottles of liquid. Matthew sat at the end of the counter, writing something on a piece of paper.

"I hope I'm not interrupting," Thomas said.

Matthew slid the paper into his front pocket. “No, that’s all right, pull up a stool.”

Thomas sat next to Matthew, their images reflected in the large panel of glass behind the counter. Side by side, they looked almost identical. Matthew had his arms folded on the counter and his jaw locked in concentration, as if something were weighing on his mind.

“You want a drink?” Matthew asked. “I highly recommend the root beer.”

“Sure,” Thomas said.

Matthew went behind the bar and dispensed two glasses of brown liquid from a machine that also provided ice. “To better days,” Matthew said, touching his glass to Thomas’s.

Thomas wondered how to explain the fact that they were returning to Coney Island without being suspicious. He decided the best approach would be to keep it as simple as possible.

“I’m sorry for barging in,” Thomas said, “but I wanted to tell you we can’t go with you to Pittsburgh. We have to go back to Coney Island.”

“It looks like it’s going to be flooded for a few more days at least. You sure?”

“Yeah,” Thomas said, taking a sip of root beer, hoping the issue was settled.

“What’s in Coney Island, if you don’t mind my asking?” Matthew said.

“It’s kind of complicated.”

“Tell me about it. Since the flood hit, seems like everything’s pretty messed up.”

Thomas nodded, relieved that he didn’t have to lie to his father. “The thing is, we lost our boat, so we need a lift.”

“No problem. I can take you in the dinghy, but we’ll have to wait till night. The scientists use it during the day, but at night it’s all ours.”

“Are you sure you don’t mind?”

"No. Just between us, I'm leaving tonight, too."

"What for?"

"I have to look for somebody."

THOMAS HEADED BACK TO the infirmary where he'd spent the night, and found his backpack at the foot of his bed. He did a quick check to see that his things were all there, including his prize possession: the model train locomotive. The mountaineer was nestled safely in in the bottom compartment, and he wondered why his father had chosen to give it to him in the first place. He would've liked to ask Matthew about it, but there was no way to do that without sounding strange. Now that they were leaving, he'd never know the answer to that or much else about his father, other than the fact he liked root beer.

Thomas went up to the roof where Eno was still in the arcade and engrossed in a holographic game that involved an army of rabbit warriors attacking a fortress made entirely of carrots. It was nine minutes before five o'clock.

"Where's Elly?" Thomas asked.

"Haven't seen her."

At that moment, Thomas looked out the arcade window to see the elevator doors open and Elly get out. He went out to the roof and met her at one of the tables near the pool.

"How's Ignatius?"

"Sleeping. The nurse said the medication will keep him out of it for a few days. It speeds up the healing, so by the time he wakes, he'll be fully recovered. Ordinarily they only let visitors stay for ten minutes, but she let me sit with him for as long as I wanted."

"How'd you manage that?"

"Turns out she grew up in San Francisco. She told me that when she was my age they still had cable cars."

Thomas smiled. "Did you ask if any were missing?"

"Ha, no. But I did ask her if any were ever stolen."

"Really?"

"No, but I thought about it," she said. "Did you talk to your…?"

"Matthew? Yeah. He's leaving tonight to look for somebody, but he'll take us back to Coney Island first."

"Did he say who?"

"No, but with any luck, you'll be sleeping in your own room tonight."

Elly nodded. But Thomas could see that the prospect of returning home didn't seem to make her any happier than it did him.

"Is everything all right?" Thomas said.

"I'm good," she said. "But there's been a small complication…"

A voice shouted across the roof. "Anybody hungry?"

They turned to see Matthew get off the elevator with a large cooler.

"Tell you later," Elly said, as Matthew approached.

"I brought some stuff from the cafeteria," he said. "I figured we should eat an early dinner so we can take the dinghy out as soon as the sun goes down."

Matthew put the container on the table. Elly helped him take out the food, a mixture of grilled fish and vegetables, when Eno appeared from the arcade looking puzzled at the set up.

"Why aren't we eating in the cafeteria with the Alliance scientists?"

"It's too depressing. All they talk about is the end of the world and this crazy idea for building an outpost on Mars."

"Mars?" Eno said, glancing at Thomas.

"Hard to believe, huh? Personally, I can't see living in a place where you can't breathe the air or go outside. I'd rather be eaten by a meg."

Before Eno could protest, Elly jumped into the conversation. "So, Matthew, Thomas tells me you're looking for somebody?"

"Yeah, my girlfriend, Kate. She went down to Washington with some friends for a protest and got stranded when the flood hit."

"Wasn't she aware that it was coming?" Eno said.

"Sure. But the computer models were off and it landed about forty miles farther south than the projections. By the time they rerouted the rescue operation from Baltimore, the entire government was stranded and getting all those people to safety became the top priority. Everybody else was told to shelter in place."

"How long has it been since you heard from her?" Elly said.

"Almost thirty-six hours. They were gonna try to wait it out in one of the monuments, but her phone died before she could say which one. I asked my dad if we could send a boat down there, but we don't really have one to spare."

"That's what your disagreement was about?" Thomas asked.

"Yeah."

"Matthew, do you have a picture of your girlfriend?" Elly asked.

Matthew pulled out his phone and held it up so that she see the image.

Elly turned to Thomas. "Can I talk to you for a sec in private?"

As Matthew finished emptying the cooler, Thomas followed Elly to the roof railing near the telescope. She kept her voice down so it wouldn't travel across the roof.

"The complication I referred to earlier is that we can't go back to San Francisco yet."

"Why not?"

"My guess is you'll want to help Matthew find his girlfriend."

"What for?"

"Because she's not just his girlfriend. She's your mother."

## CHAPTER 32

Eno let out a loud frustrated sigh, dropping his forehead into his palms.

"You can't be serious."

Matthew had gone downstairs to retrieve his duffel bag for the boat trip. The moment he left, Elly broke the news about Thomas's mother. When she was looking through his mother's books for something appropriate for Ignatius, a photo fell out of one of them. It was of Matthew and his girlfriend when they were only teenagers, not much older than he is now. The image on the phone was a perfect match for the one tucked into the book.

"So, let's say for argument's sake that mother and girlfriend are one and the same," Eno started. "I still don't understand why we shouldn't let Matthew go to her rescue."

Elly gave him a look. "Speaking as someone who grew up without a mother, we can't let Thomas pass up what may be his only chance to meet *his*. Besides, on a purely practical note, Matthew would never make it to Washington anyway."

"And why is that?" Eno said.

"Because the moment Dr. Knight finds out he's missing, he'll send the patrol boat out to bring him back. What happens to Thomas's mother then?"

Eno glanced at Thomas, who remained silent, trying to stay neutral.

"I'm not sure," Eno said. "But I doubt there's much we can do about it."

"I don't agree," Elly said. "We can convince Matthew to stay here, and we go instead."

Thomas suddenly spoke up. "How are we going to do that?"

"You have to talk to him, convince him it's in his best interest."

"I wouldn't know what to say."

"It'll come to you, Thomas. After all, you're both wired in the same way."

In the background, the elevator door opened, and Matthew appeared, duffle bag in hand. He took one look at Thomas and sensed that something wasn't right. "Have you changed your mind about going back to Coney Island?"

Thomas glanced at Elly, who prodded him with her eyes. "Not exactly," he said. "But something came up, something we have to do first."

"What's that?" Matthew said.

"Could we talk?" Thomas said. "Just you and I?"

"Sure."

They walked to the other side of the roof. The sun was almost down, laying a thick orange stripe across the river below. From sixty floors up, it's seemed like a small stream. Son and father stood shoulder to shoulder.

"I know it's none of my business," Thomas said. "But I was just wondering what will happen when your father finds out you've gone to look for your girlfriend. Won't he send the patrol boat after you?"

"I hadn't really thought about it," Matthew said. "I guess it's a good possibility. But there's not much I can do about it."

"Actually, there is," Thomas said. "Let us go instead."

"I can't ask you to do that. We barely know each other."

"But it's not like I'm a random stranger after what happened last night. The truth is, I wouldn't be alive if it weren't for you. This would give me a chance to pay you back."

"You don't owe me anything, Thomas. Besides, I have to go myself."

Thomas didn't know how to respond to that and wondered what Matthew was really thinking. And then it came to him. It was the same thing Thomas would be thinking if he was facing the same dilemma. "You think if you stay here, it's the same as doing nothing, right?"

Matthew looked surprised, as if Thomas had read his mind.

"Well, yeah."

"But don't you see, you would be doing something. The hard part."

"What's that?"

"Help us get a boat, then cover for us when we leave. If you really want to save Kate, it's your best shot."

A pigeon landed on the rail a foot away and watched them, as if waiting for the answer.

"I hate to say it," Matthew said. "But you're probably right."

"Think of it as a team effort."

Matthew raised a hand for a high-five. Thomas's palm made contact with his. The smack echoed across the roof and sent the pigeon flying.

✦✦

TWO HOURS LATER, AS the sun went down, Matthew led them to an office on the ninth floor, which was barely above the current water level. A rope was tied around one leg of a heavy wooden desk, trailing out the open window to a twelve-foot rubber dinghy. It bobbed up and down, in and out of view, advertising itself in a tantalizing way.

While Matthew held the rope, Thomas lowered Elly and Eno into the boat and then handed down their backpacks before getting in himself. Matthew followed, along with a duffel bag of his own, and sat in the stern. He pressed the ignition button, and the small outboard motor hummed to life. Separated from the river, the water was calm as a lake, and the boat glided forward easily.

"Why is there no tide here?" Eno asked.

"Actually, there is," Matthew said, as he made a turn between the rows of skyscrapers. "But the buildings act like barrier reefs, so the current's so slow you can barely feel it."

"How do you know where you're going without street signs?" Elly asked.

"Landmarks. If the Empire State Building's on the left and the Chrysler Building's on the right, you're on Fifth Avenue."

After a few minutes, Matthew turned the dinghy north. Thomas saw something in the distance and reflexively started to stand. "Look! Aren't those…?"

Elly pulled him back into his seat. "They are," she said, as a barge loaded with horses floated toward them.

"Wow," Thomas said, barely about to contain his excitement.

Matthew looked back, puzzled by the exchange.

"Thomas loves horses," Elly said. "You'd think he'd never seen one before."

Thomas shrugged sheepishly, as a few policemen on the bow waved.

"They're still evacuating all the animals," Matthew said.

"What's that?" Eno asked, pointing toward a strange looking barge covered in a dome of translucent white mesh. The letters NYCB were painted on the bow.

"The City Beekeepers."

As the barge came closer, they heard a loud buzzing and could make out the thousands of bees swarming inside.

"Precious cargo. The Keepers are moving them to a sanctuary in Connecticut."

In a few more minutes, they passed under the gothic spires of St. Patrick's Cathedral. Several people stood on the flat section of roof, looking up to the sky.

"Prayer group. When we first got here, it was full every night, a couple hundred people at least. Now it's down to a handful."

"Look," Elly said. "The Plaza Hotel. Or the top half anyway. That's where I stayed with my dad when we were here."

"It marks the beginning of Central Park," Matthew said. "We're almost there."

They came around the hotel to see that the park itself, a rectangle of four-square miles, was completely under water. Bordered on all sides by high-rise apartment buildings, it now formed an urban marina.

Matthew pointed to a penthouse terrace where an elderly woman sat at a grand piano, playing energetically. "She's here every day. Ninety-two years old."

"How do you know?" Elly said.

"I went by right after the flood hit and asked her if she needed help getting out, but she insisted on staying. 'Going down with her piano,'" she said.

"It must be very difficult to leave everything you know behind," Elly said, glancing at Eno, who gave a slight nod of agreement.

Matthew continued north, and they could see that, attached to the buildings, there were several more boats of every size and shape, their mooring ropes tied through open windows.

"Why are all those boats still there?" Thomas asked.

"Most of the rich people who live near the park got out early by plane. And the ones that stayed didn't want to risk going downriver, particularly after the megs started attacking. Even if you were lucky enough to get past them, you had the convicts to deal with."

"The convicts?" Eno said.

"A bunch escaped from the Rikers Island jail after the floods hit. They started hijacking evacuees, but I hear most of them have moved on now that there's nobody left to rob. The evacuation deadline was three days ago."

Matthew steered them into the middle of the park, picking up speed.

"I've come up here a few times, looking for the perfect boat. Yesterday, just before you got here, I found it."

Matthew pointed to a sleek black power yacht about forty feet long. An elevated bridge stood ten feet over its deck, enclosed by a protective fiberglass console. A name was written in silver script across the stern: ACQUA STELLA.

"It means 'Star of the Sea' in Italian," Matthew said.

They all nodded, transfixed by the sleek boat.

"Why is the name in Italian?" Elly asked.

"It's registered there. Built by Ferrari. And it handles like one, believe me."

Thomas remembered seeing pictures in the Artifacts Museum of the famous Italian race cars, including his favorite: the 125 Sport.

"You've driven it?" Thomas said.

Matthew smiled mischievously. "Hey, I had to test it out. I heard that the owners left the country, so they won't need it until the flood's over. I plan to bring it back after I finished."

"Yeah, we're familiar with that strategy," Elly said, winking at Thomas.

Matthew pulled alongside the gleaming vessel. Thomas tied the dinghy to the boarding ladder and jumped up to the deck. After handing up their backpacks, the other three joined him.

"Come on, I'll give you a quick tour."

Matthew led them down the stairs to the lower deck, past a galley complete with stove and refrigerator, and into a passageway with storage hatches on either side.

"Everything you need in the way of supplies is in this hatch on the left. Weather gear, diving equipment, and a signal balloon for emergencies."

He opened the opposite hatch. "This one's got the recreational stuff like inflatable rafts, wakeboards, and water skis. Too bad you won't get a chance to use them." Matthew continued down the passageway and opened a door at the end. "Staterooms are in here. The boat sleeps twelve, so there's more than enough room. But only one king-size bed. You'll have to flip for it."

Matthew brought them back out toward a center console next to the ladder leading up to the bridge. "Steering wheel's up there. And you don't have to worry about maneuvering in tight spaces. The boat is state-of-the-art and does pretty much everything automatically. Control room's full of communication equipment, so you can talk with whoever's in the captain's chair."

Matthew opened the control room door to reveal a bank of several monitors. Underneath was a master board with a touch screen. "You can operate everything from right here. This button triggers the autopilot, and this one operates a thousand feet of anchor cable. The system's linked to the International Satellite, but I haven't been able to find the weather predictor."

Eno stepped forward. "May I look?"

"You have some experience with boats?"

"None at all," Eno said.

"But he's good with computers," Thomas added.

Eno fiddled with the screen for a few moments, and a weather grid appeared.

"Wow," Matthew said. "I guess you must be the navigator."

"Actually, I am," Eno said. "What's this white button at the top?"

"That's the reason I chose the boat. It's the Hover Mode, which lifts the hull five feet above the water. Extremely handy if you run into some megs." Matthew pressed a button and a global map filled the screen. A flashing red dot showed their position in New York. He selected Washington, DC, and a route appeared, complete with distance and estimated arrival time: 6:07 a.m. "You'll be traveling in the same direction as the river, so you should easily get there on time. That'll give you the entire day to look for Kate and her friends."

Matthew pressed the ignition and the engines hummed to life. "C'mon, I'll lead you out of town. You can program the boat to follow."

Eno slid into the navigator's chair and made himself comfortable. Elly and Thomas followed Matthew to the rear of the boat, where he knelt over his duffel bag.

"There's enough food in here to get you through a few days, including enough for Kate and her friends. I also threw in a map of the monuments. I'd check the Capitol first because that's where they were headed. Oh, and there's one other thing you might need."

Matthew unzipped the bag and removed a shoulder holster attached to a leather strap. It held a larger and more primitive version of the Sonic Inducer Ignatius had given Thomas back at the Station. "You know what this is, right?"

"Yeah," Thomas said. "But won't you need it?"

"They have a bunch on the patrol boat, so they won't miss it. Unfortunately, I could only get three cartridges, so I can't give you a lesson. But it couldn't be simpler. All you do is point it into the water and pull the trigger. It's loaded and ready to go."

Thomas nodded as Matthew handed it over.

"With all the shark activity we've been having, I'd wear it at all times."

While Elly untied the mooring lines, Matthew got back into the dinghy and pulled out.

Thomas slid the Sonic Inducer into its holster and followed.

# CHAPTER 33

By the time Thomas steered the Star onto the East River, all that was left of the sun was a small sliver of yellow light. He waved farewell to Matthew, who quickly became a small dot in their wake. Shortly afterward, the East River met the Hudson to form a single, stronger waterway. Elly joined Thomas on the bridge while Eno monitored from the control room directly below them.

Seconds later, they came within a hundred feet of Lady Liberty. Elly smiled to see that she remained above the water, as if the superflood understood that going farther would be trespassing on something sacred. Her floodlights were still lit, making her an even brighter-than-usual beacon for the surrounding neighborhoods without electrical power. As they entered New Jersey, Manhattan receded into the darkness and the sky became deep black. Fortunately, the Star's running lights were bright enough to illuminate the places where the river swirled around islands of debris, and the collision warning system automatically steered around them.

At twelve minutes after nine, they put the boat on autopilot and gathered in the galley for dinner. Elly unpacked some of the food Matthew had given them and heated it in the microwave. They sat at the fold-out table and ate.

"You know, I've been wondering," Elly said. "Now that Thomas has met his father and we're on the way to find his mother, how is all this even possible?"

"You mean, in the time travel sense?" Thomas said.

"In any sense," Elly said, "that actually *makes* sense."

"I think I'll let Eno handle that one," Thomas said.

"You've heard of the multiverse theory?" Eno said.

"Of course" Elly nodded. "What's happening here in our universe is also happening in different versions in other universes."

"Right," Eno said. "Only the theory is completely wrong."

"I thought you were gonna say something like that," Elly said.

"It's not as if a version of what's happening here, in this time and place, is happening at the same time in another universe. We all happen to be on a new branch of the reality tree, which is actually an offshoot of the original branch, shaped like a 'Y,' with the original part old and the new part well…new."

"But when did that second part actually begin?"

"When we landed on Earth, and our temporal realities collided. Since we came from the future, the new branch formed out of necessity to cope with the physics of time."

"Did it start when you landed or when Thomas and I met?"

"Technically, it began when the shuttle touched down on Earth as a result of our time-travel. But there's also a school of thought that the first human interaction is actually the defining moment."

"So, by the simple act of making eye-contact, Thomas and I started a new universe."

"You could say that, yeah." Thomas nodded.

"Wow," Elly said. "That sort of makes us the time-travel version of Adam and Eve, huh?"

"I have no idea who they are," Eno said. "But if that makes sense to you, then yes."

Elly was about to respond, but kept the thought to herself and simply smiled.

✦✦

After dinner, Thomas and Elly took turns on the bridge while Eno remained at the control console. As the night wore on, the temperature started to drop, and Elly found some waterproof jackets in one of the hatches. Thomas kept his unzipped so that he could reach the Sonic Inducer in case of an emergency. But so far the trip had been sharkless.

Around midnight, the stars huddled around each other like small families, and Thomas found himself thinking about the powerful nature of the tide of time. In a matter of a few short days on Earth, it had already connected him to his father, and now it might add his mother.

Elly appeared out of the darkness on the bridge. "My shift."

"I'm not really tired," Thomas said.

"What is it with you and sleep, anyway?"

"I never needed much, even on Mars. And since I've been on Earth, I seem to need even less. Eno says it's the extra oxygen."

"I have a different theory," Elly said. "I think you just don't want to miss anything."

She was joking, but Thomas didn't smile. Elly could see that his mood had become much more serious since leaving New York. "Thomas, are you worried about meeting your mother?"

"Yes. But if what you just said is true, maybe I'm worried about *not* meeting her."

"I know it must be stressful either way, and you're gonna need to be at your best to deal with it. So, I'm ordering you to go below and shut your eyes."

"Yes, ma'am," Thomas said.

He headed down to the master stateroom and sprawled out on the king-size bed, which seemed five times bigger than anything he'd ever slept on. The pillows were so soft that his head seemed to disappear inside. Oddly enough, the round window on the opposite wall was about the same size as the portal in the cell he shared with Eno back on the Station. But his view, unlike the lifeless Martian landscape, was now the river. It gently rocked him up and down, like the chair in his mother's room, and despite his attempt to stay awake, his eyes slowly closed.

He woke to the sound of the engine throttling back and slowing down. Through the portal, he glimpsed a large object, painted in bright colors. As it drifted by, he got out of bed and ran to the bridge. He got there just in time to see that a strange inflatable creature towered over the boat. The jaws on its huge brown head were open, and painted flames flickered from them.

"What is it?" he asked Elly, who seemed completely unfazed.

"A moon bounce. Or at least that's what we called it back in the good old days of 2023. This one's supposed to be a dragon."

"Like the ones we saw on our cable car trip through Chinatown."

"Right, you know what they are?"

"I looked it up. Mythical creatures, like unicorns."

"Yeah, but they're the unicorns' big bad cousins."

The boat's wake caused the dragon to bounce back and forth as if it were bowing toward them. As they watched it recede into the darkness, a plaintive howl echoed in the dark.

"What's that?" Thomas asked.

"Sounds like an animal of some sort," Elly said.

Thomas found one of the portable lights and scanned a small cluster of nearly submerged houses. A small ball of yellow fur sat on top of a roof barely above water.

"It's a puppy," Elly said. "It must have gotten stranded. Steer us over, and I'll grab it."

Thomas took the wheel and steered in the direction of the house.

"It's all right, little guy," Elly shouted. "We're here to save you."

Thomas jumped down to the deck, grabbed the nearest mooring line, and tied it to one of the rain gutters on the house. Elly stepped out onto the roof as the frightened puppy backed away. She slowly reached out and snatched it into her arms.

"I've got him!" she yelled.

As she spoke, a floodlight hit her in the eyes and a voice rang out from the darkness.

"Don't move!"

A man appeared on the roof wearing an orange prison uniform. His face was covered with a thick black beard and he held a shotgun pointed at Elly's head. Thomas immediately thought about the convicts Matthew had mentioned.

A second floodlight hit the boat from a small barge moored to the house next door. Three more men stood along its perimeter, all wearing prison garb. The one in the middle held the lights, while the other two pointed their weapons at Thomas. "Climb down. And don't try anything, or you'll be shark food."

Elly climbed onto the barge, which was piled high with an assortment of computers, TVs, and kitchen appliances, including stoves and refrigerators. All the men had beards, except for the youngest, who was also the biggest, at well over three hundred pounds.

"We don't have any money, if that's what you're after," Elly said.

"We just want your boat. As you can see, ours is pretty full."

"You can't just leave us stranded," Elly said.

"Wouldn't think of it," he said. "You're welcome to our backup." One of the men pulled on a rope, dragging a small rowboat into view. "This should be plenty big enough for you and your boyfriend there."

As the younger man nudged Elly and the puppy into the rowboat, Black Beard turned his weapon toward Thomas.

"All right, boy, climb onto the roof and get over here."

Thomas started to do what he asked, but when he got to the top of the roof, he stopped.

"C'mon now, we don't have all night."

Thomas surveyed the barge, as if making some kind of mental calculation.

"What's a matter, afraid of fallin'?"

"No," Thomas said, locking eyes with Elly. "I'm just worried I'll make a lot of noise. I mean, a *deafening* noise."

"Trust me boy, nobody's gonna hear a thing out here."

"Just the same," he said, "you might want to *hold your ears.*"

Thomas slowly reached inside his rain slicker. Elly's eyes widened as she suddenly realized what he was doing. She shielded the puppy against her chest as Thomas pulled out the Sonic Inducer. Before the men could react, he pointed it into the water and fired.

The cartridge made a loud thunk as it sliced into the water. There was a moment of silence, and Thomas thought it might be a dud. But then a loud boom echoed from below. The surface of the water exploded, creating a wave that rocked the barge, sending Elly and the puppy overboard

"Kill him, you morons!" Black Beard shouted.

The men swung their shotguns toward Thomas, but the barge was still in motion and their shots echoed over his head. Thomas leapt back onto the deck of the Star as a dazed Eno appeared from the control room.

"What's going on?"

There was no time to answer. Thomas grabbed a lifesaver and hurled it toward Elly and the puppy. It landed close enough so that she could grab it with her free hand as more gunshots rang out.

"Pull!" Thomas shouted, as he and Eno began to pull her in.

But when she got within a few feet, they hit sudden resistance. Elly turned to see a hand gripping her ankle. Behind her, the heavyset man was grinning like a madman.

"Not so fast, sweetheart!"

Thomas and Eno pulled with all their strength, but the lifesaver was like a dead weight. Suddenly they heard a high-pitched scream, but it wasn't coming from Elly. They looked out to see the big man's face filled with terror as he disappeared under the surface. A moment later the hand that had been around her ankle bobbed to the surface still attached to its arm, but the arm was no longer attached to the man. Elly stifled a scream of her own, as Thomas and Eno pulled her and the puppy into the boat, out of the shark's reach.

They looked up to see that the barge had started to settle and Black Beard was taking aim. Gunshots ripped the water all around the boat.

"I'm gonna make a run for the bridge," Thomas said.

"No," Elly said. "Wait!"

"Wait for what?" Eno asked.

"Reinforcements," Elly said, motioning toward the water.

A giant tail fin appeared behind the barge, and it was lifted out of the water on the back of the megalodon. The barge creaked under the weight of all the appliances and then broke in half, sending the men into the water under an avalanche of stolen goods.

Thomas scrambled to the bridge and threw the Star's engine into gear. The boat lurched forward, drowning out the sound of the men shouting with its powerful motor. In a matter of seconds, the barge, along with the convicts, disappeared in their wake.

At the next bend in the river, Thomas glanced back at Eno and Elly. "Everybody all right?"

"Arms and legs accounted for," Elly nodded.

"Will somebody please tell me what happened?" Eno asked.

"We stopped to save this little guy," Thomas said, motioning toward the puppy in Elly's arms.

"We risked our lives for a dog?" Eno asked.

Suddenly, the boat tilted to one side.

"What's that?" Eno asked.

"I'm not sure," Thomas said. "We better find out."

They hurried below deck and threw open the engine room door to see that several gunshots had blown through the hull, producing four separate streams of water.

The Star was flooding.

# CHAPTER 34

Elly found a towel and cut it into short strips, which the boys rolled up to use as makeshift plugs. But the towels quickly became soaked and were spit back into the boat by the pressure of the river. To make matters worse, the water was now gathering around their ankles and rising fast.

"I don't think this is gonna do it," Thomas said. "We need hard plugs."

"Better yet, a bilge pump," Elly said. "There should be one on a boat like this. Eno, why don't you check the console while I look for something we can use to make better plugs."

Elly disappeared toward the bow while Eno headed in the opposite direction.

Thomas was standing in water up to his shins, and the Star was beginning to lose speed, when Elly returned with a boogie board.

"What's that?" Thomas said.

"Boogie board. Normally used for riding waves, but it looks like it's made from Styrofoam or something similar, so it should work. We just need something to draw holes."

Thomas dug into his backpack to find a box of crayons. "Will these do?"

"Perfect," Elly said, pulling out a black crayon.

While holding the puppy with one hand, she used the other to draw several small circles on the boogie board. Thomas used his diamond blade to cut out a circular section of board, then pushed it into one of the holes, but it was too large.

He carved the bottom of the plug to make it smaller. Then, using the handle of the Sonic Inducer, he hammered it into the hole.

The leaking stopped.

"Ah, the wonders of science," Elly said.

They quickly sealed the other holes, after which a hum sounded and an automatic bilge pump kicked in, pumping out the remaining water.

Eno appeared a few moments later. "Found it," he said.

Within minutes, the boat was dry again.

"What time is it?" Thomas asked.

"Almost one in the morning," Elly said. "Five more hours until we reach DC. We should all get some sleep. The master stateroom is big enough for all of us."

Eno glanced at the puppy in her arms. "I'm not sleeping with a dog, thank you."

"You don't know what you're missing," Elly said.

"I'll take your word for it," Eno said.

✦✦

THOMAS PUT THE STAR on autopilot and returned to the master stateroom, where Elly and the puppy were already tucked under the blankets in the king-size bed.

"Before we go to sleep, we need to name him," Elly said.

"Any ideas?" Thomas asked.

"Given the circumstances, I think we should go with 'Lucky.'"

"I like it," Thomas said.

Thomas laid down next to Elly as Lucky nestled his head on Elly's shoulder with his tail stretched across Thomas's neck. Underneath them, the Star carved a smooth path through the river. Thomas marveled at the feeling, the same one that he'd experienced for the first time on the ferry to San Francisco. It reminded him of the astonishing fact that most of the Earth was covered in water. Beautiful, precious, wonderful water. Which was about to drown the planet.

"Relaxing, huh?" Elly said.

"Yeah," Thomas said. "Why does it feel so good?"

"They say it's primal, like being in the womb."

"Ah," Thomas said, grateful for the simple explanation. But Elly's mention of the womb also reminded him that he was on the way to meet his mother, which could be much more complicated. His only real experience with girls Kate's age had been his few days with Elly, and he hoped that it would be as easy as that. In any event, there was absolutely no way to prepare for it. He closed his eyes and wished for the best.

It was just after four in the morning when he woke to feel the boat pick up speed. He went to the control console and checked the digital map. They were nearing the headwaters of the Potomac River, which ran directly through the city of Washington. Like the East River, it cut through the larger floodwaters with its faster current.

Thomas went up to the bridge. The stars hung overhead like a crown of lights. Even in the midst of chaos and destruction, he thought, the Earth was spectacularly beautiful.

Sometime after dawn, Elly woke to an alarm. The digital readout revealed they were less than an hour from their destination. But when the alarm stopped, she became aware of a high-pitched sound. She went up to the bridge and joined Thomas.

"Do you hear anything? A sort of hissing?"

Thomas cut the engines. The sound became louder.

"It's out on the river somewhere," Elly said. But in the darkness, they could barely see beyond the area of light directly around the boat.

"Let's check the monitor. Maybe it'll show something."

They came down from the bridge and entered the control room.

Eno, who had fallen asleep in front of the console, jolted awake. "Are we there?"

"No. We picked up a noise, and we're trying to figure out what it is."

"Hopefully not another dog." Eno pushed the touch screen to illuminate the weather map. "I don't see anything."

"What about this little white dot?" Elly asked.

"What dot?"

"That one, on the water right in front of us."

Elly pointed to a tiny ball of digital fuzz that spun in place. Eno leaned closer, favoring his prosthetic eye, which had an automatic magnifier when it came within an inch of any object.

"Yes, I can see it now," Eno said.

A word began to flash in red letters: OBSTRUCTION.

The monitor calculated that it was 1.7 miles away, with the distance quickly closing.

"Grab your binoculars," Thomas said, as he burst out of the control room and climbed to the bridge, where the hissing morphed into a whooshing sound.

Elly scanned the horizon.

"See anything?" Thomas asked.

"Yeah. It looks like a giant…fountain. No, make that a monster fountain."

"Eno," Thomas shouted, "let me know when we're within a mile."

"We're already there. Six tenths and counting."

Thomas and Elly leaned forward as the fountain finally came into view. A thick plume of water, more than twice the width of the boat, gushed straight into the air.

"What is it?" Thomas asked.

"No idea," Elly said. "But it looks like somebody turned on a gigantic fire hydrant under the water."

"Point four," Eno shouted from below.

As they glided closer, the water from the gusher began to pour down on them like heavy rain. Thomas put the Star into reverse to duck out of the rain as Eno reappeared below the bridge. "According to the monitor, we're only a few miles from our destination."

"Look," Thomas said, pointing to an area where a mountain of trees and boulders had accumulated against the banks of the river.

"It's the same on the other side," Elly said. "That's why the river's being funneled into that narrow chute in front of us. The water has no choice but to go straight up."

They watched the plume for a few silent moments, awestruck by its size.

"Well I suppose that does it," Eno said.

"What do you mean?" Elly asked.

"The boat's too big to go through that chute, and we certainly can't go over it."

Thomas thought about it for a moment. "Why not?"

"What are you talking about?" Eno said.

"The boat can hover, remember?"

"But only five feet," Eno said. "According to the console, the water's almost eighteen feet high."

"If we get a running start, the water should act like a ramp and take us right over it," Thomas said.

"Or flip us backward, destroying the boat." Eno said. "And us along with it."

Thomas kept his eye on the gusher. "Just run the equation."

"You're not really serious, are you?"

"Look, if we don't get through this thing, I can't rescue my mother. Not that I expect you to understand."

Elly could see that Eno was stung by Thomas's accusation. "There's no harm in running the equation, is there?" she said. "At least that way Thomas can make an informed decision."

"Of course," Eno said, his tone suddenly formal. "I can calculate our speed and distance, but I'll have to make a rough estimate about mass."

He turned and went below deck.

Thomas glanced at Elly. "I guess I didn't handle that very well, huh?"

"Thomas, we're all with you. But Eno's here for a reason. He's your Navigator, not to mention your Protector. And he takes the job very seriously."

Eno rejoined them on the bridge. "It's physically possible. But we'd have to start from almost three miles back and reach maximum velocity within eleven seconds."

"Shall we take a vote?" Thomas asked.

"No need," Eno said. "This is a decision for the mission leader. Whatever you say goes."

"Thanks, Eno," Thomas said. "I say let's do it."

"I know I don't have an official vote, but I agree," Elly said.

Eno nodded. "Consider it done."

Thomas turned to Elly. "Maybe you should get into the control room. That should be the safest place to withstand the impact."

"If we're really gonna do this, I prefer to watch," Elly said. "But I should make sure Lucky's safe." As Thomas began to turn the boat around, she went below to the control room, where Eno was focused on the screen. "You don't mind dog-sitting for a few minutes, do you?"

"Would it make any difference if I did?"

"No," Elly said. "Just this once, I promise."

Without waiting for a response, she handed him the puppy and headed back to the bridge.

Thomas tightened his grip on the wheel as she reappeared. "Ready when you are, Eno!" Thomas shouted through the intercom.

Eno's voice echoed back. "Engaging Hover Mode."

A low rumble echoed under the Star as it slowly began to rise over the water. It was a strange feeling, Elly thought, like being on a magic carpet.

Eno's voice echoed through the transmitter. "Hover complete."

Thomas pointed the Star directly at the mountain of water.

"Here goes," he said, engaging the throttle.

The Star shot forward. Within seconds, they were speeding toward the gusher. The closer they got, the higher it seemed.

Elly grabbed the handrails and tried to resist the temptation to shut her eyes.

And suddenly they were there.

"Hold on," Thomas shouted, as they made contact with the gusher. It slammed against the windshield, instantly cutting off visibility.

The front of the boat started to rise, and for a moment it seemed like they were going to take off. But they were no sooner airborne then the Star began to slow, and they started to dive, nose first, in a free fall. Thomas felt an instant pang of regret over his decision to take on the gusher. Ignatius had told him to trust his instincts, but that was in the service of the mission. Rescuing his mother was not part of the mission. It was his own selfish need.

Elly let out a scream.

Finally, the boat began to fight back against the water, its heavy bow knifing into the plume and pushing them downward. At the same time, it began to wobble precariously, throwing them off the bridge and into the wash of water that covered the deck. Elly slid toward the edge of the boat, about to be thrown overboard. But at the last second, Thomas reached out and pulled her back as the boat hit the water and twisted itself into an upright position. The gusher was behind them.

"You all right?" Thomas said.

"Yeah. I think I just lost a year of my life, but who's counting." Elly said.

They pulled themselves upright. With the gusher gone, they could finally see downriver, where a smattering of emergency lights marked the monuments of the nation's capital.

"We did it, Thomas," Elly said. "There it is, Washington DC."

"Wow," Thomas said, mesmerized by the majestic buildings shimmering against the water's surface.

"I guess we can turn Hover Mode off now," Elly said.

"Take us down, Eno!" Thomas said.

But there was no response from below deck.

"Earth to Eno," Elly cracked, giddy with the adrenalin of having survived. "You there?"

But all they could hear was the puppy whine over the transmitter.

"That doesn't sound good," Elly said.

Thomas put the boat in neutral and rushed down to the control room.

He threw open the door to find Eno on the floor, eyes closed, writhing in pain. The puppy was standing over him, licking his face. Elly arrived a moment later.

"Eno, what is it?" Thomas asked. "Show us where it hurts."

But Eno could only point downward.

Eno carefully reached for his leg. Elly gently touched it below the knee, causing him to shriek in agony. She turned to Thomas and mouthed a silent word.

*Broken.*

# CHAPTER 35

THOMAS ACTIVATED THE ANCHOR while Elly found the first-aid kit. She gave Eno some pain medication along with a few sips of peach liquor she found in the galley. To her surprise, he took it without protest.

Eno hadn't said a word since the accident, and Elly told Thomas that he was probably in shock. She propped some pillows under his head and leg while Thomas located a child's inflatable raft. After letting out the air, Elly gently wrapped it around Eno's leg. Thomas taped it together then partially reinflated it to form a protective splint. By the time they'd finished, Eno had passed out.

They carried him to a bed in one of the guest staterooms and closed the door. Elly took the puppy and went up to the deck with Thomas, who looked glum. "It's all my fault," he said.

"Actually, I'd put most of the blame on the monster gusher."

"No, I mean the whole trip. You and Eno were just doing it for me."

"If you recall, it was my idea to begin with. I'd like at least some of the fault."

Thomas didn't respond. Either he didn't get the joke or didn't find it funny.

Finally, he turned to Elly. "Maybe we should head back."

"Let me just point out that if we do, Eno broke his leg for nothing. I'd also add that we're here now, so we might as well try to find your mother. Remember, you basically talked your father into going in his place, and he's counting on you."

Thomas gave her a reluctant nod.

"Good," Elly said. "I'm glad we see eye to eye."

Thomas had to smile. Once again, Elly was right.

The sun had risen, revealing a beautiful cloudless day. Twenty minutes later, they entered the calm waters of the nation's capital. As in New York, the massive buildings formed a natural harbor. But unlike the high-rise buildings around Central Park, these had a regal bearing that made him feel that all was well with the world. Even knee-deep in floodwater, they seemed to stand for a higher purpose, like the Statue of Liberty.

"Do you know which monument is which?" he asked.

"Yeah, in third grade I built a scale model of the Capital out of Popsicle sticks. It's the big one with the dome and four tiers sticking out of the water. Looks like a wedding cake."

"Is that like the cake used in birthdays?"

"A close relative. A wedding is the official union of two people in marriage."

"For life?"

"Well, that's the idea anyway."

Thomas throttled forward. In a few minutes they were in front of the building. Partially submerged, the stairway looked like it was expressly built for the purpose of walking into the water. Thomas put the engine in neutral, leaving no other sound than the soft lapping of water against concrete. "Hello?" he shouted.

There was no response.

"It's still early in the morning," Elly said. "They could be sleeping."

As the boat drifted closer, a faint voice echoed from above.

"Hey! Up here!"

Elly looked up and saw a red-haired girl in one of the windows, waving frantically.

"It doesn't look like Kate," Elly said, "but it could be one of her friends."

"Hold on," Thomas shouted. "I'm coming!"

Thomas brought the boat alongside the monument, while Elly tied a mooring line around the nearest column. He stepped onto a ledge and tried one of the windows. It was locked, so he climbed up the dome wall to an open window on the second level, and crawled inside. He found himself on a circular balcony that wrapped around an open rotunda, which had flooded, forming a deep pool.

He looked up to see that he was directly beneath the red-haired girl, who was with five other girls her age. He hurried around the balcony to a set of stairs, which brought him up to their level.

As soon as he appeared, the girls ran to greet him. The red-haired girl seemed to be their spokesperson. "I'm Casey," she said. "Who are you?"

"A friend of Kate's boyfriend, Matthew. Is she here?"

"No. We all snuck in to see a congressman and hid in one of the bathrooms overnight. But when we came out, the flood had hit and the place was evacuated. We could see there was a staging area for an airlift at the Washington Monument, so we came up here to signal for help. But by that time, we were trapped."

"Kate volunteered to try and get over there," added a girl with thin metal wire on her teeth. "She was the only one brave enough to go downstairs."

"Because of the water?" Thomas asked.

"No, because of him." She pointed over the balcony to the rotunda pool where a massive megalodon fin cut through the water.

"How did he even get in here?" Thomas said.

"They were doing some repairs before the flood hit and left an open wall at the back of the building, We know, because that's how we snuck in." Casey said.

The girl with the metal wire on her teeth shook her head dramatically. "He won't leave. It's like he's waiting for us."

"Well, the wait's over," Thomas said, pulling the Sonic Inducer from his holster. "But you'll need to cover your ears."

✦✦

Elly heard the muffled sound charge as it blew out several windows on the second tier of the dome. Moments later, the girl with wire on her teeth climbed out and hurried toward the boat. Elly pulled her on board.

"Hi, I'm Elly. Welcome to the Star of the Sea."

"I'm Meredith."

The rest of the girls quickly followed, with Thomas bringing up the rear.

"You girls must be starving," Elly said. "We've got plenty of food in the galley. Go down and help yourselves."

"Is that your puppy?" Casey said.

"No, she's a rescue, like you guys. You mind watching her for a while?"

"Sure thing, whatever we can do to help."

As the girls went below deck, Elly turned to Thomas. "What about…?"

"She's at the Washington Monument."

Elly turned toward the concrete obelisk a mile or so behind them. It stuck out of the water like a giant candle. Other than a pair of small windows at the very top, there was no apparent entrance.

"You have to be kidding," Elly said.

"I wish," Thomas said. "Have you ever been inside?"

"Once," Elly said. "There's only one door, at the very bottom, like the elevator."

"Which are both now under water," Thomas said.

"Unfortunately. I guess you could use the steps, assuming you can get to them."

"Why don't I get us over to the monument and then figure something out."

Thomas went to the console, and Elly went below. She found the girls at the galley table, unpacking the food from Matthew's duffel while Meredith held Lucky.

"Do you think we can reach Kate?" Casey asked.

"We'll do our best," Elly said.

"We begged her not to go alone. But she organized the trip and felt responsible for us. How are we going to get her out of there?"

"Thomas will think of something," Elly said. "He always does."

"Is he your boyfriend?" Casey asked.

"No, we actually just met a few days ago."

"And who's that?" Meredith asked, looking over Elly's shoulder.

Elly turned to see Eno standing in the doorway of the guest stateroom. With the inflatable raft around his leg, he looked even stranger than usual.

"That would be our navigator, Eno."

"I see you've found her," Eno said, his words slurred from the liqueur. "Which one is Thomas's mother?"

The girls looked to Elly, bewildered.

"Eno's under the influence of some pain meds we gave him for his broken leg, suffered in the line of duty."

Eno looked at the inflatable raft as if noticing it for the first time. "My leg is broken?"

"You poor thing," Meredith said, as the others echoed their sympathy.

"Is there anything we can do?" Casey asked.

"There are some kayak paddles in the recreation hatch," Elly said. "Maybe you could rig up some crutches."

Casey jumped to her feet, ready to serve. "We can do that, can't we, girls?"

✦✦

On the bridge, Elly joined Thomas and the Washington Monument came into view. It seemed so much higher now that they were underneath it.

"How's it going down there?" Thomas asked.

"Eno's up. The girls are taking care of him and Lucky. We're free to get on with the rescue operation."

Thomas lowered the anchor and pointed up to a pair of small, rectangular observation windows at the top of the obelisk. "Those monument windows—how big are they?"

"Big enough to crawl through, if that's what you're thinking."

"I figure I can use the Porta Gill to swim up to the stairs and then walk the rest of the way."

"How much time will the Porta Gill allow you to breathe?"

"Twenty minutes or so."

"You may need more, just in case. I saw some scuba gear in the rec hatch, which would give you an hour or so if something goes wrong. But say you get up the stairs, how in the world do you plan to get her down?"

"That's the simple part. Zip line."

"Zip line?" Elly said, in obvious disbelief.

"Yeah, like the one in your backyard."

"Sorry to break it to you, but the distance between my bedroom and the tree house is sixty feet. I know because I had to measure it when I bought the cable. This is more like a few *hundred* feet, not to mention five hundred feet high. Also, my bedroom's on the same level as the tree house, but here you've got a serious angle of descent. You'll need a much longer cable."

"Matthew said the boat has a thousand feet of anchor cable, so that should be more than enough," Thomas said. "With the extra length, we could back up the boat far enough for a safe descent. Worse case, we could make a water landing."

"I hate to be negative Thomas, but since Eno's out of commission, let me say that your plan is flat-out crazy. In the first place, hitting the water from that height is like landing on concrete. Secondly, do you have any idea how much a thousand feet of anchor cable weighs? My guess is a few hundred pounds. How will you carry it up all those stairs?"

Thomas thought about her objections for a few moments.

"Okay, strike the water landing. As far as the cable goes, worse case I can take it up by one end and when I get to the top, spool up the rest. It's at least worth a try."

Elly sighed. "Believe me, I understand why you think so. In fact, I'm even a little jealous. I've dreamed of meeting my mother all my life. But it's just too dangerous."

"We're here now, like you said. I can't let my father, *or* my mother, down."

Thomas readied himself for Elly's next objection. But then he saw her expression change, and if there was one thing he'd learned about Elly, it was that she was always more interested in solving somebody else's problem than her own.

"You need a harness of some sort," Elly said. "Big enough for two people."

"Think you could rig one?"

"There's a tow rope with the ski stuff. I'll just need to find a pulley."

At that moment, Eno appeared on his new crutches, kayak paddles cushioned with pillows tied at the top. He was flanked by the girls.

"Eno, good to see you on your feet," Thomas said.

"One foot, anyway. But I've only had one eye most of my life, so I'm sure I can manage."

Thomas smiled. "Good to have you back. Now that you're here, I'll need you to take over on the bridge for me."

Eno turned to Elly. "I assume Thomas has concocted some incredibly dangerous plan by now?"

"You got it," Elly said. "In fact, I'd say he's really outdone himself this time."

"May I suggest we at least confirm that the *girlfriend* of Thomas's *friend*, is even up there?" Eno said.

"We can handle that," Casey said. "C'mon, girls."

They moved to the bow and started shouting Kate's name as loud as they could. After a few moments, a small head appeared at one of the two windows. And then a hand reached out through the barred window, waving.

Casey waved back. "That's her all right."

# CHAPTER 36

Thomas borrowed Elly's binoculars, hoping to get a better view of Kate. His eyes moved up the monument to the small observation windows. He recognized her immediately. With her long dark hair and soft features, she was a smaller, younger version of the woman in the pictures Ignatius had shown him. Despite her predicament, her face bore no sign of weakness or fear. If anything, she looked strong and determined.

Elly gathered the girls on the bow and led them below deck to the five-foot signal balloon. It came with a portable inflation device as well as a weatherproof marker for writing messages. "This is a signal balloon. Let out enough line so that it's high enough for Kate to see. That way you can keep her up to date with what's happening."

"We'll take care of it," Casey said.

"Meredith, I'll need you and the rest of the girls to take the king-size mattress from the master stateroom and haul it up to the deck."

"We're on it," Meredith said.

As they peeled off, Elly continued down the passageway to the supply hatch where the recreational equipment was stored. She opened it and crawled inside.

Back on deck, Thomas was on the bridge with Eno, who was calculating the safest angle of descent. He released the anchor cable and together they watched the monitor as it spooled out from under the boat.

"Elly's worried the cable will be too heavy for me to carry," Thomas said.

"She was no doubt thinking of the kind made back in the good old days of 2023," Eno said. "I checked the boat documentation and saw that this is a graphene version created mid-century. It can't weigh more than thirty pounds."

"Do we have enough length?"

"More than you'd ever need. The only challenging issue will be your landing."

"How's that?" Thomas said.

"Since there'll be two of you riding the zip line, you'll be coming down much faster than if you were alone. I recommend a buffer of some sort."

"Coming right up," Casey said, as she and the girls carried the king-size mattress onto the deck and laid it out to form a landing pad.

"Looks like Elly's thought of everything," Thomas said.

"Why does that not surprise me," Eno said, as she appeared on deck with a canvas bag full of equipment. She plopped it down and began to remove a variety of scuba gear, including a mask, fins, and a nylon dive belt with quick-release buckle. Finally, she brought out a blue steel cylinder no bigger than a bicycle pump.

Thomas jumped down from the bridge to join her. "What's that?"

"Oxygen tank. It's much smaller and lighter than the ones I'm familiar with back in—"

"Yes, we know," Eno echoed from the bridge. "But we probably shouldn't mention that."

"Right," Elly said, glancing toward Kate's friends. "Anyway Thomas, you might as well start getting into this stuff. I just need to get one more thing."

Elly ducked into the galley and came out with a deep-sea fishing rod. She unscrewed it into three sections and took off the reel. "This should work fine as your pulley," she said.

Elly looped it through the towrope to form a makeshift zip line harness and held out the thick bottom section of the rod, which was about two feet long. "Here, you'll need this, too."

"What for?"

"A brake. If you find yourself going too fast, you can jam it into the pulley."

Thomas slid the rod under his scuba belt while Elly tied the zip line harness around his waist. In the futuristic gear, with the Sonic Inducer strapped across his chest, Elly thought he looked like some kind of alien warrior. In a way, she thought, that's exactly what he was.

"One more thing," Elly said, reaching into the bag for a pair of small electronic devices. She slipped one onto Thomas's free wrist and the other around her own. "Walkie-talkies, so we can communicate."

"I guess that's it, huh?" Thomas said.

Elly could see the anxious look on his face. It was the same one that had overcome him before he met his father. "You've already met your father, so this can't be any more difficult."

"Yes, it can," Thomas said.

"I get it. She's the woman who'll someday give you life."

"Are you trying to make me feel better about this?" Thomas sighed.

"Just think of the upside. How many people ever get to revisit the single most important person from their past. Have you figured out what you're gonna say?"

Thomas shook his head, embarrassed that it hadn't even occurred to him.

"Just like a boy. When I was in third grade, I made up a list of questions to ask my own mother."

"But I thought…"

"Of course I knew she wasn't alive, but it somehow made me feel more connected to her. I still keep the list in my wallet after all these years"

"If you don't mind my asking," Thomas said, "what kind of questions?"

"Oh, all sorts. *How did you know what you wanted to do with your life? What was my real father like? And why in the world did you name me Elpis?"*

Elly smiled, and Thomas could see that by making a joke she was trying to distract him from the seriousness of what he was about to attempt.

"I guess I should try to think of some questions of my own," he said.

"You still have some time."

Behind them, Casey and the girls let out the message balloon. As it climbed into the sky they could see that written across the back was the message: HELP IS ON THE WAY!

Thomas slid a pair of goggles over his eyes and put the air hose in his mouth.

Elly gave the gear a few final tweaks. "Let us know as soon as you get into the tower."

Thomas gave her a thumbs up, then sat on the side of the boat with his legs dangling over the water. Elly gave him the thumb's up sign, and he pushed off.

Under the water, he swam to the front of the boat where the anchor cable was attached to the bow. He quickly cut it loose with his diamond blade. Sure enough, it wasn't much thicker than everyday wire, and even lighter. Looping it around his elbow, he pulled himself downward until he'd gathered it all and reached the anchor itself, which was embedded in the grassy lawn in front of the monument. He cut the cable free, slung it over his shoulder, and swam away.

After a few minutes, he spotted the circle of flags that marked the park surrounding the Washington Monument. In a matter of seconds he was at the monument door, but due to the water pressure he could barely budge it. He planted his feet against the side of the monument and leaned back, using his body weight to open it a few inches before it quickly closed.

Needing something to pry it open, he took the air hose out of his mouth and replaced it with the Porta Gill, then unstrapped the oxygen tank from his back. He tried the door again and managed to get it open wide enough to jam the tank inside, creating space for him to enter sideways. But as he did, a shadow darkened the water. Out of the corner of his eye, he could see a megalodon, probably the one from the rotunda, coming toward him. Before he could pull the tank away to release the door, the shark lunged forward, wedging its nose inside. It flailed back and forth against the doorway, it's gaping jaws reaching for Thomas, who quickly started to swim up the stairs.

He'd barely gotten a few feet when he heard a loud bang and looked down to see the door torn from its hinges. The megalodon now had his entire head inside and was trying to squeeze its body through the doorway. Thomas was pretty sure it couldn't get its whole body into the monument, but also knew he couldn't take the chance.

He pulled the Sonic Inducer from its holster and fired.

But in the confines of the thick monument walls, the charge reverberated with greater force than usual, the blowback slamming him against the wall, knocking him unconscious.

Fifty-nine seconds later, he found himself floating on his back two floors above the entrance. He had somehow managed to drift up the monument stairs to the waterline, his face barely submerged, the Porta Gill still in his mouth. The Sonic Inducer bobbed in the water next to him as a muffled voice echoed from below. He lifted his walkie-talkie wrist out of the water and heard Elly's voice.

"Thomas?" she shouted. "Thomas, are you there? Please answer me!"

He pulled the Porta Gill out of his mouth to speak. "Yeah, I'm here."

A trickle of blood—the result of a gash in his forehead—dribbled over his nose and dispersed in the water. He snagged the floating Sonic Inducer and put it back in its holster, then dragged his aching body onto the steps.

"Whew," Elly said. "We could hear the Sonic Inducer go off from here."

"Yeah, I had to deal with one of our friends."

"That's what I figured. I just wondered if you remember what Matthew said when he gave it to you?"

"My head's a little fuzzy right now. Remind me."

"He only had three cartridges. You used the first one on the convicts last night and the second in the Rotunda with the girls. You just used the third on that meg."

There was a moment of silence as Thomas realized what Elly was saying.

He was out of ammunition.

# CHAPTER 37

Thomas tucked the Porta Gill into his pocket and staggered to his feet, pain rippling from his legs to his back. He stepped out the water and looked up the long circular staircase. The observation tower was eight-hundred and ninety-six steps away, minus the fifty or so he'd already navigated under water. He started upward, silently counting the steps the way he used to do back in the Station. He knew exactly how long it should take under normal circumstances, and when he finally came around the last curve he was surprised to find he wasn't that far off.

Kate was standing at the window. Thomas was so relieved to have made it that any anxiety about meeting her had vanished. But still, he could only think of one thing to say.

"You must be Kate?"

"Yes," she said, turning to see him. "You must be Thomas?"

He was still a bit dazed, and for a brief moment had the strange feeling that she somehow sensed who he really was. "How did you know?"

"The girls have been keeping me up to speed with balloon messages."

Thomas glanced outside the observation window to see the message Elly had written on the front of a weather balloon: THOMAS IS COMING.

Kate pointed to his forehead. "Oh my gosh, you're bleeding."

"It's nothing, really," Thomas said, casually wiping off the blood.

"I feel terrible about making you come up here. It was so stupid of me to get us all stuck in the flood. And then I went and made matters worse by getting stuck over here."

"You were just trying to help. That's all I'm doing, too."

"The balloon said you're an old friend of Matthew's?"

"It's a long story," Thomas shrugged. "Right now, we need to get you out of here."

"Are we going back the same way you came in?"

"No. Unfortunately the door is too far under water. We have to go, uh, out the window."

"This window?" Kate said, assuming he was kidding. "Are you serious?"

"I'm afraid so. Are you afraid of heights?"

"Not at all. But I think it's way too high to jump."

Thomas laughed. "We won't be jumping. Have you ever been on a zip line?"

"Plenty of times, though not from a national monument."

"Principle's the same," Thomas said, unloading the wire and harness from his shoulder.

"Where do we land, on the water?"

"No, on the boat, where your friends are."

"What about the bars on the windows?"

"No problem. I've got a special tool."

Thomas pulled out his Tetrascope and cut the bars away with a few quick slashes of the laser. He looped the anchor cable through the bars on the second window, knotted them several times, and leaned back with all his weight to make sure it was secure.

"Can I help?" Kate asked.

"Actually you can," Thomas said, handing her the other end of the cable. "Start lowering this out the window."

Kate did as instructed, but glanced over at Thomas dubiously.

"Don't worry, this is gonna be fun."

"Fun?" Kate laughed. "I can see why you and Matthew are friends."

Thomas looked out the window to see Eno maneuver the boat toward the observation window. The cable snaked down the side of the monument, and Elly reached across the bow to grab it. She walked it to the bridge and tied it off, so the zip line would deliver Thomas and Kate onto the large front deck, where the mattress was strategically positioned.

"Cable's ready," Elly said through the walkie-talkie. "We're moving into position now."

Thomas and Kate watched as Eno put the boat into reverse and the zip line slowly rose into the air. In a matter of seconds, it became taut.

"How does that look?" Elly shouted through the walkie.

"Perfect," Thomas said.

Beside him, Kate's eyes widened at the prospect of what they were about to undertake.

"Just so you know," Thomas said, "I can slow us down if we start going too fast."

"It's not the speed I'm worried about," Kate said, glancing at the water below. "But the giant shark down there is another story."

Thomas looked down to see the megalodon that had tried to attack him at the door circling the monument.

"Don't worry about him," Thomas said, tapping the Sonic Inducer. "The noise this thing makes drives them away." He knew he could no longer rely on the weapon, but if they were to pull off the harrowing descent it was important for Kate feel as confident as possible.

Thomas attached the harness and pulley to the cable. He then climbed up to the window and put his legs through the towrope as if it were a swing. Lastly, he held out a hand for Kate.

"All right, climb aboard."

Kate squeezed onto the swing next to him.

Thomas looked down to the boat and could see Eno on the bridge and Elly at the bow. Behind her, the girls were lined up on both sides of the mattress, holding it in place for the landing.

Elly lifted the walkie to her mouth. "How you guys doing?"

"Good to go!" Thomas said, with as much confidence as he could muster.

"Whenever you're ready!" Elly said.

Thomas glanced at Kate, and she nodded her readiness. "Here we go," he said.

Thomas pushed off, and they began to move, slowly and steadily, downward. Kate gripped the sides of the harness so tight that her knuckles went white, but managed to put on a brave smile. The pulley slid along the anchor cable with ease, making the ride surprisingly smooth, and Thomas felt a rush of relief that the worst part was over. As long as the harness didn't become unattached, there was little that could go wrong, he told himself. On the way up the monument stairs, he tried to think of a question he might pose to his future mother, perhaps something about her hopes or dreams for the future. But they were nearing the halfway point of their descent, and he couldn't think of a single question that wouldn't seem strange, unless he was willing to admit the bizarre truth of who he was and why he'd come to help her. As the zip line hit the halfway point, Thomas could see the boat rushing up at them, with the group of fearful faces gathered in hushed anticipation.

Everything was going according to plan. Until suddenly it wasn't.

Thomas realized they were going too fast for a safe landing. It was exactly what Eno had warned him about, the weight of two people as opposed to a single rider.

He pulled the fishing rod from his belt and jammed it into the pulley, preventing it from moving faster. For a few moments they began to slow, but the friction quickly caused the rod to splinter and then explode into a shower of small pieces. They immediately began to speed up again, hurtling toward a certain collision.

Thomas knew there was only one thing he could do now to slow them down. He grabbed the top of the harness and pulled himself up so his feet were on the tow bar.

"What are you doing?" Kate shouted.

"We're going too fast," Thomas said. "There's too much weight."

And with that, he leapt into the air.

As Thomas fell, he heard the scream erupt from the boat and knew it was for him. The journey downward seemed like it took forever, his body twisting uncontrollably in the air, until he hit the water. The impact produced a sickening crack as he plunged downward in a cocoon of bubbles. A stinging pain shot through his body, and he remembered what Elly said about the water being like concrete.

At some point his downward motion finally stopped, though his body was too stunned to react. But after a few moments, he slowly began to float upward and finally broke the surface with a gasp, his ears ringing painfully. The blood from his forehead dripped into his eyes, and he pushed it aside to see Kate's friends huddled around her, screaming with joy.

But then he saw Elly.

She was standing at the railing, screaming with something that looked very much like panic. She was waving at Thomas with both arms, frantically pointing behind him. He swiveled around as much as the pain would allow, to see the huge black fin. His brain told him to swim for the boat, but his body, still numb from the fall, wouldn't move.

Back on the Star, Elly looked up to the bridge and screamed. "Eno! Help him!"

But Eno didn't even look her way. He was frozen on the bridge, too intent on whatever he was doing to respond. There was nothing left to be done.

✦✦

THOMAS LOCKED EYES WITH the giant shark as it zeroed in. Helpless, he pulled the Sonic Inducer from its holster. He knew that he was out of cartridges, but hoped that the very sight of it might trigger a reminder of their last encounter in the shark.

Unfortunately, it only seemed to make the beast speed up.

Thomas went limp, prepared to meet his fate.

That's when he heard the muffled roar of the Star's engine, and saw that it was moving at full speed, five feet above the water, in full Hover Mode. From his perspective, the shimmering boat seemed almost dreamlike. It was heading directly toward the shark as the beast was heading toward him. Neither one showed any signs of changing course, as if the two were rivals in one of the medieval jousting contests Thomas had often read about.

The only problem was that he was in the middle.

But it was too late to move now, as the megalodon rose up out of the water for a final lunge at Thomas. At the exact same moment, the Star flashed over his head, hanging in the air for a brief moment before boat met beast in a loud clash of flesh and fiberglass.

The momentum sent the shark spiraling backward, landing it in the water with a tremendous splash. The victorious Star hit the water with a loud whack and then turned back to pick up Thomas. Despite the the ringing in his ears, he could still hear Eno and Elly.

"You saved his life!" she said.

"What did you expect?" he said. "I am, after all, his Protector."

# CHAPTER 38

By the time they started back to New York, the pain in Eno's broken leg had returned, and Elly gave him a double shot of peach liquor, as he requested. He passed out in his stateroom and the girls circled the bed protectively in case the Star hit rough water.

With Thomas back on the bridge, Elly took Eno's place in the control room. They soon noticed that the endless plain of floodwater had receded to the point where land was visible. Even more surprising, the massive gusher that once blocked their path was barely higher than the boat. Using Hover Mode, the Star passed over it so easily that the deck barely got wet.

Thomas pushed the boat to its maximum speed, while Elly checked the depth finder to discover that the river was now several feet lower than the previous day. The reduced volume, along with the weakening current, allowed them to make much better time on their return trip.

By late afternoon, the air started to cool slightly. Eno woke just before eight o'clock, and the girls helped him up to the deck, where they witnessed a spectacular orange-blue sunset. A spontaneous cheer erupted at the sight of Lady Liberty's gold-covered torch reflecting the sun's last rays. Elly was thrilled to see that the lady herself was now standing firmly on her pedestal, at least twenty feet above the water.

By the time the Star docked at the Science Alliance headquarters, it was almost ten o'clock. The building seemed much taller than when they left, and Thomas noticed that the waterline had dropped down to the fourth floor.

Matthew, who'd been keeping vigil from the big windows at the bar, was there to meet them. After a joyful reunion with Kate, he woke one of the doctors to set Eno's broken leg. Matthew and Kate accompanied them to the infirmary. Afterward, Thomas, Elly, and Lucky passed out on some empty beds.

The sun was just beginning to rise when Matthew and Kate woke them.

"Sorry to get you up so early, but I thought you'd better see this."

They led them to the windows facing uptown and were shocked to see that the waterline on the surrounding buildings was down to the third floor. Up in Central Park, the bigger elm trees were peeking out of the water like tiny islands of shrubbery.

"This is good, isn't it?" Thomas asked.

"Good for us, but not for you if you're still planning to go back to Coney Island," Matthew said. "The water's receding fast, but it's really warm, so a lot of it's being sucked into the air. That's fuel for a big storm."

"Matt told me you had to leave," Kate said, "so you might want to get out before it hits."

"You guys can take the dinghy and leave it at Coney Island," Matt said. "Kate and I can take the Star back to Central Park and hitch a ride later this morning to pick it up."

Thomas nodded, slightly disappointed. "I was hoping to spend some time with you guys before we left."

"Us, too," Kate said. "I'd love to hear more about how you got here or where you're going. Elly filled me in on some of it, but I still have a few questions."

Thomas gave Elly a quizzical look, but she just smiled as the two girls gave each other a sisterly hug. "Hopefully we can talk more the next time we get together," Elly said. "But I have a farewell present from Thomas and I." She handed them Lucky, who was still asleep.

"We promise to take great care of him," Kate said. "Are you leaving Eno with us, too? His fan club will be crushed if you take him away."

"I guess we could loan him to you for a few years," Elly said, and Thomas laughed.

✦✦

ENO WAS IN THE same bed Thomas had occupied after his attempt to save Ignatius a few nights earlier. He had a fresh cast on his leg and was surrounded by the sleeping girls.

"Eno," Thomas said. "Time to go."

Eno opened his eyes. Thomas and Matthew helped him up.

"Did the doctor say how long I'd have to have this cast on my leg?"

"You got a lucky break," Elly said. "If such a thing exists."

"Elly's right," Thomas said. "If this happened back in the good old days, I understand you'd be looking at six weeks minimum. But the doctor gave you some of these new super-calcium pills, and he swears your leg will be completely healed in twenty-four hours. All we have to do is release those clips on the side of the cast, and you'll be good to go."

Thunder rumbled outside as they took the elevator down to the third floor. Matthew and Kate led them to the room where the dinghy was now moored outside.

"Thanks for all your help," Thomas said.

"Hey," Kate said, "*we* should be thanking *you.*"

She gave Thomas a long hug, and he held onto her for an extra moment, a meager attempt to make up for a lifetime lost. As Elly watched the two of them, she did her best not to shed any tears.

"Take care of this guy," Kate said. "He's very special."

"You don't know the half of it," Elly said.

Another thunderclap echoed in the distance. Thomas and Elly climbed out the window, and Matthew and Kate lowered Eno into their arms. Thomas positioned him at the back of the boat, and Elly nudged him.

"What?" Eno replied, still grumpy from having been awakened too early. Elly pointed up to Meredith, who stood at a nearby window, waving.

"I got her number, just in case you come back this way," Elly said.

Thomas started the engine, and Matthew leaned out the window.

"Hey, Thomas. Hopefully we'll see each other again."

"I hope so," Thomas said. But he knew that even if he were to cross paths with Matthew in 2071, he probably wouldn't even recognize him. They waved their final farewells.

Thomas steered the dinghy around the building and into the river, where they were greeted by a surprising sight. The Brooklyn Bridge, along with its roadway, was now above water and revealed in its full majesty. Thomas was sorry he wouldn't get to walk across it, as Elly did with her father.

They scanned the horizon and spotted the cable car, perched atop the roller coaster. "Number twelve is still there," Elly said excitedly.

"With any luck, we'll have you home by bedtime," Thomas said.

Another thunderclap echoed above them, and the sky darkened as if someone had turned down the lights. Thomas steered the dinghy through the main entrance of the park and was shocked to see that the water was so low they could almost walk. But while it was too shallow for the megalodons, the roller coaster now seemed to be several times its original height.

Elly looked up anxiously. "How are we going to get Eno up there?"

"No doubt Thomas has devised some terrifying plan," Eno said.

"I'll need your help on this one," Thomas said.

He pulled the dinghy up next to the roller coaster car, which was parked on the lower tracks, well above water. Holding the mooring line in one hand, he jumped out of the boat and into the car and tied it off on the tracks behind him.

"What are we gonna do?" Elly said. "Hotwire the thing?"

"If *hotwire* means start the motor, yes," Thomas said. "But this is Eno's territory."

"If it's as primitive as everything else on this planet, it shouldn't be that difficult," Eno said. "But I'll need my kit."

Thomas helped Eno into the coaster car while Elly retrieved Eno's case from his backpack. As Thomas transferred the rest of their gear to the car, Eno took out some tools and fiddled with the engine. The car came to life.

Elly helped Eno into his seat then sat next to him and pulled down the protective bar. Another thunderclap boomed above, much louder than the last. A light rain started to fall.

Thomas gave the car a push and hopped in. It crawled slowly along the tracks to the first hill, but as they came over the peak, it began to gather speed. Elly gripped the bar tightly, while Eno closed his eyes.

Thomas leaned back and opened his arms to the rain, as if to surrender to the ride.

"I can see why these things were so popular," he shouted over the clatter.

But there was no agreement from Eno or Elly.

The roller coaster car raced along the tracks, building speed. They roared up and over the second peak into the straightaway at the very top of the structure. Elly saw that they were headed straight for the cable car.

"I hope you also have a plan for slowing this thing down," she shouted.

Thomas leaned out the side of the car, reached underneath, and pulled up a handful of wires. They abruptly lost power, and slowly rolled toward the cable car.

"Ride's over," he said.

"Not a moment too soon, from the looks of it," Elly said.

Thomas glanced up at the storm clouds, which were moving into position directly above. The rain started to fall in thick sheets. Elly and Thomas helped Eno into the cable car, then gathered their backpacks.

Thomas removed the Time Globe, and Eno went to work installing it. Outside, the wind rattled the cable car noisily against the tracks. A lightning bolt flashed in front of them, warning them they had little time.

"Eno?" Elly said, "I'm not asking you to get me back to the same day or even the same week. But please, can you at least make it the same year?"

"I can if you'll let me concentrate," Eno said, as he finished setting the globe. "The countdown has begun. Prepare for transit."

They put on their helmets and strapped themselves into their restraints.

Elly took Thomas by the hand. With her other hand, she grabbed Eno's. Surprisingly, he didn't pull away.

The countdown meter hit three and another lightning bolt blew out a section of track with a loud bang and a cloud of smoke. As the track tumbled hundreds of feet down the structure, the cable car lurched to one side, and for a moment Elly thought they were falling to their deaths. She closed her eyes and squeezed Thomas's hand with all her strength.

The storm, along with the sky itself, disappeared.

# CHAPTER 39

Thomas opened his eyes to a sliver of light. The platform window on the cable car had cracked slightly, allowing the moonlight to peek inside. It illuminated the multicolored particles that accompanied every jump, giving them a golden glow. But the crackle of energy they normally emitted was missing, and they were strangely silent. Thomas recalled the Mastership's bombardment of the Returner Compound when they time-jumped from the Station and couldn't help wondering whether the silence might be a sign that something had happened to Ignatius.

A groan echoed from the dark, and Eno sat up.

"How's the leg?" Thomas asked.

"Awful, thank you. And it's not even the broken one."

Elly got to her feet and opened the window. "Look. The moon. It's a waxing crescent, just like when we left."

Thomas opened the door to reveal the cable car was sitting at the edge of a bluff several hundred feet above the beach.

A loud bang echoed in the distance, and a shower of color burst over the horizon, illuminating the skyline of San Francisco.

"Hey, we caught the fireworks after all," Thomas said. "With any luck, I'll get you home before your father gets back from his party."

"And with any luck," Eno added, "I'll get to stay right here."

✦✦

Thomas set up one of the sleeping bags in a corner of the cabin while Elly gave Eno some pain medication. As they left the cable car, Thomas looked back to see that the timeflies, which were normally gone by now, still lingered in the cabin, huddled around Eno.

"It's like they're keeping him company," Elly said.

Thomas nodded. It looked that way to him as well.

With the light from the fireworks to guide them, they made their way down the steep hillside to the road, where the firework finale was underway in the distance.

They paused to watch, and when it finally ended, Thomas couldn't take his eyes away.

"It's over," Elly sighed.

Thomas nodded, but wondered if she was referring to more than the fireworks. Now that she was headed home, perhaps this was the end of her time with him. They took a taxi the few miles to town in time to make it onto the last ferry of the day, which was crowded with families who'd been watching the fireworks. He noticed that Elly was uncharacteristically silent during the trip across the bay. It was only after they got off the boat and into the taxi that she finally spoke. "Have you given any thought to when you'll leave?"

"Not really," Thomas said. In an ideal world, he'd spend the rest of the summer in San Francisco, hanging out with Elly in Muir Woods, going to the beach, maybe even learning to ride a surfboard. Perhaps he could take Elly's father up on his offer to stay at the house. But the last thing he wanted to think about right now was leaving again.

"I figure Eno will need some time for his leg to mend."

"Yeah, and we'll need to get you some different supplies for the next time-jump: some serious camping and climbing gear, an inflatable boat, at least a dozen kinds of dehydrated food, and, oh, some stuff to cook with. That's just for starters."

Thomas smiled, grateful that Elly was always thinking about the mission. But something else was on his mind. It had been weighing on him ever since they left New York.

"Hey, I almost forgot to ask you, what did Kate mean when we left? She said you filled in her on some stuff?"

"Yeah. She wanted to know all about us, how we met and wound up traveling together."

"What did you tell her?"

"I had to dance around the real story, so I stuck to the Iceland angle, meeting in Muir Woods, etcetera. I skipped time-travel, the lost shuttle, Mars, and of course the mission."

Thomas was silent. Elly looked over at him.

"Well, aren't you gonna ask?

"What do you mean?"

"C'mon Thomas, it has to be on your mind. It's what we call the elephant in the room."

Thomas knew what she meant. "Did she say anything about me?"

"Actually she did. She said you were incredibly brave, and…"

Elly paused, as if she was either reluctant to say the rest or saving the best for last.

"And what?" Thomas said.

"If she ever had a son, she hoped he'd be just like you."

"Really, she said that?"

Elly crossed her heart. "She did. Seems like you made a bang-up first impression. I think she'll remember you for the rest of her life."

Thomas beamed. And couldn't stop smiling for the rest of the ride.

✦✦

THE TAXI PULLED UP at Elly's house, which was dark except for the light outside the front door. She paid the driver and they got out.

"Doesn't look like Dad's home yet. You want to come in and get something to eat?"

Thomas hesitated. There was nothing he'd like more, but Eno was alone in the cable car. "Thanks, but I should get back to Eno."

"Here, take this," Elly said, pulling out a candy bar that was still wrapped. "I got it in the Alliance cafeteria but forgot to eat it. It's food from the future."

"Thanks," Thomas said, sliding it into his pocket.

She pulled out some crumpled bills and handed them over. "You'll need bus money."

"I promise to pay you back," Thomas said.

"Hey, I owe you. After all, you took me to New York and Washington, all on your dime. I can't even guess what that costs in future dollars."

After the din of the fireworks, the street seemed particularly quiet, and Thomas had the sense that he was trapped in the same bubble of silence as Elly on the ferry, unable to come to grips with what had happened during the last few days.

"Elly, I'm sorry for dragging you along on all of this."

A sheepish look came over her face. "Well, if I'm being brutally honest, you didn't."

"What do you mean?"

"When I was running from the police outside the Cable Car Barn and you grabbed my hand, there was a split second when I knew I could still let go. But I didn't. In fact, I held on even tighter. I wanted more than anything to go with you. And now that it's all over, I'm having a hard time believing it happened. Fortunately, I've got the scar to prove it." Elly patted her arm in its clean bandage.

"At least we got you back without any broken limbs."

"Actually, you did more. Remember that weird thing I get in my head all the time?"

"Yeah?"

"Well, it never happened, not once. And I have a theory why."

"What's that?"

"Maybe I belong in the future."

Elly chuckled, and Thomas couldn't tell whether she was serious or not. In any event, he wished it was true. After everything that had happened, he couldn't imagine continuing without her. At the same time he knew that wasn't possible. She had a home and a father and a dog. A life in the present. He had to accept the reality that their time together had come to an end.

"Dad will be home soon," Elly said. "I should go in."

"I should get to the bus," Thomas said.

"You still have the phone I gave you?"

Thomas pulled it out of his pocket and held it up.

"I'll call you in the morning."

"Great," Thomas said.

Elly gave Thomas a quick kiss on the cheek and ran for the door. He waited until she got safely inside before he turned to go. After a few steps, he looked back to see Elly at her bedroom window, with Charlie. She waved again. He waved back. Charlie gave him a good-bye bark.

Thomas started walking down the street. He couldn't avoid touching the spot on his cheek where Elly had planted a kiss. It felt like the one that Lina had given him back at the Returner Compound but also different in a way he didn't quite understand.

He was halfway to the corner when a car turned onto the block. The glare of headlights obscured the color of the car, or who was inside, so he flipped up the hood of his sweatshirt in case it was the FBI.

The car pulled over to the curb next to him and stopped. The window rolled down and the driver peered out of the darkness.

"Thomas?"

Thomas recognized the face. "Mr. McAllister?"

"I hope your stay went well?"

"Yes, sir. I just brought Elly home from the…fireworks."

"Thank you for returning her safely."

"Actually, she had a little accident, but she's fine now."

To Thomas's surprise, Mr. McAllister didn't seem upset in the least. "You'll find that she's incredibly resilient."

"That's true, sir."

"I wish I could take some of the credit, but it's all her mother's genes, or so I'm told. I never met the woman, though I understand she was a remarkable person. I suppose Elly mentioned that she's adopted."

"Yes, sir, she did."

"I didn't come by fatherhood naturally, so I take it much more seriously than most. I lost my own wife before we had the chance to have children."

"I'm sorry."

"As it turns out, fate had another plan for me. And it was far more amazing than anything I could've dreamed of on my own." Mr. McAllister shook his head as if he was still amazed by it. "Elly was an unexpected gift, so it's hard not to be overprotective. But like all of us, she has her own destiny to fulfill. I'd be the worst kind of father if I stood in the way of that."

Thomas nodded, though he wasn't quite sure what Mr. McAllister was talking about.

"The world's not getting any better, Thomas, and I'm sorry that my generation has failed you so badly. I'm afraid it's up to you now."

"Me, sir?

"You and Elly. You're our future." Mr. McAllister reached out to shake Thomas's hand. "Good luck in your continued travels, wherever they might take you."

"Thank you, sir."

Mr. McAllister drove on toward his house. Thomas watched him go, but when the bus appeared across the street, he sprinted toward it, arriving just a moment before the door closed.

Thomas plopped into the empty back row, exhausted. He wanted more than anything to close his eyes and sleep, but something nagged him. There was something odd about the conversation with Elly's father, but he couldn't quite put his finger on it. It was as if he were trying to tell Thomas something without coming right out and saying it. One sentence in particular jumped out at him: "*You're our future.*"

It was the exact thing Ignatius had said to him before he left for Earth.

Maybe it was a simple coincidence. He racked his brain, but he couldn't come up with anything that hinted at an explanation. He put it out of his mind, and as the Golden Gate Bridge appeared in the distance, he drifted off.

When he woke up, the bus was on a deserted two-lane road bordered by forest on both sides, like a tunnel of trees. There was only a few passengers left on the bus, and the moon gave the woods a sinister glow.

A headlight flashed in the window behind him, and Thomas turned to see a single car behind them. It was hard to tell in the dark, but it looked like the color of the one driven by the FBI agents who'd visited Elly's house.

As the bus pulled around a winding curve, its brake lights illuminated the two men in the front seat, and it was clear. They were the agents that had questioned Elly.

In a few stops, he'd be getting off the bus, and he couldn't risk the possibility of the agents following him back to the cable car, where Eno was barely able to walk, let alone run. The bus pulled over again and the last of the passengers filed toward the front. Thomas glanced at his wrist pod to see that he was still four miles from the cable car. But if he waited until then to get out, it would put the FBI agents within striking distance of his location.

The bus started to move again.

Thomas bolted out of his seat and shouted to the driver. "Hold on! Sorry, I fell asleep."

The annoyed driver reopened the door, and Thomas jumped out.

As the bus pulled away, Thomas glanced back to see the FBI car, which had pulled over about twenty yards behind, its engine idling.

Thomas had two choices. He could either cross the road and go up the hill toward the cable car or go into the woods right in front of him.

Thomas darted into the woods.

He heard the car's engine rev up, and its headlights flared behind him as it sped past. Thomas hoped it might be driving away, but it turned onto a fire road parallel to his path.

Through the trees, he could see the agents getting out of the car. As he turned his head, his foot caught a fallen log, and he flew through the air, landing face down. The agents moved in his direction, their flashlight beams slashing all around him.

Thomas jumped to his feet and stumbled forward. Another grounded tree obstructed the path, but this time he used it as a springboard to pick up speed.

The agents continued to close in around him when a flash of blue light suddenly illuminated the forest. He turned to see that the agents seemed to have stopped.

And then he heard gunshots.

Recalling Ignatius's Tetrascope demonstration, he pulled the device out of his pocket and aimed it overhead. A hundred feet of translucent wire shot into the air before the neodymium barb made contact with a branch. Thomas hit a second button and it pulled him into the upper section of the tree, hidden from sight. A pop of light flashed nearby, flooding the forest with yellow smoke.

And then the gunshots stopped.

Thomas stayed perfectly still as the footsteps of several men thumped across the forest floor toward him. He gripped the Tetrascope, ready to use the laser to defend himself, but to his surprise, the men continued past him.

The woods were silent again.

The only sound he could hear was the thumping of his heart.

He waited almost ten minutes before he thought it safe enough to lower himself to the ground. The area was still filled with the residue of yellow smoke. But as it began to clear, he could make out the shape of two limp bodies lying on the ground. It was the FBI agents.

He crept closer and knelt down to confirm that they were still breathing. A whisp of smoke drifted into his face, and Thomas recognized the smell from his encounter with the Commandos back in the Station tunnel. Knockout gas.

The light that had distracted the FBI agents suddenly made sense. *Blue shift.*

That could only mean one thing: the arrival of a Time Transport.

But how could that be?

Perhaps it was Ignatius, using one of the other Time Globe prototypes in an attempt to join he and Eno? Thomas got to his feet and noticed a sinister shadow nestled in the trees. Slowly, he took a few steps forward and froze.

Lying directly in his path was the Mastership, its probe stretched toward him like a metal stinger. Had he gone another step, it would have impaled him. Tucked into the woods, its skin reflected the dark green trees, making the ship look like it was covered with scales.

Thomas felt a wave of panic. If the Mastership was here, it could only mean one thing: that Balthazar had somehow stolen Ignatius's time travel technology.

He thought back to the time the High Governor and Bron had visited Ignatius to talk about the legend of the boy who would lead the Returners back to Earth. The governor insisted that the boy be eliminated so that the myth couldn't take on a life of its own. Thomas suddenly realized what the Mastership was doing on Earth.

It had come for him.

Without waiting another second, he sprinted toward the deserted road, dashed across it, and disappeared into the forest on the other side. He jogged up the steep incline for what seemed like an hour, though his wrist pod revealed it was half that. Finally, he reached the ridge line and made his way to the cable car where Eno was asleep. Surprisingly, the timeflies were still hovering around him, as if waiting for Thomas to return before taking their leave.

He sat on the platform to catch his breath and looked out to the ocean. Smooth as a mirror, it was covered with starlight and seemed to reflect the entire universe. In the distance, he heard the muffled sound of waves breaking against the beach. Slowly, his breathing returned to normal. But instead of feeling relief, he was overcome by a sudden sense of disappointment. More than that, failure. In only a few days on Earth, he'd gotten Eno wounded and Elly nearly killed, and attracted the attention of the FBI. If that wasn't bad enough, he'd brought the Mastership to Earth to hunt him down and return him to Mars. And during that time, he hadn't come close to Colorado, let alone accomplishing his mission.

Thomas flopped back against the tree, physically and emotionally drained. In the background, he heard a faint buzzing sound and turned to see the timeflies rustling with agitation. They drifted through the platform window, gathering at Thomas's head.

He could hear the muffled voice of Ignatius, broken and barely audible, as if he were in some form of distress. His words were punctuated by painful pauses, and Thomas had to lean in to the timeflies to hear what he said.

"*Don't. Ever. Forget. You're. Our. Future.*"

The timeflies slowly began to fade, exhausted by the completion of their own mission, leaving Thomas with nothing more than a sense of guilt. He closed his eyes and wondered if he had made a terrible mistake by taking on the mission in the first place. On the brink of sleep, he was startled by a flutter and looked up to see a flash of blue emerge from the darkness and land on the branch above him. It was the Steller's Jay he'd spotted after he first landed in Muir Woods. Thomas noticed that the blue on its back was actually streaked and seemed to sparkle with silver in the moonlight. How incredible, he thought, that such a thing could even exist. A creature who flew through the sky and brought good luck to humans. Only on Earth.

Suddenly, the sense of hopelessness Thomas had felt seemed to disappear, leaving behind a new clarity. Perhaps the last few days hadn't really been wasted but were a necessary part of the mission. He'd gained a valuable understanding of Earth, and not just from a dictionary. He'd felt the sun and the sand, seen the fog and the rain, tasted the ocean and breathed the air. On a personal level, he'd met his father, rescued his mother, and saved Ignatius's life. To top it all off, he'd gained an amazing friend and ally in Elly.

It was a good beginning. While it might take months or years or even a lifetime to accomplish his mission, the tide of time was on his side.

He understood for the first time that his destination truly was his destiny.

And after years of dreaming about the planet of his birth, he was finally home.